Praise for C

"A fascinating look at shipb... characters are delightful and inspire anticipation for the next story."
—*RT Book Reviews* on *The Wedding Journey*

"This well-written, sweet love story has lots of romance and adventure."
—*RT Book Reviews* on *To Be a Mother*

"A charming love story with a plausible storyline and characters who are firm in their beliefs."
—*RT Book Reviews* on *Marrying the Preacher's Daughter*

Praise for Sherri Shackelford

"Shackelford's latest features imperfect but likable characters whom readers can connect with. Watching the progression of their slow-building relationship is enjoyable and makes this book a perfect treat for Christmas."
—*RT Book Reviews* on *The Rancher's Christmas Proposal*

"With sparkling dialogue and a perfectly matched hero and heroine, along with an intriguing mystery, this Prairie Courtship story makes a highly entertaining read."
—*RT Book Reviews* on *The Engagement Bargain*

"A lovely marriage-of-convenience story, the interaction between the two main characters is a joy to watch, and the hero's acceptance of love is well done."
—*RT Book Reviews* on *The Marshal's Ready-Made Family*

CHERYL ST.JOHN

Cheryl St.John's love for reading started as a child. She wrote her own stories, designed covers and stapled them into books. She credits many hours of creating scenarios for her paper dolls and Barbies as the start of her fascination with fictional characters. Cheryl loves hearing from readers. Visit her website at cherylstjohn.net or email her at SaintJohn@aol.com.

SHERRI SHACKELFORD

Sherri Shackelford is an award-winning author of inspirational books featuring ordinary people discovering extraordinary love. A reformed pessimist, Sherri has a passion for storytelling. Her books are fast-paced and heartfelt with a generous dose of humor. She loves to hear from readers at sherri@sherrishackelford.com. Visit her website at sherrishackelford.com.

Cowboy Creek Christmas

CHERYL ST.JOHN

SHERRI SHACKELFORD

HARLEQUIN® LOVE INSPIRED® HISTORICAL

Thanks and acknowledgment are given to
Cheryl St.John and Sherri Shackelford
for their participation in the Cowboy Creek series.

LOVE INSPIRED BOOKS

Recycling programs
for this product may
not exist in your area.

ISBN-13: 978-0-373-28383-5

Cowboy Creek Christmas

Copyright © 2016 by Harlequin Books S.A.

The publisher acknowledges the copyright holders of the individual works as follows:

Mistletoe Reunion
Copyright © 2016 by Cheryl Ludwigs

Mistletoe Bride
Copyright © 2016 by Sherri Shackelford

www.Harlequin.com

Printed in U.S.A.

CONTENTS

MISTLETOE REUNION

Cheryl St.John

Mistletoe Reunion is lovingly dedicated to my friend and critique partner of over twenty-five years. You may have seen Barb Hunt's name in book dedications, mine and others. You may have met her.
She supported my career in every way possible.
We knew each other's families and shared our faith.
She was there when I got the call that I'd sold my first book. We celebrated every victory and supported each other through the rough times.
She was a loyal and loving person, and I'm fortunate to have had her as a friend for as long as I did.

Though I miss her all the time, I'm assured she is seated at the right hand of God and having a really good time—likely even a better time than all the Friday nights with the girls put together... and we have laughed a lot! Donna Kaye, Debra Hines, *lizzie starr, Sherri Shackelford and I continue to celebrate Barb's life and honor her memory. While it's difficult to think of this natural world without her, she will always have a place in our hearts. She knew how much she was loved—by her family, her friends and her Heavenly Father, and that gives me peace.

All flesh is grass, and all its loveliness
is like the flower of the field.
The grass withers, the flower fades,
because the breath of the Lord blows upon it;
Surely the people are grass.
The grass withers, the flower fades,
but the Word of our God stands forever.
—*Isaiah* 40:6–8

Chapter One

Kansas, late October 1868

The bell over the door rang, and Marlys Boyd glanced up to see her scheduled patient arrive with a bright smile. "Good morning, Doctor Boyd!"

Pippa Kendricks removed her coat and hung it on the rack inside the door. After using the mat Marlys provided to wipe her wet boots, she took a pair of bright pink slippers from her bag and changed footwear.

"Good morning, Pippa. I have the water heated, and I'll fill the tub."

Pippa followed her toward one of the bathing rooms on the north side of the roomy office building. "You know I enjoy this room with the windows near the ceiling. It's bright and cheerful."

"I had those windows added after I purchased this place," Marlys told her. The frosted glass had been etched with leaf and berry scrolls, and was one of the ever-practical lady doctor's few splurges.

Pippa turned her back to Marlys for help with the hooks and buttons on her dress, then stepped behind the painted pine dressing screen. "There are so many exciting things happening of late. I'm actually glad winter came early, so Gideon and I can stay until spring. We would have been gone before all these rousing things happened. Truthfully, I'm going to miss everyone here."

"We will miss you, as well. I read in an edition of the Philadelphia paper that President Johnson has declared a national day of thanksgiving, so you will be here for that."

"Yes!" Pippa exclaimed. "In fact I was asked to be on the committee to organize a town celebration. I suppose because I know so many people. You should volunteer for the committee and get to know your neighbors."

"Oh, I don't know. I'm not very good at things like that."

"Nonsense. You've done a marvelous job organizing things here for your medical practice. You'd be an excellent addition to the committee."

"But I'm still so new to town. Surely the committee is meant for more established townspeople."

Pippa laughed. "Established? In Cowboy Creek? Why, the town is practically brand-new. There are always new townspeople. Like the new newspaper owner. Any day he'll be putting out his very first edition," Pippa told her as Marlys filled the tub and added oils and minerals. "I've already asked for an interview about the upcoming play at the Opera House. We're doing *The Streets of New York*." The petite redhead came from behind the screen, tying the sash of the flannel robe, and eyed Marlys. "Have you done any acting, Dr. Boyd?"

"No, I haven't." At the speculative look on the actress's face, Marlys added, "And I have no interest in trying. My focus is on building my practice."

Getting people to take her seriously as a lady doctor was difficult all on its own, but the situation only worsened when people discovered she did not practice traditional medicine, but instead took a homeopathic approach. She had hoped that establishing her practice out West would give her access to patients with the enterprising, pioneer spirit who might appreciate unconventional treatments. She'd been eager to learn more about the people of different cultures and ethnicities who had settled in this Kansas boom town.

Nearly two weeks after Marlys had opened her practice, Pippa had been the first resident of Cowboy Creek to inquire about her medical techniques, in reference to a skin rash. When Marlys suggested they try a few different herbs and oils, the flamboyant ginger-gold redhead had been elated. She'd been in a couple of times a week since, so Marlys had adjusted to the young woman's dramatic speech and manner.

"So, the newspaper editor will give your play editorial support?"

"Yes, and he seemed quite pleased to have news for his first edition."

In August Pippa had married Gideon Kendricks, the agent who sold stocks for the railroad. They were planning to travel west after the weather cleared in a few months.

Marlys needed all the advertisement she could get. The townspeople hadn't exactly flocked to her practice. But if she could convince a few more residents like Pippa to give her a chance, she believed she could win them over, and word of mouth would spread.

"I'll go see about an interview myself after we've finished here." Marlys checked the temperature of the water in the porcelain tub and stirred one last time to assure the minerals were well dissolved. "Your bath is ready. Take your time and relax. You have towels on the stand there. I'll let you know when you've soaked long enough, but should you need the water reheated, ring the bell."

"Thank you, darling! You've saved me from a winter

of dry skin and made me look dewy fresh. I will glow at my performance. I am singing your praises to the other ladies—lilting notes on a sweet high C."

Marlys smiled and left the bathing room. She'd had two of those deep bathing tubs installed in comfortable private rooms, funded—along with the rest of her practice—by selling the jewelry and townhome she'd inherited from her mother. After working multiple jobs to pay for her degree from an unconventional school of medicine, selling her property had been her only option. Her father had supported her early desires to learn languages and world history, but had never approved of her medical studies. Immediately after she'd made the decision to become a doctor and not marry, he'd cut off all support.

As soon as Pippa's session was over, Marlys emptied and cleaned the tub, hung the towels to dry, and dressed in her wool coat and fur-lined boots. She tugged her collar up around her neck and tied a scarf over her hair. Winters in the East had prepared her for cold, but not for the relentless wind that caught the hem of her skirt and whipped the end of her scarf across her face. She held it over her nose and trudged along Second Street.

She passed Dr. Fletcher's office on the corner of Second and Eden, crossed the street and passed Sheriff Hanley's office and jail to reach the newspaper. The previous owner had been sent to prison for crimes against the local business owners. While evading arrest, he had deliberately set fire to his own building. The quick response of the townspeople had saved the jail and the boarding house on either side, but the *Herald* had been gutted.

Shortly after her arrival, Marlys had learned that an Eastern journalist had bought the gutted building and renovated it so quickly her head had spun. She imagined a fresh young fellow eager to make a big name for himself in the quickly growing cattle town.

The exterior had been freshly painted, and the new door didn't show any wear. On the other side of the enormous pane of glass, a bespectacled man was painting bold gold letters, scrupulously edged with black, spelling out *Webster County Daily News*. Beneath the name of the paper, the artist's brush had scripted *Owner & Managing Edito*…and was midstroke on the *r* when he spotted her and quickly opened the door to usher her inside. A bell rang above the door as he opened and closed it. "It's too cold to stand out there for longer than a minute," he said. "Come inside and warm yourself by the stove."

There was a new stove surrounded by wooden chairs in the corner of the front open area, a space obviously designed to welcome visitors and perhaps encourage local gossip. A blue-speckled enamel pot sat atop the stove, and pegs holding half a dozen tin cups lined the wall.

A four-foot-high wooden room divider with a half-door separated the back portion of the room, where desks had been haphazardly deposited and crates stood against one wall. Two enormous printing presses took up the space in the rear, and there were two doors leading to rooms beyond, one with the door open, the other closed.

"Coffee's hot. I just made it." The painter gestured to the stove and pushed his glasses up his nose.

"Are you the editor or a journalist?" she asked.

"Forgive my manners. I'm Pete Sackett. Just here to do this lettering. I'm sure the owner heard the bell, so he'll be out in a moment."

Marlys used the predicted moment to survey the impressive array of framed front pages along the interior wall of this area. *The Progressive*: LINCOLN ELECTED, *New York Illustrated News*: RICHMOND IS OURS!, *Dallas*

Morning News: LEE SURRENDERS, *The Daily Intelligencer*: LINCOLN ASSASSINATED were a few headlines she had time to read before a greeting came from behind her.

"Welcome to the *Webster County Daily News*."

At the instantly recognizable rich voice, her hands stilled on the scarf she'd been about to remove, and she turned.

At the sound of the bell, Sam Mason wiped ink from his fingers and stood, dropping the rag to the floor beside his journeyman. His knees cracked as he straightened, and the lanky young man grinned. They'd been cleaning type block since early that morning, arranging the blocks in orderly sequence in stained wood trays. "Your knees would protest, too, if you'd slept on the cold ground for months at a time while marching through Virginia. You were still on your mama's knee by the fire, and a good thing for you."

"I'm not *that* young—you're exaggerating," the younger man disagreed. "I was running my family farm on sweat and prayer. Where do these uppercase script letters go?" Israel asked.

"In that tray." Sam pointed to the tray behind Israel. "Starting third row down and ending row seven in the middle."

Israel nodded and loaded the first letter block. Sam's uncanny memory for details astounded most people, but Israel was used to it. He'd apprenticed under Sam in the city and had been honored that Sam had asked him to accompany him on this new venture.

The appearance of the outer room gave Sam a jolt of pleasure every time he walked into it. The work area still smelled like new wood and plaster, but soon the combined smells of ink and paper would remind him of the history of years of journalistic endeavors and indicate a job well done.

A woman in a practical gray coat and red scarf stood facing away from him, perusing his collection of front pages. Pete was still painting letters and had just outlined the *S* for Samuel's name. "Welcome to the *Webster County Daily News*."

The woman pushed the scarf from her chestnut brown hair as she turned. The winter sun chose that moment to stream through the freshly cleaned and shined window, silhouetting her form and sparking glistening gold variations of color in her unfashionably short wavy hair, reaching only below her ears in casual disarray.

She wore no jewelry and hadn't rouged her cheeks, but her skin glowed, and her beauty needed no ornamentation. Her gaze riveted on his face, intense, probing, *familiar*. He experienced a jolt of awareness akin to the nervous anticipation of an impending skirmish. Why he dredged up that feeling puzzled him for only seconds. She narrowed her gold-brown eyes. They recognized each other at the same time.

"Samuel?" she intoned.

Her voice was a confirmation. He'd never forgotten the lilting sound of it. *Marlys*. "Miss Boyd. Or—is it still Miss Boyd?"

"Yes." His former fiancée's astute gaze took in his shirt and trousers, the ink on his hands. "I had no idea it was you who had taken over the newspaper. I thought you'd long been settled in Philadelphia."

"The war changed a lot of plans." He determinedly collected himself. "May I take your coat? You'll get too warm."

She unbuttoned the garment and let it slide from her shoulders. She wore a pale blue blouse without ruffle or lace and a dark blue skirt. She was still as narrow and delicate-looking as the girl he remembered, but she'd blossomed into a lovely woman. He took the coat, sweetly perfumed with the scent of her hair, and hung it on a hook near the stove. His olfactory senses had not forgotten her, either. "Have a seat. There's coffee."

"I'm fine, thank you." But she moved to perch on a chair, and her formal manner drove his discomfort up another notch.

The air crackled with more than the snap of the kindling in the stove. There were years between them, and he didn't know her anymore. He had never truly known her.

She glanced behind him and back to meet his eyes. "Are you the editor?"

Perfunctory as always. "I am."

"A piece on my new practice would help spread the word and let people know I'm ready for business."

No small talk or girlish chatter. Her blunt and business-like manner didn't surprise him, nor did it offend him. Perhaps he knew her better than he thought. Sam tilted his head and went to gather paper and pencil before settling on a chair across from her. "I guess you're the lady doctor who built on Second Street?"

"I am."

"We lost touch quite a while ago," he said, the first one to mention their previous relationship. "And we maintained no mutual acquaintances, so you'll have to fill me in on your background, and we'll make the piece interesting."

"Will you interview me right now?"

He spread his fingers in question. "Do you have a few minutes?"

"Yes, yes, of course." She smoothed her skirt over her knees.

"I recall you're fluent in several languages. That's an interesting fact. Four, is it?"

"Latin, French, German, Portuguese, passable Chinese,

and I can communicate somewhat in Choctaw, Chickasee and Cherokee."

"More than I thought." He added a note on the paper. "And your education?" He kept his voice studiedly neutral as he mentioned the reason she'd called off their engagement.

"I attended the Philadelphia School of Eclectic Medicine."

His pencil paused. He glanced up. "Did you learn conventional medicine there?"

"If by conventional you mean cutting, purging, administering harmful chemicals, and adding tar to drinking water, I did not."

He sensed he'd opened a can of worms. "By harmful chemicals, you mean…?"

"Mercury, arsenic. Even in small doses they are harmful at their worst and placebos at best."

The pieces he'd read about reformers and botanical physicians had not been favorable. The majority of the population looked upon them as quacks. "So you studied the teaching of…" He'd read the news from all major cities for years, and he had perfect recall. "Wooster Beach?"

"As well as John King and John Milton Scudder."

He nodded. It shouldn't come as a surprise that she'd followed their practices. She'd always had unconventional ideas and questioned everything.

"Eclectic medicine promotes botanical therapies with the belief that the body heals itself. I studied medicinal plants of European and American origin to learn remedies. I was encouraged to explore how medicine should work with nature to harness its intrinsic healing capabilities."

Marlys was passionate about her studies, about her practice. He didn't doubt for a moment she believed her methods could help people. She was as caring and compassionate as she was strong-willed and outspoken. She was also the same woman who had broken off an engage-ment with him, left him to explain to friends and his so-cial circle, wounded his masculine pride and left a crater in his self-respect.

Sam kept his expression neutral. He was a journalist, and no matter their history, it was his job to report the news in an impartial manner. He offered up a silent prayer for guidance to handle this situation without emotion or prejudice. "Do you have any followers yet?"

When she didn't reply immediately, he glanced up. She was eyeing him with a guarded expression. "Don't you mean *patients*?"

"I do mean patients," he answered firmly.

"Yes, I do."

He held the pencil at the ready.

Any previous warmth had fled her gold-flecked eyes. "I sense your hesitation to shed a positive light on this subject."

"It's my job to report the news impartially, Miss Boyd."

"If you can't call me Marlys, it's Dr. Boyd. I don't expect you to endorse my practice. Your concern is not unfounded—you haven't seen the effectiveness of this type of medical practice firsthand. A lot of people don't understand the benefits, but education is power. I can educate them."

"You're not wrong. I am definitely interested in an ar-ticle. Maybe more than one. It could give you a chance to share information. I'll choose language carefully to in-form readers without insulting Doc Fletcher's practice."

"That sounds fair. It's not my intention to insult anyone. I'm more interested in education and advanced medicine."

He asked her several more questions, and she supplied answers.

"What was your first impression of Cowboy Creek?" he asked.

She thought a moment. "The town is laid out efficiently. I had no problem finding my property or locating help to work on my building. The stores are more than adequate, and the boardinghouse is sufficient for my needs until my quarters are ready. I've spent all my time and energy on my office and supplies."

"What about people? Have you made friends?"

She flushed a little, which made Sam frown. Had people been unkind to her? He could understand if the townsfolk preferred to continue going to Doc Fletcher rather than try-ing something new, but that was no excuse for rudeness. She seemed to be struggling for an answer, so he hastened to say, "It was not my intention to make you uncomfort-able. You spoke of locations and not of the people. I was attempting to interest the readers who like to hear about their friendly town."

Her posture relaxed, and she faced him. "A lot has hap-pened since we were last…together," she said. "You know me well enough to know I'm socially awkward. I'm no good at inconsequential chatter—which can make it hard for me to make friends in a new town."

"You're good with patients, I assume."

"I try to be." She stood. "And now, I really should go." She took her coat from a hook, and he stepped to hold it as she slid her arms into the sleeves. Her shiny waves didn't touch the collar. She turned and faced him. He didn't back up, so only two feet separated them.

He never had the slightest idea what she was thinking behind those golden-flecked eyes, one of the things that had intrigued him from the first. He'd never been certain if she'd broken his heart or injured his pride.

"I read some of your articles during the war," she said. "You were in Pennsylvania, Massachusetts, Maine?"

"And Virginia, too. I pretty much saw it all."

"And your parents? How did they fare?"

"My father died shortly after I enlisted. Mother is well. She's currently traveling abroad. And your father?"

She absorbed the information. "My father is alive."

Her lack of further information spoke volumes. "He disapproved of your aspirations."

"Along with everyone else."

Did she mean him? "I suppose that was a strain on your relationship."

"We no longer have a relationship."

"I'm sorry."

She turned to watch Pete edge the letters of Sam's name with a neat gold line, giving him a moment to study her profile. She looked less girlish, of course, but even though she wore no jewelry and her hair lacked sophistication, she was as lovely as he remembered. She still fascinated him, but he'd learned the hard way she wasn't carved out to be a wife. Even if she'd changed her mind about that—which he doubted—he'd know better than to trust her with his heart again.

Her gaze wavered, and she lifted her brows in curiosity, drawing his attention to the door where Hannah Johnson and a shivering August peered in. Pete stepped back to allow them entrance, and Sam's eight-year-old son shuffled in ahead of their neighbor, Hannah, ushering in a gust of cold air.

"How was your day at school?" Sam said as they approached.

August glanced uncertainly at Marlys and then up at his father. "Fine. Mrs. Johnson made a pie for our supper. She let me help."

Sam knelt and awkwardly touched August's cold cheek. The child smelled like fresh air, chalk dust and flour. Things had been strained between them ever since he'd returned to his mother's home at the end of the war. Thanks to his years in the Army, they'd spent too long apart—too many years he'd missed getting to know his son. He believed bringing August here where they could start a new life together would be the answer to bringing them closer. The boy had never known his mother, and his grandmother had been his caregiver until a few months ago. Sam's mother deserved the opportunity to travel and see friends. And Sam needed time with his son to re-create and repair their relationship. But the relationship was slow to heal. August was reserved and withheld feelings and affection. Sam's heart ached at the chasm of years and uncertainly between them.

"Dr. Boyd!" Hannah said, drawing his attention back to Marlys. "It's nice to see you."

Sam straightened. Hannah was a seamstress with her own dress shop, so it wasn't unusual that Marlys would already have met her during her initial weeks in town.

"Mrs. Johnson," Marlys acknowledged, but her attention was on August.

"Hannah, please." The other woman glanced at Sam and handed him a covered pie. "My husband came home to be with the baby, and I thought a brisk walk would do me well, so I accompanied August."

"Thank you. And thank you for getting him after school and keeping him for a time."

"My pleasure," she assured him. "I need to stop by the mercantile before heading home, so I'll take my leave." She nodded at Marlys and departed.

"August, this is Dr. Boyd," Sam said. "Dr. Boyd, this is my son, August."

August politely removed his wool stocking cap, and his dark hair stood up in disheveled curls. "How do, ma'am."

Chapter Two

The boy child's shy expression was enchanting. He had shiny black hair and thick lashes like his father. Who was his mother? If things had gone differently, Sam's son might have been her child. Nearly a decade had passed since she and Sam had been engaged. He had wanted a family. Of course he had married.

What kind of woman had Sam chosen? Surely someone with all the admirable feminine qualities Marlys's father wanted her to possess. Someone focused on a marriage and not schooling and a career.

Marlys remembered meeting her father's colleagues as a child, recalled her self-conscious feelings of inadequacy and the discomfort of being stared at. "It's a pleasure to meet you, August. How old are you?"

"Eight, ma'am."

"Do you enjoy school?"

"Yes, very much. Miss Aldridge lets me bring home her very own books. I'm careful with them."

"I should like to meet Miss Aldridge."

"Do you have any boys or girls?"

"No, I don't. But if I did, I'd be proud if they were smart and liked to read, like you."

August tilted his head to glance up at his father.

Sam clamped a hand on his shoulder and grinned. "Why don't you hang your coat and go see if Israel needs a hand sorting the type."

"Yes, sir." August dutifully hung his coat and headed toward the room in the rear with the open door.

Marlys caught the wistful expression on Sam's face. "He's a bright boy," she said.

"Yes. He is."s

"Do you have other children?"

"No. My wife died when August was born. My mother helped care for him. He stayed with her during the war, and she continued to look after him when I returned. Until just a few months ago actually."

There was a whole history of love and loss in those few words. "I'm sorry to hear about your wife." She wrapped her scarf around her hair and buttoned her coat. "I will return tomorrow. I would like to pay for an advertisement."

"I'll look forward to seeing you."

She lifted her gaze to his midnight blue eyes, puzzled. Fascinated in some unexplainable manner. "Your wife must have been..." She grasped for something comforting because it was expected. Yet she was always at a loss for words in these situations. "Just what you wanted in a life mate."

"She was a lovely young woman."

"Will you want to do another interview then?"

"Yes, perhaps in another week or two. We'll generate interest with this first article, and with your advertisement, and then follow up so people don't forget."

"I read your book," she said. She hadn't been going to admit it, but there was no reason to withhold that bit of information. "It's not my usual reading material, but it held my interest. You're a very good writer."

"I don't know whether or not that's a compliment. Your

usual reading material is medical journals and field experiments."

"I read history and—" She stopped abruptly. He was teasing her.

He was smiling, the corners of his dark-lashed eyes crinkling. The resulting flutter of anticipation was one she'd only experienced when facing a particularly stimulating curative challenge. How strange. But maybe she was responding to the challenge of convincing him to write about her in a way that would help grow her practice? Sam was no inexperienced journalist looking to make a name for himself. He'd been a city editor in New York, and the book he'd written about his Army experiences had been highly successful. He was well-known and admired.

"I'll see you when you return to schedule your advertisement," he said.

Pete held open the door for her, and she stepped onto the boardwalk, where the frigid air stole her breath. She glanced back into the newspaper office in time to see Sam's tall form disappear into the back room where his son waited.

When faced with the choice between a life as someone's wife and the challenge of learning and a career, she'd made her decision. She rarely paused long enough to consider what she may have missed. The past was the past, and both of them had moved on. She was satisfied with the path she'd chosen.

And now here he was, back in her life. Samuel Woods Mason. Still fascinating. Still charming. Still enigmatic and charismatic.

Still her one regret.

In the days that followed, Marlys's plans didn't go as expected, but such was the life of a doctor. She was surprised but gratified when three uniformed soldiers showed up in her office.

The shortest soldier removed his hat upon seeing her. "How do you do, ma'am. Is the doctor in?" A second man was occupied keeping the third fellow upright, with no free hand available to remove his hat. The patient grimaced and stood on one foot, leaning all his weight on his friend.

"I'm Dr. Boyd." She hurried forward. "What is the injury?"

"You're the doctor?" the first man questioned, but was cut off by his comrade.

"It's my leg and foot," the man in pain barked. "Horse reared and crushed me against a building."

"Let me take a look at it." She gestured to a narrow hallway. "Take him into the first room."

"You sure about this, Ben?" his friend asked, eyeing Marlys.

"Get me to the room like she said," Ben demanded, and hopped forward.

"His name's Benjamin Cross," the first man told her. "That's Enoch, and I'm Jess. There was a note on Doc Fletcher's chalkboard saying he'd be out all morning. Sheriff told us you were here."

"Are you able to remove your trousers, Mr. Cross?" she asked.

Pain wasn't enough to dull his discomfort with the suggestion, because the patient flushed, glanced around but finally unbuttoned his uniform pants. His friends helped him remove them and got him situated on the examining table. Marlys took a pair of shears and cut the leg of his gray flannel union suit from ankle to knee. "How long ago did this happen?"

"Happened right in front of the sheriff's office," Jess said. "Took us maybe ten or fifteen minutes to find you."

"You're fortunate, Mr. Cross." She probed the area of his ankle, which was beginning to swell. "I don't believe anything is broken. And I can encourage blood flow away from your foot to prevent more swelling and to help the soft tissue heal faster."

"How are you going to do that?" Ben asked, looking at his purpling foot. Sweat beaded his forehead.

"While Enoch goes to the Cowboy Café for ice, I'll give you something for pain, and then we will soak your foot in warm water, and I will massage the blood from the injury, upward back toward your heart. When Enoch gets back, we will ice it."

"I never heard of such a thing," Enoch said. "My pa got a crushed foot, and the doc put it in a cast."

"How did he walk afterward?" Marlys asked.

"Well, he limped and used a cane."

"Exactly. I don't think Mr. Cross is ready to retire from his Army position and take to using a cane. I'd rather treat the injury and enable his body to heal the damaged tissue."

Enoch just looked at his companions.

"It's up to you, Ben," Jess said.

Ben didn't waste any time making his decision. Pain was a strong motivator, and the prospect of losing mobility— and employment—obviously added fuel. "What she's saying sounds better than being a cripple," he answered. "Go."

Enoch turned and headed out.

Marlys diluted a pain remedy and gave it to her patient. He grimaced but swallowed it all. She heated water, dissolved Epsom salt, along with drops of hyssop, cypress, yarrow root, parsley and fennel oil, in a pail and had Ben soak his foot and ankle. After a few minutes he was resting somewhat more comfortably on the padded table. Using the oiled water, she massaged his foot and ankle in firm upward motions. He winced once or twice, but for the most part remained at ease.

"What did you give him?" Jess asked.

"It's a boiled mixture of bark, roots and leaves to help with pain."

He looked at his chum and then at her. "Seems to have worked."

She nodded. "This procedure would have been quite painful without it. It's necessary, though—motion will help the healing process and prevent his ankle from becoming stiff."

Ben opened his eyes and attempted to sit up.

"Stay lying down, Mr. Cross. You're doing very well."

"Good thing Dr. Boyd was here," Jess told his friend. "You're going to be just fine." Jess gave her a nod.

"What is the Army doing in Cowboy Creek?" Marlys asked.

"Delivering food to the Cheyenne."

She paused her work on her patient's foot momentarily. "Nearby?"

"To the south."

"I read General Sherman had ordered provisions until a more permanent arrangement could be made by the peace commissioner." She continued her effort to massage blood upward. "Have you seen their camp?"

He nodded. "Saw it last time we were through. They're doin' some farming."

That made sense, since the tribes didn't have freedom to travel, and their hunting was limited. The settlers would claim they had rights to the land if the Indians weren't going to farm it. "Could you give me directions to get there?"

"Respectfully, Doctor, it's not safe for you to ride into their camp alone."

"I want to help them."

"They don't know that. Do you speak Cheyenne?"

She shook her head. "I don't, but I can speak other languages, and there might be someone to interpret until I pick it up."

He cast her a doubtful glance. "All the same, not a wise idea."

"Perhaps you could take me with you."

"I'm afraid not, ma'am. These distributions have to be handled delicately. Our orders are to send in as few men as possible while guarding the perimeter, deliver our parcels peaceably and leave. Taking a woman along would land us in hot water."

"Of course." She didn't want to get the soldiers in trouble. But she wasn't going to give up on the idea, either. *I'll just have to find an escort.*

Enoch arrived with ice. The sound of additional boots on the floor in the waiting area caught her attention. "Are there patients arriving?"

"No, ma'am," Enoch said. "I mentioned Ben's treatment when I was at the café, and some of the men wanted to see what was going on."

She blinked, gathering her thoughts. "What exactly do they want to see?"

"This here hot and cold treatment."

"I carried ice!" someone called from the other room.

"Watch Mr. Cross a moment," she said to Jess. "I'll be right back." Enoch followed her out of the exam room.

It had begun to snow, and four cowboys hung dripping dusters on hooks inside the door. "I'll wipe that up," one of them told her. "Wanted to see the soldier's foot."

She'd never had an audience before, and she didn't know what to make of this one. She looked from face to face, seeing only sincere curiosity. "If Ben doesn't mind, I'll allow you in, two at a time."

Enoch accompanied her back to the room, where he relieved Jess, and within minutes Jess was relaying what he'd witnessed to the group of cowboys.

Ben shrugged his acquiescence, and she had no lack of help chipping and dumping ice into a tub. She wrapped Ben's foot in a wet cloth and instructed him to lower it into the tub. He winced and cursed inventively. "Sorry, ma'am."

"Would you like another dose of the pain medicine?"

"Yes'm, please."

She diluted and administered the herbal mixture, and it didn't take long for her patient to relax.

The observers were surprisingly quiet, occasionally whispering among themselves. Soon she asked Ben to remove his foot from the tub. "We're going to do hot water mineral therapy again and then one more round of ice. Are you doing all right?"

"Ben, your ankle is already half the size it was when we brought you in," Jess told him. More men clambered to get a look as Marlys dried it off and rubbed oil into the flesh.

"Would this treatment work if a horse stepped on ya?" one of the men asked.

"I need more water heated, if a couple of you don't mind," she said. "There are kettles on the stove. I'll answer your question when the water is ready."

Within minutes her helpers had emptied the deep bucket and replaced it with steaming water. Collective silence ensued as she added oils and Epsom salt. With her damp sleeves pushed up over elbows she began the massage.

"What good does that rubbing do?" one of the men asked.

"It works the blood back toward his heart and supplies oxygen to his injured muscles and tissues. I first made certain he had no broken bones or cuts that needed treatment," she explained. "If he had, I'd have cared for those first and then assessed whether or not this procedure was safe. Since I believed there were no underlying problems, I felt it was harmless to treat the crushed area."

"And what did you add to the water?"

"My own mixture of oils. The smell helped him be more calm, and the oils contain healing properties."

"Will he be able to walk on that foot?"

"He'll need to keep it elevated and rest until the bruising goes away, but I believe he'll be just fine."

"Are ya done gawking?" Ben asked.

"I'm going to go clean up your floor," the man who'd promised told her. "Glad you're going to be all right, soldier. Thank you, ma'am."

"I'll let Sergeant Calhoun know about Ben," Enoch said as he left.

The few remaining men departed until only Jess remained.

"Where is the rest of your regiment?" she asked.

"Camped outside town."

"Mr. Cross can stay here as long as needed," she told Jess. "I have passable quarters set up in the rear, so I can stay and check on him during the night."

The next morning brought the Army sergeant, who thanked her and paid her generously for her services. He arranged to have meals for the soldier sent from the Cattleman Hotel. Several new patients ventured in with various complaints, from foot fungus to stomach aches and coughs. She suspected one or two were there merely to see the recovering soldier, but she treated them anyway.

By the end of the day it was clear that if business continued at this pace, she was going to need help. Just running the dirty laundry out and picking it up left her waiting room unattended. She needed time to restock supplies and clean, as well. But despite the difficulties, her day had been exhilarating. Obviously this influx of patients was a result of yesterday's news, so it could slack off at any time, but while the surge lasted, she was relieved to use her skills.

She hadn't had time to return to the newspaper, so at the end of the week she wrote out her advertisements, made certain Ben was settled, and trudged along the snowy street. Her research about Kansas had revealed freezing temperatures and snow any time in late October, but she hadn't learned about the wind until she'd climbed down from the train and chased her hat across the platform. She got a firm hold of the *Herald*'s doorknob and pushed, so she didn't lose hold of it, and entered.

The interior was warm and smelled of oil and ink. The desks and filing cabinets had been organized and arranged, and it looked like a place ready for business. Sam stood from where he'd been seated at a desk and motioned for her to come behind the divider. "Dr. Boyd."

"Mr. Mason." She removed her wool mittens, unbuttoned her coat and took the papers from her skirt pocket, unfolding them and joining him to spread them flat on his desk. "How much for these two advertisements?"

"May I take your coat and get you a cup of coffee?"

"I won't be staying long. I have to get right back. One of my placements is a request for an assistant."

"Sounds like you've already been busy. I heard talk about the soldier you're treating." His deep blue eyes still held a measure of reserve.

"How much do I owe?"

"I charge by the word as a rule." He took a pencil from behind his ear and quickly calculated the words on her two notices, then gave her a price.

She paid him. "When can I expect these to run?"

"Tomorrow. I'll be printing five issues a week to start. Would you like your advertisements in consecutive issues, as well? As long as I have the type set, I'm happy to do that for free for, say, another week? Or until you find your assistant, if it takes less time than that."

She blinked in surprise. "Yes, thank you."

He wrote her a receipt and handed it to her. "My pleasure."

"Also," she said, "you've probably met more townspeople than I have since you're gathering news. Would you know of a guide or anyone who would be willing to escort me on a short trip outside of town?"

"Where do you want to go?"

"There's a Cheyenne encampment to the south. I want to visit them."

"Visit the Cheyenne?" Lines formed between his brows when he frowned. "Tensions are high between the Army and the Indians. There's only a tenuous balance of peace. I don't know that that's wise."

Her determined gaze locked with his, and she hoped he could see that she would not be dissuaded. "I'm going."

Chapter Three

"The soldiers are unable to accompany me," she continued. "They said I'd need an escort."

"Indeed you will if you persist with this plan. If you don't mind me asking, why do you want to go there?"

"I want to see if they need medical attention."

"They're Cheyenne, Marlys. They have their own medicine."

His use of her given name startled her, and she looked at him more closely. His ebony hair had a disheveled look, as though he'd run a hand through it recently. His furrowed brow showed only concern. He had a half-inch-long curved scar on his cheekbone under his left eye that she hadn't noticed before. It was still pink, as though it was fairly new.

"That's another of my reasons for wanting to meet them," she admitted, tucking the receipt into her pocket.

He nodded, but his look of censure remained. "It wouldn't be safe. Relations between the Army, the settlers and the Indians are touchy. There are entire regiments assigned to protection when those provisions are delivered. It's not unusual for the Sioux to try to steal goods from the Cheyenne."

"I don't have anything to steal, and they have no reason to fear me."

"That's naive thinking, doctor. You don't want to land yourself right in the middle of unexpected danger."

She gave her head a little shake. "You're entitled to your opinion."

"You're a bullheaded woman."

"Which is why I will ask for a guide at the hotel and the sheriff's office if you don't have any better suggestions."

"You've made up your mind you're going."

"I have."

"I'll find a scout and go with you, then."

"You?"

"Is that so hard to imagine? I spent the whole of the war in the Army. How about you? Do you ride well?"

"I do."

"When would you like to go?"

"Thursday?"

"I'll meet you here at seven, then."

Ben's sergeant was with him when Marlys returned. "Is Private Cross able to be moved to the hotel?" he asked. "I will engage another private to stay with him."

"Mr. Cross should be fine as long as he keeps his weight off that foot for at least another few days. I have crutches he can borrow until then, so he can get around unassisted. I've learned they have two small rooms on the ground floor, so ask for one of those."

"I have to admit I wouldn't have believed how good his foot looks in only a few days if I hadn't seen the difference myself."

"He was fortunate," Marlys replied. "Nothing was broken, and his friends got him here quickly."

"He was fortunate you were the doctor they brought

him to." He took bills from a flat purse on his belt and handed them to her.

"You already paid me," she said.

"Even this amount is inadequate for your services. He will be back with the regiment soon. He may have been forced to leave the Army had you not healed his foot."

"God created the body to do the healing itself. I simply treat the symptoms in a manner that best advances the process." She accepted the payment. "Thank you." She gathered Ben's belongings and ushered them to the door.

A minute later, she patted the cash in her pocket. She now had the time and the funds to have some additional work done to her office. First thing she would do was find someone to install a secure lock on her medicine pantry. Many of her tinctures and oils could be harmful if used improperly. She gathered the laundry and headed out. After dropping off yet another heavy bag, she paid to have it delivered, then carried her clean clothing items to the boardinghouse. After putting them away in her temporary room, she found Aunt Mae bustling about the kitchen.

"Hello, dear," the short, round woman said with an easy smile. "There's certainly a lot of talk in town today, and you're the topic of one choice tidbit."

"The soldier's injury, I presume," she said.

"Yes, that." She sliced two loaves of bread in deft strokes. "How is the fellow doing?"

"Quite well. His sergeant just took him to the hotel to finish recuperating."

"And have you heard all the talk about Quincy Davis's mail-order bride?"

Marlys puzzled over that one. "Wasn't he the previous sheriff who was killed?"

"Precisely. But unbeknownst to everyone, he'd sent for an Austrian bride, and she arrived ready to give birth.

Leah, the midwife—do you know her?—attended to her, and the blacksmith married her on the spot so her baby would have a name and a father."

That seemed like a hasty decision, but she addressed the medical aspect. "Is she faring well?"

"Seems it was touch and go for a long while. Doc Fletcher couldn't be reached."

"Someone should have sent for me."

"Leah's a competent midwife."

"I'm sure she is."

"Stay for lunch as long as you're here. I made a hearty soup and this warm bread. You skip too many meals, and they're included in your rent."

"Thank you." She carried the basket of bread to the dining room, where the boarders were just settling into their places.

Old Horace was probably in his seventies, and wore his long gray hair in a tail down his back. Gus Russell had a white beard and was probably about the same age. In summer the two of them played horseshoes in the lot behind Booker & Son. Sunny days in winter afforded them afternoons on a bench in front of the mercantile. They knew all the comings and goings of the residents and newcomers. Though they often contradicted each other, their friendship was obvious.

"Howdy, Doc Boyd. Heard about the little German baby born last night?" Horace asked.

"He ain't German. He's Austrian," Gus corrected.

"Same thing, ain't it?"

"Same language, but different countries," Marlys said. "There are different inflections in their dialects."

Gus licked his lips at the steaming bowl Aunt Mae sat before him. "You speak German?"

"I do. I'm looking for someone to teach me Cheyenne."

Gus squinted at her.

She seated herself and thanked the proprietress. She tasted the hearty soup. "I'm also looking for someone to install a lock on a storage pantry. Is there a local locksmith?"

"The farrier does locks," Horace told her. "Colton Werner's his name."

"He's the blacksmith who married the Austrian woman," Aunt Mae explained.

"So, I'd find him at the livery to the north on this same street?"

"That's the one," the woman replied. "Speaking of newcomers, we have a new boarder. Georgia Morris is her name. She's here to make a marriage, so she won't last long." She eyed Marlys. "Are you making friends in Cowboy Creek?"

Sam had asked the same question. Why did everyone want to know? While she wasn't averse to having friends, she had simply never had the time. "I haven't been here long enough."

"Maybe, but you've stayed to yourself for the most part. There's church service on Sundays, and this week there's a gathering afterward. You should go. Just meet people. They'll be more likely to trust you with their medical concerns if you've made their acquaintance."

Marlys studied the older woman thoughtfully. As a doctor, she had a lot working against her, to be honest. She was a woman in a man's profession in a man's land. She didn't practice conventional medicine. She had never been outgoing or personable. She didn't care about fitting in, but perhaps giving the appearance of fitting in would make her more appealing and earn trust. Aunt Mae was genial and well-meaning, and she had no lack of helpful opinions. Marlys appreciated learning, so perhaps there was something to be learned from this woman everyone liked.

Marlys finished her lunch and thanked her landlady.

The blacksmith was a large man with a nice face and scarred hands. He listened to her explain what she needed, and told her he'd be able to do the work the following day.

She stopped at Godwin's boot and shoe shop, and a thin brown-haired woman wearing a print dress and a white apron greeted her. "Good afternoon. I'm Opal Godwin. Can I help you?"

Marlys removed her scarf. "I hope so. My boots get wet so often, they're never dry by the next time I go out. I need another pair."

"It's going to be a long winter," the woman said with a smile. "Have a seat and I'll draw your foot for my husband." She knelt and unlaced Marlys's boots. "Are you Miss Morris?"

"No, I'm Dr. Boyd."

"Oh, I've heard about you from Pippa. Sorry I haven't made it over to welcome you. I've been busier than usual."

The fact that she'd meant to stop over heartened Marlys. "That's quite all right."

"Your boots are very well-made."

"And comfortable. I want practical and comfortable."

A thready high-pitched cry arose from the rear of the room. Opal placed a hand over her breast and glanced up. "It never fails. He cries as soon as I'm busy. And I'm always busy."

"Bring him to me while you do that. I'll hold him."

"Are you sure you don't mind?"

"Not at all. It's practical."

Opal returned with a baby wrapped in a white crocheted blanket. He looked to be only a few weeks old. Marlys looked him over, even listened to his breathing and held him up to rest her ear against his chest. He flailed his arms, so she tucked him snugly back in the blanket. "His heart and lungs sound healthy. He appears to be a sturdy child."

Opal blinked at her, and then smiled. "I was extremely exhausted while I carried him, but Richard's a good eater and is growing."

"You probably needed more minerals and protein in your diet. Nourishing him depletes your own reserves. Are you eating well now?"

"Yes."

"Drink as much milk as you can. I can make a supplement that will help you, too."

Opal appeared somewhat uncomfortable with her suggestion.

"I suppose you've heard things about me."

"No, it's just that Leah is my friend…"

"And the midwife, I understand."

Opal nodded.

"Well, talk to her first, and then come to see me if you choose."

Opal drew patterns of both of Marlys's feet on brown paper and wrote on them. She showed her leather samples, and Marlys chose a supple dark brown.

"And we'll make you a sturdy heel. Just enough to be fashionable, but not so much as to lose comfort."

"Perhaps another fur-lined pair as well as a pair for indoors," she decided.

Opal looked pleased. "I'll show you the styles we have."

Marlys chose a style, and Opal wrote notes for her husband.

Baby Richard had fallen asleep in her arms, and Marlys took a moment to admire his downy hair and tiny rosebud lips. What had Sam's son looked like as an infant? She imagined wispy black hair and round cheeks.

"Your first pair should be ready in less than a week."

Marlys looked from the baby to the eyes of the new mother. She remembered what Aunt Mae had said about people trusting her if she made friends. Her heart beat faster against the weight of the baby, but she opened her mouth to speak. "It's a lot to get used to caring for a new baby, isn't it?"

"It is, but he's a blessing."

"If you come by my office, I'd love to prepare a mineral bath for you. Just to relax for an hour or so. I'll make a bed for Richard, or I'll hold him. My treat."

Opal's brown eyes showed her surprise, but also appreciation. "Thank you, Dr. Boyd. I've heard only good things about your mineral bath treatments from Pippa."

Marlys stood and, after another tender look at the baby, handed Richard to his mother, then laced up her boots. Maybe it wouldn't be all that difficult to make friends. It would be nice to feel accepted—and a little less alone. "I'll check back next week."

"If they're finished sooner, I'll bring your boots to you."

Marlys smiled and headed back to her office.

The first edition of the *Webster County Daily News* came off the press the following day. Sam and Israel folded, stacked and bundled papers. The sun came out as though in celebration of the big day. Accompanied by August, the three of them traveled the streets of Cowboy Creek, where melting snow formed ruts of oozing mud. Sam cleaned his boots on the iron scraper in front of Remmy Hagermann's mercantile. He'd already made arrangements with as many stores as possible to keep a stack of newspapers until he replaced any old ones with new.

Remmy greeted him with a smile and a wave. "The first edition, eh?"

"It's here."

"I'm looking forward to actual news. Our last newspaperman skewed everything to make situations look bleak. We all figured it out too late. He was undermining the town for his own cause. We're glad to have you. You're a newspaper legend. When we learned you were coming to Kansas, I ordered a couple dozen copies of your book, and they all sold."

"Much obliged, Mr. Hagermann."

Remmy picked up the top newspaper and read the headlines. One eyebrow climbed his forehead. "'Cowboy Creek's First Female Doctor Sees Results with Progressive Medicine.' The Boyd woman, I reckon."

"Yes, Dr. Boyd is a most interesting woman."

"I heard she learned Chinese medicine at a peculiar university."

He had his own doubts about her education and practices, but he would stay neutral. "You'll find the article about her education informative. She's quite forthcoming about her beliefs. And statistically, the Chinese are remarkably healthy."

Remmy glanced up from the paper and eyed Sam. "Yeah?"

"I'll be doing another article in a couple of weeks. After reading about her you may find that many of her treatments are more logical and humane than commonly accepted practices. Cowboy Creek is growing. There's more than one mercantile. I suppose there's enough patients for two or more doctors."

Remmy had opened his mercantile after Zimmerman's and cleverly catered to women to attract a good share of customers. He didn't argue with Sam's reasoning. Instead he looked over the other articles. "Like I said, nice to have a paper again. Suppose I'll run an advertisement in the next one."

"I'll give you a discount on your first ad," Sam assured him.

Remmy glanced through the front window at August waiting on the boardwalk. "That your boy?"

"Yes, that's August."

"Works with you on the paper, does he?"

"Mostly he's adjusting to a new school. Hannah Johnson watches him a couple of afternoons until I finish work."

"Reverend Taggart's daughter, the dressmaker?"

"That's right. I was surprised when Hannah offered to take August for a few hours a week, but I'm grateful." Sam headed for the door. "Come see me for that ad."

Sam pulled the cart holding papers over the muddy ruts, and Israel joined them. He had taken papers to the railroad station. The three made their way north on Lincoln Boulevard, so they would pass Dr. Boyd's office on their way back to Eden Street. August grabbed a paper, and Sam pushed open the door, which rang a bell. Israel followed.

A pleasant mixture of unusual smells hung in the air. A row of plain wood chairs lined one wall, all empty. A large rug, obviously new, covered the varnished wood floor in the waiting area.

Marlys stepped from an open doorway to greet them. "Good morning."

August extended the newspaper he held.

"We brought you a paper so you could see the article," Sam explained. "Israel, meet Dr. Boyd. This is Israel, my journeyman."

Marlys leaned toward the young man. Israel removed his heavy glove and shook her hand. "Pleased to meet you, Doctor."

"My pleasure. Let me grab a coin so I can pay you."

"No, this one's complimentary," Sam said quickly.

"Thank you." She unfolded the paper and studied the

front page. She couldn't have missed the caption about her practice, but she read aloud another. "'President Johnson Proclaims a Day of Praise, Thanksgiving and Prayer.'" She glanced up at him. "It sounds like Andrew Johnson believes our country has turned a corner, politically, economically. He's giving people permission to hope again."

Sam nodded. "In his proclamation he talks about the abundance of jobs, crops, harmony in this country."

Marlys read aloud, "'I therefore recommend that Thursday, the 26th day of November next, be set apart and observed by all people of the United States as a day for public praise, thanksgiving, and prayer to the Almighty Creator and Divine Ruler of the Universe, by whose ever-watchful, merciful, and gracious providence alone states and nations, no less than families and individual men, do live and move and have their being.'"

"What does it mean, Papa?"

Sam looked into his son's curious blue eyes. "It means even though we've been through a lot as a country, losing family and friends in war, that we have a lot to be thankful for. Like our freedom. So there will be one day set aside when everyone is thankful together."

"The town is putting together a celebration. Mrs. Kendricks suggested I volunteer for the committee," she said. "Perhaps it's not a bad idea. I do need to meet people, so they will learn to trust me."

"That's good advice. I made up my mind to delve into town projects and affairs as soon as I arrived, so people learn to see me as one of their own."

"While you're here," she said, "I've made something for you. Follow me."

She turned and left them standing.

Chapter Four

"I'll wait here," Israel said.

Perplexed, Sam followed Marlys into the room behind the waiting area, August trailing behind. They followed a hallway into the first room, which held a desk, shelves lined with books and a small wooden rack on a cabinet.

She took a squat bottle from the rack and applied a dot of glistening liquid to her little finger.

"What's that for?" he asked.

"Lean toward me."

He hesitated, but slowly leaned.

She trailed her finger under his eye.

Her closeness and touch made him unexplainably unsettled.

"I can't promise this will completely remove that scar, but the skin growth appears new enough that this might greatly improve its appearance."

He'd received the injury while unloading the presses and parts a couple weeks ago. Sometimes he noticed the mark when he shaved, but hadn't paid much attention to it after the cut had healed. Apparently she'd noticed. He wasn't sure how he felt about that. A surprising curl of gratification spiraled in his chest. It had been a long time since someone had tended to him like this. But she was a doctor, so he'd be foolish to read anything more into the gesture. "Smells good. What's in this?"

"Sandalwood powder, honey, lavender, aloe plus a couple drops of other oils." She put the cap back on the bottle and handed it to him. "Dab it on a couple of times a day."

Their fingertips grazed as he accepted the bottle. "Thank you."

"Our plans for Thursday still stand?"

"Yes. I found someone who knows the area to travel with us. He speaks Cheyenne."

Marlys's eyes opened wide. "You did? That's perfect. Thank you."

"You're dead set on doing this. If I can't talk you out of it, I'll first make it safe and then make it advantageous to your cause."

"I can't be talked out of going."

"I know." They returned to the front of the building where Israel waited. "Thank you for the balm."

"My pleasure. That should be plenty."

He took an awkward step back, gave her a nod and turned away. Their cart was half-depleted, so Israel walked ahead, and August sat on the remaining newspapers, hanging on and laughing when they crossed the ruts.

Sam had the urge to caution him about falling off, but instead smiled at the unfamiliar sight of his boy's gap-toothed grin and the joyful sound of laughter. His son hadn't derived much pleasure from their relocation.

Sometimes thinking about his son's remoteness made Sam sick to his stomach. August had been only a year old when Sam had enlisted. Upon his return Sam had been a stranger to the five-year old. Little wonder the boy had barely warmed to him, preferring his grandmother's company and tutelage over his father's. But Sam's mother had done more than her part in raising and caring for her grandson. It was time she had the freedom to travel and enjoy friends. And now that they were settled in their new home, it was past time August and Sam learned to make the best of their threadbare family.

But it seemed the more he tried to draw him close, the more reserved August became. Sam was at a loss, and he prayed continually for a breakthrough.

His thoughts skipped back to Marlys, strangely pleased that she'd had the inclination to make something for the scar under his eye. He glanced at his reflection in the window of the sheriff's office as they passed, then grabbed a paper and entered to give the lawman a copy.

Marlys was still an enigma. He'd never understood what made her tick, and he still didn't. He needed to create a stable life for his son, perhaps marry and establish a family if God saw fit to make that happen. He'd be wise to remember she wasn't that woman, and no attraction or friendship was going to change that. He'd already learned the hard way that hoping for a piece of her heart was futile.

But for some reason, he did value her friendship, and he felt unexplainably responsible for her. She was the smartest person he knew, but she was also headstrong and naive, and those two qualities could mean trouble. He meant to keep his guard up where she was concerned—for her protection and for his.

Dressed in sensible boots, a slim split riding skirt and a warm coat with a fur hat, Marlys approached the livery and opened the single door. November had arrived with more sun and less snow, but she'd been warned that the weather was unpredictable, so she was prepared.

Sam stood beside a shiny mahogany horse in the wide open area, wearing a suede coat and boots, with a revolver holstered to his thigh. He tightened the cinch on the saddle, patted the horse's rump and turned to spot her. "I thought we were meeting at the newspaper office."

"I was ready so I walked," she replied.

"You look warm and ready for the day."

"Amos Godwin made these boots for me," she told him. "I ordered two pair, and he finished these warm ones first." She glanced over her shoulder. "We will need to go back to my office, though. I have items to bring that I couldn't carry."

"I wondered about that. Do we need another horse?"

"I believe so."

The door opened again, and a young man in a heavy coat joined them, spurs jangling. "Sam." He tipped his hat to Marlys.

"Marlys, this is James Johnson, Hannah's husband. James, this is Dr. Boyd."

"How do, ma'am. I've heard about you."

Marlys greeted the young man with a warm smile. "All good, I'm sure."

He grinned. "You arrived in town a little too late to hear all the gossip about me and Hannah. And there were a lot of tongues wagging so I was relieved about the new topic of interest."

"You have me curious now," she said.

"We'll have plenty of time to talk," he replied.

"How much are you taking?" Sam asked her. Then, without waiting for a reply, he said, "James, would a wagon make the trip?"

"No hills or rivers," he answered. "One creek, not too deep. A wagon will fare well."

"We will probably need it," Marlys agreed.

"I'll hitch horses," Sam decided. "And I'll drive the wagon. You can ride ahead, James."

Their scout headed back into what appeared to be the tack room. "I'll help with the animals."

It didn't take long for the two men to have the wagon ready. Sam assisted Marlys up to the seat and climbed up to take the reins. Back on Second Street, they loaded her crates and bags from her office, and covered them with a tarp.

"I brought food, too." She handed him a basket with a lid, and he tucked it under the covering.

The weather cooperated, with partial sun breaking through the clouds, but the air was crisp. She was glad she'd bundled for warmth and brought her scarf for her neck and face. James rode ahead as they made their way north out of town.

"No patients today?" Sam asked.

She raised an eyebrow and slanted him a glance. After the incident with the soldier, she'd had a few patients by default, and Pippa liked the mineral baths, but her waiting room was still a good place to be if one wanted quiet time.

"Was that a no?"

"There was a rush of curious people after I treated the soldier, but only a few since then. Perhaps there will be more patients tomorrow," she said.

He gave a nod of agreement. "The piece I wrote didn't do any harm, I hope."

"You stated the facts," she replied. "At least no one has applied for the assistant position, so I'm not paying a helper yet."

He glanced up from beneath the brim of his hat, and she followed his gaze to see a hawk gliding on a current.

"From what you said earlier, though, it sounds like you've grown accustomed to getting by on very little. Your father cut you off financially after you called off our engagement, did he not?"

"Most definitely."

"How did you pay for university?" When she didn't answer right away, he said quickly, "I'm sorry. That was a rude question."

"I appreciate forthrightness," she replied honestly. "I worked several jobs to pay my way. I cleaned every evening for a barber. I did laundry for a family. I stayed with a statesman's elderly mother and had a small room in her home with meals included."

"When did you study?"

"Every chance I got. Mostly at night."

Sam looked at Marlys, and his admiration hitched a notch higher. He'd always known she was smart and ambitious, but her fortitude and passion equaled that of the great men he'd known. The strength and determination that shone on her face made her even more striking, with her beautiful porcelain skin and winged brows a shade darker than her bright chestnut hair. Little wonder he'd been smitten with her, but had she ever felt drawn to him? She'd accepted his proposal to appease her father, but now he believed she'd never felt anything beyond a sense of duty. No man wanted to feel like an obligation.

He didn't really blame her. They were too different. They wanted different things. He'd wanted to marry and start a family. She'd been ardent about her education and medicine. It was better she'd been strong enough to end it than to allow them to make a mistake and enter an ill-fated marriage. "And once you'd graduated, you started looking for a place to locate?"

"I shared a practice with a colleague for a time, but we struggled. Most city people who appreciated advanced medicine already had established doctors. I'd followed the articles and ads about Western locations for some time. The more I looked into the new towns, the more I saw the possibility of pioneer communities being open to new and unconventional practices. Once I had the idea, I couldn't let go of it. I saw several advertisements encouraging brides and business owners to Cowboy Creek. I wrote the town council, and the town clerk sent me a map and a list of available properties."

"How did you select your location?"

"Because of my need for water, it wasn't difficult. I wanted access to the well between the bath house on Second and the laundry on First. Also it's only three businesses in from the main thoroughfare."

"Maybe I could include more of your personal story in the next article."

"I forgot for a moment I was speaking to the journalist. I'll think about it."

"Being a journalist is a big part of who I am. Like being a doctor is an important part of who you are. A person's passions are part of them."

"Like being a writer also makes you eloquent."

"Am I?" He glanced over to find her looking up at him. For the first time he felt self-conscious in her presence.

"You have the ability to reach people. You're able to inspire sympathy or understanding of anything you're focusing on."

That was quite a compliment. "You said you'd read my book."

"And several articles."

His book was a personal account, and it perhaps revealed more about him than he was comfortable with her learning. He didn't know why her opinion was different than anyone else's. People across the nation had read his book, and he wasn't concerned about their reactions.

Sam couldn't afford to expend any energy in the direction his thoughts kept leading. Enough was enough.

* * *

They rode in silence for a while. James rode back to let them know they would be arriving at the Cheyenne camp before long. Anticipation quivered in Marlys's stomach. She'd been looking forward to this for so long. Meeting the indigenous people was part of her reason for leaving the East.

"James will test the temperature with these people before we approach," Sam warned. "Strangers can be a threat to them, and we don't know their situation today. They may welcome us, they may not."

"Understood."

They drew near the village, where smoke trailed out the tops of tipis arranged in an encampment. Two skinny dogs ran forward, one barking, the other sniffing the horses. Half a dozen braves stood facing them, as though they'd been alerted to the visitors. They wore deerskin leggings, moccasins and coats and hats made of fur.

James signaled for Sam to halt the wagon and rode forward. "*Haáahe.*"

"*Néhetáa'e. Nétsėhésenėstsehe?*" the tallest of the Indians called out.

"He asks if I talk Cheyenne." James nodded. "*Héehe'e.*"

"*Tósa'e néhéstahe.*"

"He asks where we're from." James spoke several more words, gesturing to Sam and Marlys. She heard their names, and James mentioned Cowboy Creek.

The Indian seemed to ask more questions and pointed at her.

James turned. "He wants you to climb down so he can look at you."

"I'll help you." Sam climbed down and came around the rear of the wagon to assist her to the ground.

With one of the dogs sniffing at the hem of her riding

skirt, Marlys took several steps toward the Indian. Sam remained right beside her.

"*Nétsêhésenêstsehe*," he said to her.

"Red Bird asks if you speak Cheyenne," James said. She shook her head.

"*Má'heóná'e*," James told them. "That's the word for medicine woman," he explained.

"Tell him I have medicine. Soap and blankets. Are there any children?"

James spoke with Red Bird and then turned to her. "There are about twenty children. A few are sick. Their medicine woman is old and feeble, and her helper died."

"I can help them."

James relayed her message, and Red Bird pointed to the wagon.

"He asks to see," James said.

Marlys gestured for Red Bird to follow and led him to the back of the wagon, where she climbed up onto the bed to open crates and show him the contents.

Red Bird looked down at her. His eyes were so obsidian they shone, his dark skin lined from the sun, though he didn't appear old. He had a broad nose and a long scar from his lower lip across his chin, but in his uniqueness she found him strikingly beautiful.

"*Ho'eohe*," he said, and gestured for her to join him. Sam was right there to help her down, and she followed Red Bird toward the encampment. Red Bird spoke to James on the way past.

"Leave the wagon, but bring the supplies," James said to Sam.

The other Indian men picked up crates as well and followed.

Red Bird led Marlys to the largest tipi, called out before entering and held the flap aside for her. She took a deep breath and followed him into what appeared to be their chief's dwelling. A man whose long, coarse black hair was shot with steel-gray exchanged words with Red Bird. Red Bird led Marlys forward. *"Né'seéstse'hena."*

"Take your coats off," James interpreted.

The three of them did so, and the chief gestured for them to sit near the fire.

Among those in the tipi was a woman who was perhaps the chief's wife and two women not much older than Marlys, as well as several children, ranging in ages. All the children sat quietly behind their mothers.

"Éhame." The chief pointed to Sam.

"Chief Woodrow Black Snake asks if you are her husband," James explained before he answered for Sam.

Red Bird spoke to Chief Black Snake, and apparently the chief asked to see the contents of Marlys's crates and burlap bags. The men who had accompanied them displayed the contents.

Marlys explained that the blankets were gifts and that the bundles and jars contained medicine.

The chief sent for someone, and after several minutes a brave helped an aged woman into the tipi. She inspected the herbs and opened jars to sniff and taste, then she spoke to the chief. He signed for her to take a seat, and Red Bird helped her lower herself before the fire. Her cloudy black eyes surveyed the newcomers with keen interest.

The chief directed the two young women, and they brought the guests water, roasted nuts and jerky. Marlys instinctively understood they were being treated as honored guests, and the impoverished Cheyenne's generosity brought swift tears to her eyes.

She asked James to tell her the Cheyenne word for every item in her sight, even the women and children's names.

The women nodded, and the children smiled shyly when she said their names.

"*Néá'ee*," she said, thanking them. "Tell them it's our pleasure to give them blankets."

James spoke and got up to take the stack of blankets and place it before the oldest woman. She in turn handed one to each of her daughters or daughters-in-law, kept one for herself and instructed Red Bird to give one to the elderly medicine woman. The old woman touched the plain gray wool and nodded at Marlys. "*Néá'ee*."

The chief's wife spoke to one of her daughters, and the younger woman went to a huge woven basket under the slant of the tipi and returned with a folded item she placed before Marlys.

The blanket the old woman had given her was woven with colorful stripes, obviously made from the dyes of berries and plants. The edges had been sewn with short, soft leather fringe. Marlys blinked. She wasn't an emotional person, and she understood these proud people's honor depended on an equal trade, but this poignant communion between people of different languages and skin colors touched her heart and soul. *Thank You, Lord, for showing me their hearts and giving me this important moment.*

"James, please tell her it's beautiful and will keep me warm for many years."

James translated.

The woman raised her chin, and her daughters smiled. She then spoke directly to James. "*Teke' váótséva éháomóhtâhéotse.*"

They conversed for a moment.

"She says a girl is sick with a fever. She asks if your medicine is powerful enough to heal Little Deer."

Marlys's heart leaped. She wanted nothing more than to help these people. She'd touted herself as a great healer—

now was her chance to prove her worth. "I know little of their needs or the diseases common to this land and the native tribes," she said aloud in an uncommon moment of self-doubt.

"Most likely they are immune or have cures for the sicknesses common to them, but the ones that baffle them are those they've contracted from the whites." Sam gave her an encouraging nod.

She stood. "Take me to her."

After a brief interaction, one of the braves who had accompanied them to the chief helped the old woman stand and gestured for Marlys to join them. Sam got her coat, and he and James stood. "Bring those two crates and my bag," she said, and they left the chief's tipi.

The brave spoke to James, and James told them his name was Gray Cloud. They referred to the medicine woman as *Hausisse*.

"What does it mean?" Marlys asked.

James spoke to the woman. "She said to some it's *She Knows*, to others it's *Old Woman*."

Marlys followed them, trudging through trampled-down snow to another lodge, this one painted with animals and figures of women and children. "I like *She Knows*."

Inside, there were several children, three lying under fur robes near the fire in the center.

"*Teke' váótséva éháomóhtâhéotse*," She Knows said.

"This is Little Deer," James interpreted. "She has been sick for many days. The fever doesn't leave."

"What have you given her?" Marlys asked.

After a discussion James replied with the remedies the old medicine woman had given the child. Marlys instructed Sam to open the crates. He did as she asked and then took a seat away from the patients.

Marlys asked for water and used it to wash her hands.

The child's mother gave her a concerned look. "I want to help Little Deer," Marlys said.

James interpreted their conversation.

"I am Blue Water. My child is not strong. She does not eat."

"May I uncover her and look at her?"

Blue Water nodded and pulled the fur robe away.

The child's tongue was cracked. She was painfully thin, her skin hot and dry. Marlys examined her for rashes or cuts, even checked the bottom of her feet, which were peeling.

"Are her feet sick?"

"No. The fever causes her skin to peel. We need to cool her down. Sam, bring me water that isn't too warm, please." She got cloths from her a crate. "Let's move her away from the fire."

With a minimum of effort she relayed her desire to find a vessel large enough to hold the girl. Gray Cloud brought an enormous but surprisingly lightweight bowl-shaped tub carved from a wood she'd never seen before.

Marlys and Little Deer's mother made a secluded spot away from the heat by draping a blanket from the lodge poles and bathed the child in the tepid mineral water. They carried her to her relocated bed, and Blue Water attempted to cover her. Marlys stopped her with a gentle touch on her arm. "Let's allow her skin and body to cool."

Blue Water settled back with a nod.

Marlys draped only a light covering over her torso and gave Little Deer spoonfuls of water. Roused by the cool bath, the girl swallowed thirstily.

Marlys dissolved fermented soybean and coriander into water, as well as a combination of honeysuckle and forsythia powders, and spoon-fed it to her. She Knows came and watched, asked to sniff and taste. Marlys explained the curative properties of the mixture. Although she didn't understand the cause of Little Deer's fever, she'd learned this restorative Chinese fever remedy as a last resort, and it seemed She Knows had already used her vast knowledge of medicines to try the more common options.

Marlys had the education to remember and apply therapies for symptoms, but she'd never felt as humble or inadequate as she did at that moment. "Lord, You are the Great Physician. Help me understand how to treat this child. Touch her with Your hand of mercy, in Jesus's name." She glanced at the dividing blanket and called softly, "Sam."

"I'm here."

"Pray."

Chapter Five

$\diamond$

At the unaccustomed qualm in Marlys's voice, Sam experienced a thread of concern. She now understood the magnitude of coming here and claiming an ability to help these people. If her treatment didn't help the Cheyenne girl, and she worsened—or even worse, died—the Cheyenne could perceive it as intended harm on Marlys's part. Right now there were more lives than Little Deer's at stake.

"I'm praying," he answered. "I have every confidence in you, and confidence in God to guide you and to heal the girl."

He prayed. Time passed slowly. He took his journal from his satchel and wrote for an hour or more. James's and Marlys's quiet voices blended with the sound of the other children and their mothers and the crackle of the fire, and he may have dozed.

Becoming aware that the log had burned down, he went out and found a pile of cut wood and put another log on the fire. Unaccustomed to a stranger in their tent, the Indian women watched him warily.

There was nothing to do but wait right now, and his body grew tense from inaction. With a dozen eyes on him he went to his horse and unsheathed an ax, walking toward a stand of trees, where he pulled brush and fallen limbs into a pile and chopped a log into pieces. Periodically he left the ax in a limb to check on Marlys and James. Marlys was methodically checking each child and their mother for signs of sickness. She was treating a small boy when he went back to his task.

Eventually, a woman brought a sling and piled all the wood he'd chopped. It was the women's job to find and cut wood, so she probably found his actions curious. But she did not protest. She carried the sling filled with firewood back to their communal pile several times. On her return, she brought him a steaming wooden bowl and handed it to him.

He nodded, drank the hot broth, and returned the bowl.

She wiped it out with snow and walked away.

Sam glanced at the sun. It was late afternoon. If they stayed much longer, they would be traveling home in the dark. He trudged back to the lodge and entered. The children were seated at the fire eating savory-smelling roasted meat. His belly rumbled. That broth hadn't been filling.

"Marlys, we need to think about eating and leaving. We can't travel in the dark."

"You must be hungry. Get the basket I packed and share it with James." She came around the side of the draped blanket. "I'm not leaving."

He swallowed the first words that sprang to his tongue and pursed his lips in frustration. "We can't stay. I have to get back to August."

"You go. I'll stay."

"I'm not leaving you alone here."

"I am not leaving tonight."

James was seated far enough away to give Marlys, her patient and the girl's mother privacy, but close enough to interpret. He got to his feet and stretched his legs. "What if I go back, keep August with Hannah and me overnight and come back in the morning?"

"I've learned enough words to communicate well enough," Marlys agreed.

Sam ran a hand through his hair. Short of throwing her over his shoulder, he wasn't going to get her to go back until she was ready. He might have figured as much. He glanced at the other children in the lodge, at James and back to Marlys. He raised a hand in defeat. "All right."

She hurried toward him. "Thank you."

"You didn't leave me much choice. Let James know if there's anything you want him to bring tomorrow. James, I'm going to get the basket of food. You'll eat with us before you leave."

Once the basket was opened, the curious children crept from their places and sat close. Sam broke off pieces of rye bread and piled them into a woven bowl. He gave away all the hardtack, and James passed on it, as well. In the Army, he'd eaten enough of the tasteless unleavened biscuits to last him a lifetime. The Cheyenne youngsters got over their shyness to accept the food and join them. Marlys unwrapped smoked fish, and the aroma drew the women forward, too.

The Cheyenne women gave their guests wooden bowls of roasted game and tender cooked roots. Marlys cut a dried apple pie into a dozen slivers, so each child and mother had a tiny piece.

James made them a pot of coffee with a dented pot he carried in his saddlebags, emptied it and packed to leave. "I'll bring more food in morning."

Sam walked to the edge of the camp with him.

"Nothing else we could've done," James said.

"She's immovable when she has her mind made up. I'll pay you double."

"Once we got here it didn't seem like a job," James admitted. "After seeing those children, I was thankful she planned this."

Sam couldn't disagree. "Safe trip home. Please tell August I'm well, not to worry, and I will be home tomorrow."

He watched James ride away, said a prayer for his safety and another for August to feel safe that night, and trudged back to the lodge.

After the meal was cleared away, Marlys continued her examinations of the other children. None were as sick as Little Deer, and some were only there with a sibling who suffered from symptoms. She Knows had settled onto a pallet of furs, her watchful gaze on Marlys, but had seemingly acknowledged the white woman was there to help.

Marlys and Blue Water bathed Little Deer one more time as night fell. The child roused this time and watched Marlys with uncertain black eyes. Her mother spoke softly, soothing her. They had her settled for the night when a brave entered the lodge and swiftly crossed to the child's side. He knelt beside her and spoke to Blue Water. She replied, and the Indian's eyes settled on Marlys, taking in her hair, her now-wrinkled apron and the array of her supplies.

He returned his attention to what Marlys now assumed was his daughter, and gently touched her face and hands. The girl's temperature had cooled considerably, but she was still warm. After a few minutes he left.

After tending to the fire, the mothers settled their children down for the night and lay beside them.

Marlys gave Little Deer more water and another dose of the remedy she'd prepared. Blue Water unrolled two pallets and gestured to Marlys and Sam.

"*Néá'ee,*" Marlys thanked her.

She glanced at Sam.

"I'm not leaving you alone," he said. "I'll be right here."

"Nor do I want you to go."

He slid one of the pallets several feet away from hers, in plain sight of all the women, and stretched out on top of the comfortable furs.

He listened more than watched as Marlys washed her face and hands and used what looked like a porcupine tail that one of the women handed her on her hair. She was a curiosity. She didn't conform to what their society would consider feminine fashion. Her hair was uncommonly short, and her clothing functional and undecorated. He'd never seen her wear jewelry or drench herself in perfume. Instead, she smelled always like lavender and hyssop and other natural scents. Her movements, her voice, everything about her was feminine, even without ornamentation or fripperies.

Back during their short engagement in Philadelphia, they had discussed literature and politics, and he'd learned she was intelligent. She'd never hidden her desire for education or her interest in medicine, so he'd understood her ambition. But he'd never seen her as she'd been today. Fearless. Impervious. Undeterred. *Compassionate. Kind.*

He reeled those thoughts in as soon as they'd slipped into his consciousness. This was the woman who had broken off their engagement because of her ambitions. She didn't have time or patience for a relationship. She wasn't inclined to set her career aside and focus on a marriage. It was plain that she was still as determined as ever to broaden her scope of understanding and knowledge, to discover as much of the world as was possible.

People were who they were. She couldn't be expected to change for him. He hadn't expected it then. He didn't expect it now.

She had needed his help to travel here, to make this happen. Another protector would have done just as well. She didn't specifically need Sam.

That fact reached a nearly forgotten, well-guarded portion of his heart and carved a fresh slice. He closed his eyes against the shimmer of her hair in the firelight. The interior of this lodge was surprisingly warm, the skins beneath him soft. He dozed and dreamed of summer during his childhood.

Marlys slept lightly, checking on Little Deer and finding her sleeping more restfully. Before dawn she woke to sounds of the community outside the tipi and went to find the child's fever gone. "Thank You, Lord."

She woke Blue Water by gently touching her shoulder. The woman's dark eyes opened in fear, and she sat, her terrified gaze darting to her child.

"No, she's better," Marlys told her. "Come see. *Ho'eohe.*"

The woman scrambled from her bed and leaned over Little Deer. She touched her face and neck, rolled back her covering and examined her arms and legs. Tears of joy formed in her eyes, and when she looked at Marlys, they fell unheeded. "*Néá'ee. Éévaéše'továho.*"

She touched her breast with the tips of her fingers and then touched Marlys's chest.

Marlys smiled. She didn't need a translator to understand Blue Water's mother's heart was grateful. She was no different than any other mother of any other people or skin color. Her heart was no different. Love knew no boundaries. Love translated into any language.

Sam and the other Cheyenne in the lodge woke and came near to see what was happening for themselves. She Knows shuffled forward in her fur boots, and Blue Water helped her lower herself to sit beside the child. She listened to her heart. Listened to her breathing, looked in her mouth, examined the bottom of her feet. She turned and spoke to one of the older children.

He pulled on a robe and darted from the tipi. Several minutes later he returned with Little Deer's father and the chief. Woodrow Black Snake held a conversation with She Knows and Blue Water. They all nodded and gestured. He exited as suddenly as he'd arrived. Sam left the lodge while the Cheyenne mothers washed and groomed themselves and their children.

Blue Water brought Marlys fragrant mint water and twigs and indicated she should brush her teeth. She and another woman they called Neha brushed Marlys's hair, while coating the strands with an unknown substance they lathered on their hands. They spoke in hushed tones, and Marlys guessed they wondered why her hair was cut so short. The process was disconcerting. Marlys's mother had died when she was very young, and she'd taken care of her own needs for as long as she could remember. With persistent focus, however, they managed to secure short braids and fasten them with beaded leather strips.

They brought her coat and led her from the lodge across the encampment in the crisp morning air. The aromatic smell of cooking meat made her mouth water. Together they entered the chief's tent, where Sam already waited. He raised his eyebrows in surprise at her appearance.

"I have no idea what's going on," she said. "I wish James would arrive."

"I have a feeling it's a celebration of some sort, and you're the guest of honor."

His assumption made sense after the women's ministrations. "It's a whole lot better than what I was imagining last night."

He brought his gaze to hers. "You never let on that you had any doubts."

She nodded. "No. I never let on." She turned her gaze

back to the gathering of Cheyenne before looking to Sam once more. "Thank you. For bringing me."

He made a noncommittal sound.

They were seated across from the chief at the fire, and others crowded around them. The women served them roasted meat on a wooden platter, which they shared. Marlys tasted it and found it unlike anything she'd eaten, but tasty and tender.

"What is it?" she asked.

"Maybe elk or antelope," he replied.

"Do you think sharing this food is a sacrifice for them? I mean, are we taking away from their winter supply?"

"They have meat hung in trees. If there's no big game on the land where they're allowed to hunt, the Army probably brought it to them."

"They're buffalo hunters, aren't they?"

He nodded. "This tribe seems to have been left on their own and not relocated. The Army knows they're here, so the Army is in a difficult situation, protecting the tribe while safeguarding settlers, as well. When the Indians are unable to hunt, they have to travel or starve. So if the Army is delivering supplies, they're hoping to keep them here so they know where they are."

Their discussion continued until James arrived and was given food.

"Red Bird told me the little girl is better today."

"Our prayers worked," she replied.

"And your Chinese remedy," James added.

Sam nodded, surprising her.

"How did August fare the night?" Sam asked.

"He ate supper and played with the baby. Ava laughed and smiled at him. Hannah read to them for a while, then she made him a bed, and he went right to sleep. She was planning to walk him to school this morning."

"Thank you," Sam said.

It had been a sacrifice for Sam to remain here with her and not go home to his son. Marlys wouldn't have blamed him for leaving last night, but she was thankful for his company and protection. She felt doubly indebted. Hannah had taken on additional duties for her sake, as well. "I will be happy to prepare a mineral bath treatment for Hannah to thank her." She gave James a thankful smile. "She can bring the baby, and I'll care for her while she relaxes."

Before long James went out and returned with a crate holding jars of peaches. He opened several and indicated the mothers should share them with the children. The Cheyenne spoke among themselves, smiling and obviously enjoying the treat.

"Where did you get peaches?" she asked.

"I stopped at Remmy's and bought all that Mrs. Herne had left for sale."

"Thank you," Marlys told him. "I'll repay you."

"No. This is my pleasure," he said.

Two of the women took the jars and returned with them washed clean and set them before James. James spoke to them, and they nodded and smiled at each other, carrying away the basket of glass jars.

"I'm going to check on Little Deer and two other children, and then we can head home," Marlys said.

They were headed back toward Cowboy Creek by midmorning. The ride home didn't seem as long as the trip getting to the encampment. Marlys was justifiably satisfied with the experience. She had told She Knows that she would come again to bring her herbs and to learn about the roots and leaves the medicine woman used.

She offered to pay Sam and James, but both refused.

"Thank you, James," she said as the two men unloaded

crates at her office. "I couldn't have made the trip without you."

"I'm glad I joined you."

"Perhaps you'd be willing to spend a few hours teaching me more Cheyenne?"

"Sure. I can meet whenever you want." He mounted his horse and headed for the livery.

"You owe two days for the wagon," she said to Sam. "I'll pay."

"I'll let you pay for that," he replied.

She took money from a metal lockbox and gave it to him. "Thank you for agreeing to go. And for taking the night away from August. I'm not much of a cook, but maybe I could take the two of you to supper one evening."

"That would be nice." He tucked the coins in his pocket.

News of her trip to the Cheyenne camp spread through town that week. When Marlys stopped at Booker & Son general store for supplies midweek, the skinny young man behind the counter held up one hand. "How."

She gave him a puzzled frown.

"You heap big Injun doctor? Need something to smoke in your peace pipe?" He laughed heartily at his own joke. "Don't see why you're wasting your time with them anyway."

She narrowed her eyes. "What's your name?"

"Eugene. You're the lady doctor, right?"

She held her irritation and asked, "Who is the owner of this establishment?"

"That would be Mr. Booker."

Mr. Booker came out of the back, where the portly man had apparently overheard her question, and pushed his spectacles up his nose. "I'm Abram Booker. What can I do for you?"

"Young Eugene here seems to think it's humorous to disparage potential customers."

He turned to his employee. "What have you done now, Eugene?"

"I was just havin' a little fun with the lady doc."

"I didn't find it fun or funny at all. And I can just as easily take all my business to Mr. Hagermann's. He's always respectful."

Mr. Booker clenched his jaw. The store owner's face turned red, and color crept all the way into his thinning hair. "Apologize to Dr. Boyd, Eugene."

Eugene didn't appear very pleased to submit to the demand. He lowered his chin to his skinny chest and held his body tense. Through tight lips, he said, "I'm sorry, Dr. Boyd. I didn't mean no offense."

"I accept your apology, Eugene. I strongly advise you to consider your words before speaking. It's my belief that we have much to learn from other cultures, and when people respect one another, the exchange of information benefits everyone. You might find it ironic that I treated sick Cheyenne children with a Chinese remedy. Those children didn't seem to mind when they got better."

"Yes, ma'am."

"Eugene, go sweep the back room now," Mr. Booker instructed him. "What can I help you with today, Doctor?"

"I'd like to order an array of jars, similar to something you would use to display candy."

"I can show you what I ordered for my own use."

Abram Booker was helpful and courteous, and she didn't see Eugene again while she was in the store.

Her next stop was to pick up the second pair of boots she'd ordered at Godwin's. Opal was pleased to see her. "I want to accept your offer for a mineral bath," she said. "What would be a good time? I don't want to inconvenience you."

"Any time is a good time," Marlys replied. "Come right now if you like."

"Well…" Opal glanced around the small boot shop. "Let me just check with Amos."

Her husband was pleased to see his wife take time for herself and waved them off. It was a short walk to her office, with Opal carrying the baby, and Marlys let them in and put wood in the stove to heat water. It didn't take long to fill one of the tubs.

"I've never seen bathing tubs like these," Opal told her.

"They're made deep and yet narrow, so the entire body can be immersed without using as much water as a larger oval tub takes." Marlys added oils and minerals and dissolved them in the water. "I'll take the baby and sit just outside. We'll be fine." She showed Opal the towels and told her to relax and take her time.

"Well, Richard, we're getting to be friends, don't you think?"

The bundled baby opened his eyes at her voice but soon closed them again. He squirmed a bit, and instinctively, she bounced him in her arms until he stilled. She'd been around more babies in her short time here than in her whole prior life. It was reassuring that after all the death and sorrow of the brothers' war that civilization was now replenishing itself. It didn't take a scholar to understand the psychology of bringing their country back to life with a new generation.

She felt a grave responsibility to the children, to August and all of these little ones. She had knowledge to share, skills to teach, and she needed to impart as much as she could—to leave her mark on history and make a difference.

She'd always been a hundred percent confident of her choices. She was still confident she'd been true to herself and her ideals. But a barely discernable question rose in her thoughts. Was she missing out on something? Would she eventually live to regret she had turned her back on relationships, on friendship, on marriage…on Sam?

Chapter Six

Rather than eat at the hotel again, Sam prepared a meal of sliced ham and boiled potatoes for himself and August. They sat at the tiny table in their long one-room quarters behind the newspaper office, and Sam said grace.

"I miss Grandmother," August said.

"I know you do."

"Why couldn't she have moved to Kansas with us?"

"She has her own life to live, son. She has friends, and she likes to travel."

"I could have gone with her."

"No, you couldn't have. We belong together, you and I. We're a family."

August looked at him, his eyes wide and dark and still filled with the same pain and confusion Sam had prayed to know how to erase. "But there's only you and me."

Sam ignored the ache in his chest and resisted placing a hand over the spot. "Two can be a family."

August ate a few bites and laid down his fork. "May I be excused?"

Sam steepled his fingers over his plate and studied his son. "Two more bites of your ham."

August took the two bites and lifted his gaze.

"You're excused." Sam cleared the table and washed the few dishes.

August was lying on his narrow cot when he'd finished. "Let's start a new book," Sam suggested.

"I can read by myself."

"I know you can, but if we read together, we can both enjoy the story."

August didn't respond, so Sam went to the shelf of books and perused a few titles. *"Life of Dr. Benjamin Franklin,"* he read. "I like this one. You like history, and it's interesting. It's written by Mr. Franklin himself."

"I already know he invented the glass armonica and that he experimented with electricity and that's how he got famous."

"But did you know he was a newspaperman?"

August shook his head.

"Benjamin was about fifteen when his brother started the first newspaper in Boston that did more than reprint articles from overseas. *The Courant* did opinion pieces, advertisements and printed ship schedules."

He pulled a chair close to where his boy lay. "Benjamin wanted to write for the paper, too, but he was only an apprentice, so at night he secretly wrote letters to the paper and signed them Silence Dogood."

"Who was Silence Dogood?"

"A name he made up. In these letters he gave advice and criticized what was going on, like how women were being treated. Then Benjamin would sneak the letters under the print shop door during the night. Everyone liked the letters and wanted to know who Silence Dogood was."

August's interest had perked up. "Did he tell them?"

"He finally confessed. Benjamin's brother James's friends thought Ben was clever and funny, but his brother was jealous."

"Then what?"

"Why don't we read it together, and you can learn all about Benjamin's interesting life."

"Yes, let's read it. Will we finish it tonight?"

Sam chuckled. "It will take a few evenings, but we'll read it all, I promise."

August nodded his agreement. "All right."

"'Imagining it may be equally agreeable to you to learn the circumstances of my life, many of which you are unacquainted with, and expecting the enjoyment of a few weeks' uninterrupted leisure, I sit down to write them. Besides, there are some other inducements that excite me to this—'"

"What's inducements, Papa?"

"Things that spurred him to write."

"Oh."

"'—that excite me to this undertaking. From the poverty and obscurity in which I was born, and in which I passed my earliest years, I have raised myself to a state of affluence and some degree of celebrity in the world.'"

"What is affluence?"

Sam stopped reading and couldn't help a smile. It might take longer than he thought to read this book.

It was a sunny day the following week, but cold with a bitter wind when Marlys entered the laundry and stomped snow from her feet on the mat inside the door. She took all her sheets and towels to the laundry behind her own office, but brought her personal items to Mr. Lin's. She liked the way he rinsed clothing and pressed it so it smelled fresh.

A pretty woman with a green felt hat covering most of her blond hair stood at the counter. She smiled at Marlys. "Are you Dr. Boyd?"

"Yes," Marlys answered.

"I'm Leah Gardner. I've heard so much about you from Pippa, and I've been meaning to come introduce myself, but I've had a young mother and baby to look after, plus caring for my own newborn…"

"Please, don't apologize. You must be speaking of the Austrian woman? Aunt Mae mentioned her to me."

"Yes, that's her. Do you have a few minutes to get better acquainted right now? Perhaps we could have tea and pie at the bakery?"

Surprised, Marlys thought only a moment. "I do have time."

"Good." She turned to Mr. Lin, who had wrapped a bundle and set it on the counter. "Mr. Lin, Dr. Boyd and I will be back for our laundry after we've had tea. Thank you."

Understanding, Mr. Lin bowed. "I have it right here when you come back."

Marlys spoke to Mr. Lin in his own language, and he smiled and shooed them away.

"You speak Chinese?" Leah asked on the way out the door. "I sure could have used your help when I was first bringing my laundry. Mr. Lin does an excellent job, but I don't want my kitchen towels starched."

Marlys laughed.

The bakery was on the next corner to the west, so it took only minutes to arrive and find one of the six small tables that lined the wall. Marlys removed her scarf and hung it on her coat on the back of her chair.

"Your hair is extraordinary," Leah said on an appreciative breath.

Marlys touched the hair that barely reached her shoulders. Leah had a head of wavy golden curls she had somehow swept into a knot, with feminine wisps that hung against her neck and around her ears. "I haven't done anything with it."

"The color is so rich. I'd give anything to not be so pale."

The young woman was anything but pale. She was exquisitely golden and lovely. "You have a new baby?"

"Yes. She's at home with Valentine. The woman is a jewel. My husband hired her because I was on bed rest before Evie's birth. She can cook. She keeps the household running smoothly, and she likes to have Evie for an afternoon every so often, so I have time to run errands and see friends."

"It sounds like a perfect arrangement."

"It is. I came to Cowboy Creek as a mail-order bride. I hoped to find work as a midwife and make an adequate match for a husband. I was widowed and pregnant, and who should show up at the station but Daniel Gardner, one of my childhood friends? He proposed to me right off, and after a rocky start we realized we were in love. He's the kindest, most generous man I've ever known."

Leah fairly glowed when she spoke of her husband.

"That's quite a story."

"Good afternoon." A man in an apron greeted them and set cups and a steaming pot before them. "What kind of pie would you like?"

They ordered, and Leah poured the tea. "Tell me about you."

"I studied in Philadelphia," Marlys said. "I wasn't successful in establishing a practice there, so I came here hoping my methods of healing would be appreciated."

"Are they?"

"Quite a few people are curious about me, but not many are actually patients so far."

"I'm sure they'll warm to you the longer you're here. Do you have family back in Philadelphia?"

"I have only my father, and we're…not close," Marlys finished.

Leah sipped her tea.

"I didn't conform to his ideals or wishes. I've always been interested in many types of studies, including languages. He indulged me for a time, but when I was of an age, he put his foot down and demanded I marry. Against my better judgment I accepted suitors. I even accepted a proposal for a short time."

Leah's blue eyes widened. "You were engaged, and you called it off?"

Marlys nodded.

"Did you learn something about the man that displeased you?"

She shook her head. "No. Not at all. He's smart, educated, interesting."

Leah prompted her to elaborate. "Kind?"

"Yes."

"Handsome?"

Her cheeks warmed. "Very."

Leah splayed her hand flat on the table. "But...?"

"But I simply didn't want a husband or children. I wanted to go to university."

"So, you were true to yourself. There's nothing shameful about that."

"My father disagreed."

"So you studied and became a doctor. That's an accomplishment to be proud of."

Marlys gave her a weak smile and picked up her cup. "Yes, I thought so."

The aromatic tea was strong and hot.

Leah tilted her head. "Do you have any regrets?"

The thought-provoking question made Marlys uncomfortable. "I regret entering into the engagement in the first place." She considered for a moment and then admitted. "Telling the man I made a mistake was difficult."

"I'm sure it was." Leah made a sympathetic face with her pretty lips drawn down at the corners. "What else could you have done?"

"I had two choices. Marry him and feel that I'd missed out on the rest of my life—or tell the truth." Her father had accused her of being spoiled and selfish. He'd said unkind things.

Sam, however, hadn't made one accusatory remark. "Sam told me he didn't hold my decision against me," she revealed softly. "He said if I wasn't one hundred percent sure I wanted to be his wife, it was better he learned it right then and not later."

"Of course." Leah nodded. "He wanted someone completely sure about marrying him."

"I told you he was a nice man."

"Do you know if he found someone?"

"He married."

"Do you know his wife?"

"We never met. She died in childbirth, so he's a widower."

"Oh, my. The poor fellow. And the baby?"

"He's eight already."

Leah touched the pot, testing the temperature, and poured them each another cup. "You certainly know a lot about the man. Have you kept in touch?"

Was this what making friends was like? Marlys stared at her cup and measured how she was feeling about telling Leah about Sam. Truthfully, she wasn't uncomfortable. The other woman was clearly concerned for her and interested in her story. Her stomach dipped in a peculiar fashion as she formed her next words. "We didn't keep in touch at all." She lifted her gaze. "I hadn't seen him in all those years until a few weeks ago."

"Until before you left Philadelphia?"

"No." She shook her head. "After I arrived here."

The pretty blonde sat up straight. "He's here? In Cowboy Creek? The kind, handsome, interesting man? Do I know him?"

"I don't know. Have you met the new newspaper owner?"

Leah blinked. "Samuel Woods Mason, the author? *He* was your fiancé?"

"That's the one."

"I've read his book. I told you I spent a lot of time resting before the baby came. You've read it, of course."

"I have," she admitted, feeling lighter somehow, as though she'd just had a weight lifted from her shoulders. Leah didn't seem to think Marlys had been selfish or spoiled. "It seems, Leah, that you truly understand. How can that be when our lives are so different?"

"Perhaps not as different as you think."

"What do you mean?"

"I didn't mention I'd broken off an engagement, too. For an entirely different reason, though it turned out to be the right choice. I was once engaged to Will Canfield."

Marlys had heard all about the three men who had founded this town. Leah's husband, Daniel Gardner, was one of them, and Will Canfield another.

"We were all childhood friends—Daniel, Will and I— and when we grew old enough for romance, Will and I fell in together. It was puppy love, but it felt real enough for us to get engaged. Then the war came, and Will went off to fight. I believed I would have more security if I married an Army officer rather than Will. It didn't turn out well. I lost several babies, and my husband died before I discovered I was carrying Evie. Now Daniel has accepted her as his own child, and I'm thankful every day that the Lord led me here. But you see, I understand the paths we take aren't always straight and flat. There are plenty of curves and valleys while getting to where we're supposed to be."

Leah had asked Marlys if she had any regrets. Sometimes, lately, when she spent her evenings alone, she wondered if she'd made the right choice. She'd always been so confident, so sure she was fulfilling her one true destiny. These unfamiliar new doubts were insidious, hovering barely outside her consciousness, waiting for an opportunity to inject themselves and become real.

She couldn't acknowledge them, or she might have to admit to cracks in the armor around her confidence. But she would not lose hope.

"How can I pray for you?" Leah's voice was tender with genuine concern.

No one had ever asked that before. She thought a minute. "Things might change if people could give me a chance and trust me."

"I can ask and believe God for that change," Leah said with a smile.

"Thank you for this. The talk, I mean. I appreciate that you took time from your day for us to get to know each other. I've never been very good at making friends."

"Why don't you join us for dinner after church on Sunday? I'd love for you to meet Daniel."

Her new friend's generous invitation took her by surprise. "Well. Yes. Yes, of course. I'd love to."

"We're east of here on Lincoln Boulevard. You can't miss it. My husband built an enormous house, and it sits at an angle on the corner of Third Street. In fact, why don't you just ride home from church with us?"

Marlys hadn't been to church yet, but it was high time she got out and met more people. "It would be my pleasure."

She picked up her laundry and walked home feeling

different somehow, as though by sharing her story she'd found a way to feel not quite so alone. She'd never minded being alone, but since she'd been here, the isolation was more pronounced. Not for long, she reminded herself. She was making friends.

Marlys woke early as usual and made herself breakfast. She'd officially moved out of the boardinghouse, and had taken plenty of time to arrange her small but adequate living area and unpack. She'd ordered a plain pine wardrobe from Mr. Irving, the furniture maker, and he'd finished the wood with a golden stain and varnished it to a sheen. Her garments barely used a third of the space. None of her dresses or skirts were as pretty or as feminine as those Leah and Pippa wore. She'd before never given her attire much thought, purchasing clothing for practicality and function. What would the other women at church think of her?

She paused in front of the mirror, experiencing a moment of rare uncertainty. Did she look like someone people would want to get to know? She recalled Aunt Mae's advice about people being more likely to trust her with their medical concerns if she made their acquaintance. Being part of the community would be helpful. It had been easy to talk with Leah; in fact she'd shared more things with her than she had with anyone ever.

People could like her or not. That had always been her philosophy, and she hadn't lost any sleep over being unpopular. But now it mattered that people liked her. It mattered that they trusted her. She put on her new boots and her coat and headed west, toward the church. Others were walking the same direction, and a carriage passed.

The church, a white frame building with a steeple, was on Second Street. She stepped in line behind a family and climbed the wooden stairs. The interior smelled of new wood and plaster. Stained-glass windows lined the east and west walls, and the morning sun streamed through those windows and reflected colorful rainbows on the polished wood pews and floor.

"Dr. Boyd!" The first person to greet her was a smiling Pippa, dressed in a bright jade dress with gold ruffles over her shoulders and layers of matching ruffles cascading down the skirt. Her bright ginger-gold hair was elaborately curled and fashioned, and jade earbobs dangled from her ears. "I'm so delighted you've joined us this morning! I've told my husband all about you, and I couldn't wait for you to meet him. Dr. Boyd, this is my husband, Gideon Kendricks. Gideon, this is Dr. Boyd."

Gideon was tall, with a shortly cropped beard and his hair combed back away from his forehead. He smiled and accepted the hand she offered.

"You'll sit with us, of course," Pippa said. She glanced over Marlys's shoulder. "Mr. Mason. It's a pleasure to see you this morning."

Marlys turned to discover Sam and August standing just behind her left shoulder.

Chapter Seven

"Dr. Boyd," Sam said.

She nodded. "Mr. Mason."

He held August's hand, and the boy gave Marlys a bashful grin.

"Hello, August."

Melodious notes filled the air as the organist played "O Worship the King."

"Greetings, brothers and sisters," Reverend Taggart called, and people took their seats. Marlys followed Gideon and Pippa. Sam ushered August ahead of him into the same row, so August was seated between the two of them. The boy glanced bashfully up at her and then looked away.

"O worship the King, all glorious above, o gratefully sing His power and His love; our shield and defender, the Ancient of Days, pavilioned in splendor and girded with praise."

Her discomfort inched up a notch, feeling as though the eyes of the townspeople were on her. Voices lifted in song around her, Pippa's stunning soprano, and Sam's mellow baritone, and gradually her self-consciousness dropped away. The music and the lyrics spoke to her, and she enjoyed adding her voice to the others.

"O tell of His might, o sing of His grace, whose robe is the light, whose canopy space. His chariots of wrath the deep thunderclouds form, and dark is His path on the wings of the storm."

The congregation took their seats, skirts rustling, children whispering, and Marlys was taken back to her childhood. She'd spent many Sunday mornings beside her father in church. He'd been a respected leader in the community; she'd been his awkward, studious daughter.

Reverend Taggart read a Psalm and then taught from the book of Matthew. He was a personable speaker, sharing his own experiences, occasionally using humor. He had a huge mustache and smiled often. By the time the service ended, she felt as though she'd known him for a long time. He greeted her as the congregation filed out the door. "It was a pleasure to have you worship with us this morning. I assume you're the lady doctor I've heard about."

"Yes, I'm Marlys Boyd. I enjoyed the service, Reverend Taggart."

"I hope you'll get involved by volunteering. That's how you get to know people."

She thanked him and joined Leah and her husband, who held a blanket-wrapped bundle. "I've got a carriage for the ride home," Daniel said after introducing himself.

"Marlys, this is Evie," Leah told her with a beaming smile.

The infant had fair golden hair and full rosy cheeks. She was wide awake and looking up at Daniel with bright blue eyes. "She's beautiful," Marlys told her honestly.

"I tell both of my girls that every day," Daniel said with a grin.

Leah cast an adoring look at him, and Marlys almost felt as though she was witnessing something private.

He helped the ladies into the conveyance and handed up the baby. Leah settled onto the seat and cuddled Evie.

"I hope you won't be bothered I've invited a few others for dinner as well."

"No, of course not."

The Gardner home was one of the largest in Cowboy Creek. Daniel ushered them in and hung their coats. Leah unwrapped the baby. "She's going to need to be fed right away, so make yourself comfortable in the parlor, and I'll be back in a few minutes."

"Of course." Marlys admired the carpets and furnishings. A photograph of Leah and Daniel in their wedding attire sat on the mantel. Her lace dress was exquisite. Leah had been a stunning bride.

Voices came from the entryway as Daniel greeted more guests.

"Thanks for having us. We haven't had a home-cooked meal since we've been here."

At the familiar voice, she turned.

Sam and August entered the room. August took in his surroundings, acknowledged her with a nod and settled on an ottoman. Daniel invited her into the conversation.

"Is this your first home-cooked meal since Philadelphia, Dr. Boyd?"

"I've enjoyed Aunt Mae's cooking at the boardinghouse," she answered. "Also, the elk or antelope or whatever it was we ate with the Cheyenne was home cooked, so we can't discount that."

"You're right. I'd forgotten."

"How are you, August?"

"Just fine, miss."

"Are you enjoying school now that you've been here a few weeks?"

"Yes, miss."

"What's your favorite subject?"

"I like them all, but I like history the best."

"What's your current study?"

"The travels of Marco Polo."

"He's a very interesting historical figure."

Judging from the enthusiastic smile on August's face, he clearly agreed. "When he was little, his father left him for nine years to go exploring."

"That's a long time."

"But the next time he got to go along. He was seventeen then."

"And traveled to China, didn't they?"

August's brows rose and he nodded. "There were elephants there. And paper money. No one had ever seen paper money before then."

Marlys smiled. "And Kubla Kahn traded with coal, which we use for fuel. I'm sure Marco found that puzzling."

After giving her an appreciative grin, August chattered on about Marco Polo's story and about the book he'd written of his life, which no one believed.

"Until the facts were proven true by other explorers years later," she agreed.

"How do you know so much about Marco Polo?" August asked.

"I've studied history, art and languages since I was your age."

"You did?"

She nodded. "My father indulged me by sending me to boarding school."

August frowned. "Weren't you lonely away from home?"

A normal child would have been, but she wasn't like other children. After her mother's death, she had nannies and tutors, and one instructor was much like another. Her father devoted little time to her whether she was home or not. Boarding school was structured, had purpose, and she felt accomplished and worthwhile when she was learning. She looked into his curious chocolate-brown eyes. "I wasn't lonely. I was happy when I was learning."

"Papa's reading *The Life of Benjamin Franklin* to me every night," he told her.

"Another interesting and very smart man," she replied with a nod.

August gave her a look of admiration. "You must know a whole lot if you're a doctor, too."

"And she speaks more languages than I can keep track of," Sam added.

She glanced at him and noted his relaxed expression. He had seated himself on a divan.

"You do?" August asked, his face bright with interest. "You know other languages? What are they?"

She ticked through the list, and then added, "And a little Cheyenne, thanks to James Johnson."

"Could you teach me Chinese?" August asked.

"I've never taught anyone, but I suppose I could. I have some texts."

August looked to his father. "Can Dr. Boyd teach me?"

Sam exchanged a look with Marlys. He hadn't seen August this interested about anything or anyone before. Their quick connection wounded him slightly, but he cast away the twinge of jealousy. He loved his son dearly. He didn't begrudge him anything, not even this particular friend.

"If Dr. Boyd is willing to teach you, and it's something you want, I don't see why not."

Will Canfield and his pretty redheaded wife, Tomasina, arrived, thus ending their private conversation. Will helped her remove her coat, bringing into view the girth of her belly. Mrs. Canfield looked to be expecting very soon.

"Make yourselves comfortable," Daniel said.

"No such thing," Tomasina replied and stood with a hand at the small of her back. "I'll just stand for now, and that way I won't have to get back up to go to dinner."

"Well, you don't have long," Leah told her. "Valentine is bringing out the food now."

When Leah led them into the dining room and showed them to their seats, he noticed that he and August and Marlys were seated in a row, with Marlys at his side. She obviously noticed, too, because she darted him an uncomfortable glance.

A white wicker bassinet on wheels sat on a side wall in the dining room, and Leah checked on the baby sleeping there before taking her own seat.

"Your china is beautiful," Tomasina commented.

Beside him Marlys touched the edge of the sparkling ivory plates double-edged in gold with a circle pattern of lilies of the valley around the outside.

"Thank you. They were my wedding gift from Daniel. He remembered my mother had dishes just like them when we were young, and he somehow found a whole set."

"Leah, you said you grew up with Will and Daniel, didn't you?" Marlys asked.

"Our parents were close friends, and we were inseparable as children," Leah replied.

"Leah was a tomboy," Daniel added.

"I wouldn't have guessed it," Marlys said.

Leah gestured to Tomasina. "Tomasina there was raised by her father, riding along with cattle drives. She used to have a rodeo show that she ran under the name of Texas Tom. She's a sharpshooter and can ride and rope as well as any man."

Marlys stared at the pretty redhead. "You *can*?"

Her surprise amused Sam. Seeing Tomasina heavy with child, dressed in a rust-colored jacket with white piping and a feminine white blouse underneath, it was hard to imagine her roping a steer, but he'd already heard the stories of her show-stopping arrival in town and her rodeo show performances.

"Well, I won't be doing it anytime soon, but yes, I can," Tomasina said with a wry smile.

The Gardners' housekeeper, Valentine Ewing, served succulent roast beef with vegetables and warm bread. Even August ate with more enthusiasm than Sam had seen from him for a long time.

After the meal was cleared away, she carried in a baking dish, and Leah served them hot rice pudding. The pleasant texture and cinnamon flavor was a treat unlike anything he and August had eaten since his mother had last cooked for them. August ate all of his and glanced at Sam's dish. Sam was prepared to give it to him, when Leah said, "August, growing boys always get seconds when they've cleaned their plates."

He grinned. "Thank you, ma'am."

She served him another helping, and the adults shared a grin.

When coffee was served, they retired to the library and seated themselves on the comfortable overstuffed furniture. Will helped Tomasina lower herself on to an upholstered chair and brought an ottoman for her feet.

Daniel moved the bassinet holding the sleeping baby into the room. He'd built a large home, and he and his wife had filled it with heavy pieces of furniture and attractive carpets and draperies. Sam couldn't see himself with a house as massive or as well-furnished, but he wanted to have a suitable home for August.

His son stood before the rows of shelves and studied the spines of the books.

Daniel joined him. "Are you a reader, young man?"

"Yes, sir. My teacher lets me bring home her own books to read. I take care with them and return them after I've read them."

"That's not surprising since your father is a writer." Daniel glanced over his shoulder. "It's crossed my mind a few times that Cowboy Creek needs a library."

"Perhaps we could hold a fund-raiser," Tomasina suggested. "Like a Wild West show, come spring."

"Of course you'd think of that," Will told her with a smile.

"You're welcome to read any of the books," Daniel told August. Within minutes the boy had chosen one and made himself comfortable on the rug before the fire.

"Thank you for inviting us," Sam told Leah and Daniel. "This is a treat for August. And for me, as well. We haven't eaten a meal like that or enjoyed a relaxing afternoon with pleasant company for a long while."

Marlys sat perched on a velvet divan. "You're kind to include me, too," she added.

Tomasina studied her. "James Johnson and I drove cattle for my father's outfit for years," she said. "I think of him as a brother. He told me about your visit to the Cheyenne camp. He was pretty impressed that you treated a sick child, and she improved right off. Most people don't care about the Indians, or they want to run them off. What made you go to them?"

"Part of the reason I came here was to learn about the plains tribes. I believe we have a lot to learn from them."

"You didn't mention that in your piece on Dr. Boyd, Sam," Will brought up. "Did you deliberately avoid the topic?"

"To be honest, yes," he answered. "I'd hoped to appeal to the broadest audience possible with the first article. And then later fill in information that might be considered controversial. The way news travels in this town, I may have made the wrong decision. An interview with Marlys herself is probably the best way to present her."

Marlys gave him her full attention, and he gave her an apologetic glance.

"Dr. Boyd tends to come on full throttle, and people either appreciate her approach or they don't," he added.

She raised her eyebrows and leveled her gold-flecked gaze on him.

"Would anyone like their coffee refilled?" Leah asked. Everyone declined.

"Who is in charge of the planning committee for the day of thanks?" Marlys asked.

"That would be Grace Burgess," Will told her. "Tom and Leah are on the committee, too, along with Pippa and one or two townsmen."

"We required them to have a couple of men so the party wouldn't be too heavily weighted toward the ladies," Daniel added with a grin. "Are you interested in helping? There's only about a week and a half left, but I'm sure they would appreciate another person. It's going to be a banquet at the Cattleman Hotel."

"It's going to be a grand time," Leah told her. "I'm looking forward to it."

"Definitely," Tomasina seconded. "We're having a meeting tomorrow evening at our home, as a matter of fact. Please, join us."

Marlys tilted her head. "Thank you."

The baby woke, and Leah took her upstairs, returning after she'd been changed and fed. Daniel reached for the fair-haired infant and cradled her in the crook of one arm. "Isn't she the prettiest thing you've ever seen?"

"Indeed she is," Tomasina replied and shared a glance with Will. He gave her a look of such warm affection that

Sam had to turn away. August had never had a doting mother, though his grandmother had been his caregiver and loved him as her own. August had grown attached to her, and Sam understood why the recent separation had been difficult.

The afternoon stretched out late before the Gardners' guests excused themselves, with fond appreciation.

"May I give you a ride home?" Daniel asked Marlys.

"We'll walk her home," Sam offered. "She's only around the corner from us."

"Thank you," Marlys told him.

They said their goodbyes and headed out into the brisk air. The day was sunny, but a cold wind had picked up since that morning.

"I had a good time," August said. "I like their house and especially Mr. Gardner's library."

"It is an especially nice home," Marlys agreed. She draped her red scarf over her head, and covering her hair made it seem as though someone had dimmed the sun.

August ran ahead and kicked at clumps of snow along the street.

"Made me think I shouldn't wait to buy a house for August and me. He seemed quite at home there, didn't he? Maybe it reminded him of being at my mother's."

The chill wind caught her scarf, sending a shiver down Marlys's spine. The day had grown continually colder, and patches of ice glistened on the bricks. She lost her balance on a slick spot, and Sam instinctively reached for her, holding her up with an arm around her.

She glanced up, and their faces were only inches apart. Her heart did an unexpected shimmy in her chest, and the sensation wasn't caused by the near fall. His eyes were a deep sapphire, his lashes black and thick, and his gaze bore into hers. The vapor of their breaths mingled in the air.

Chapter Eight

She closed her eyes against the intensity in his. Her heart beat impossibly fast. "I'm all right," she whispered.

He released her waist but held her arm until he was sure she'd found her footing. They moved away from each other and followed August, who hadn't noticed.

A few flakes fell from the sky, increasing in volume as they reached Second Street. Marlys unlocked the door to her office and stepped inside. It was barely light enough to see the interior. "Thanks for walking with me."

"Our pleasure. Have a good evening."

She locked the door after them and lowered the shades, then made her way to the back, where she lit two lamps and hung up her coat, setting her boots to dry. She added kindling to her small stove and warmed the room while heating water to wash.

She took a book off the stack beside her narrow bed and got comfortable with a soft afghan. She admired the blanket on her bed that She Knows had given to her. Every night she folded it carefully and set it aside. She had received only a few gifts in her lifetime, and the blanket held deep meaning. She was determined to take good care of it.

She'd never had aspirations for a big house or nice

dishes or furniture. She still didn't. Her needs were met, she had earned the freedom to do as she pleased, and she'd found what she'd believed was contentment. But that elusive something she'd begun to wonder about, that glimpse into the impossible concept of "more" had begun to take on shape and substance.

She'd had no concept of wedlock when her father had demanded she marry. There had never been an example in her life, no standard. If he'd loved her mother, if she'd loved him—Marlys had no idea. Reacquainting with Sam had made her uncomfortably curious. Seeing Opal with her baby had been like looking at life through a foggy window. Watching Leah and Daniel, observing Will and Tomasina had made the mystery clearer.

She was an outsider. An anomaly of nature. She had no one to blame but herself—and she didn't want to be a different person. She liked Dr. Marlys Boyd. She took pride in her accomplishments, so she was confused by the feeling that something was missing.

She picked up the book in her lap and opened it. She was strong. She would shake this off and move forward, satisfied with her choices. If she let herself have regrets and started doubting herself, she would lose a part of her identity, and she couldn't let that happen.

The women in Cowboy Creek were respected and honored—and deservedly so. Unlike the society debutantes she'd grown up with back in Philadelphia, women in Kansas served on committees, advised their husbands, ran businesses, planned events. They were not window dressing. But they were feminine in a way she had never bothered with, wearing their hair mysteriously curled and upswept, dressing in pretty, fashionable clothes.

She'd always thought it didn't matter if she adhered to

fashion. She was a doctor. People came to doctors for help, not to admire their clothing. But not many people were coming to her, anyway. She was smart enough to change tactics. A little more attention to her hair and clothing might improve her chances of appealing more to potential patients.

On Tuesday morning Hannah welcomed Marlys into her spacious shop. It smelled of new fabrics and lavender sachets. Two headless mannequins wore elaborate dresses, trimmed in ribbons and lace. Nerves fluttered in Marlys's stomach. She knew nothing of these womanly things.

"Your face is white, Dr. Boyd," Hannah said. "Come sit for a moment, and I'll make you a cup of tea. We'll chat."

Marlys took a seat on a wooden folding chair at a small round table. Hannah scurried about, boiling water in a kettle on her tiny stove, pouring it over leaves and letting it steep. "I even have a few cookies Aunt Mae sent."

She poured their tea into matching china cups painted with tiny sprigs of violets and sat across from Marlys.

"I'm so glad you've come to me to help you brighten up your wardrobe. Choosing clothing to highlight your beauty will be easy. You have such lovely hair and skin. The color of your hair and eyes are striking."

Marlys touched a tendril self-consciously. Leah had paid her a similar compliment. "Thank you."

"You must look marvelous in golds and greens. Probably blues, as well."

"I have mostly gray and brown skirts. I do have a blue one. The dark colors are practical."

"Pooh on practical," Hannah said. "Women deserve beautiful things. You deserve to feel attractive and confident."

"I am confident."

"About what?"

"My abilities. Knowledge. Skills."

"And rightly so. But what about your femininity? Your appearance?"

"I've never set much store by appearances."

"Each woman is unique and beautiful in her own way. Your confidence lends you an intriguing air of mystery. Woman are in awe, and men admire you."

"Does this flattery work on everyone?" she asked.

"It's not flattery if it's the truth." She urged Marlys up from the chair. "Come with me." She led her to another room with a settee, a cheval mirror and racks for clothing and accessories. Hannah had wisely chosen wall lamps for this area, so the light was flattering, and she could draw aside curtains to let more light through a window.

She stood Marlys before the full-length mirror. "Tell me what you see."

"I see a person I would trust," Marlys answered.

Hannah carried a lamp close and held it just above shoulder height. "What about your hair?"

"It's unruly and gets in the way."

"What about the way the light brings out all those shimmering highlights? Your hair is healthy and shiny. It looks soft and feminine."

"Feminine?"

"Most definitely." She set down the lamp and used her hands to span Marlys's waist. She was taller than Marlys and stood behind her shoulder. "And what about this tiny waist? Mine didn't look like that even before Ava was born. You were made to wear lovely clothing. Let's get you out of that skirt and measure you."

Marlys was uncomfortable standing in Hannah's dressing room in her cotton underclothing, but Hannah behaved as though she did this every day, which she probably did. She carefully tried on a dress that had been basted and pinned, and Hannah urged her back in front of the full-length mirror. "You're not a woman for whom frills will work. They would only detract from your striking appeal. But in flowing lines and jewel colors you are stunning."

Marlys studied her reflection, arrested by the change a simple dress made. She caught herself wondering what Sam would think when he saw her in a dress like this. She wasn't doing this for Sam. She was simply changing her image to enhance her vocation and her livelihood. "Will you be able to complete a dress by the twenty-sixth?"

The following week included the National Day of Thanksgiving and Prayer. Marlys dressed in her new garment and carried the covered dish she'd had Aunt Mae help her make the short distance to the Cattleman Hotel. The festivities were to begin at noon, and as she approached the corner, the bell in the tower clanged to announce the celebration. The bright sound rang loud across the countryside, and she shivered in expectation. Carriages and wagons were already lined along the street, and a glance to the west showed people had left their conveyances in the churchyard and the empty lot behind Booker & Son, as well.

She felt more at ease than she would have had she not joined the last two committee meetings, met more people and knew what to expect from this day. Reverend Taggart had been right about the benefits of participating.

The previous night she'd helped arrange tables and set up the adjacent parlor for children, so she knew the location and layout of the ballroom. The level of voices had already risen to a loud blur of noise, punctuated by occasional laughter.

An older gentleman in a gray suit greeted her. "Owen Ewing, miss. May I take your coat?"

He held her wrapped covered dish while she shrugged out of her coat, and they exchanged items. "Thank you, sir."

She carried her dish into the ballroom and made her way through the crowd, recognizing a few people here and there.

They'd erected a stage at the far end of the room and situated row upon row of tables and chairs lengthwise from that point. The centerpieces were heaps of gourds and cornucopias brimming with nuts. Candles scattered throughout the space gave the room a warm glow along with the light from the enormous sparkling glass chandeliers.

She made her way to the banquet table, where Leah spotted her and motioned her forward. "Marlys!"

"There are so many people here," Marlys observed somewhat nervously.

"The weather held, and we scheduled this event early enough in the day for people to come from all across Webster County," her new friend replied. "Oh, look here are the Werners."

Marlys turned to see the enormous blacksmith in a gray suit and string tie, holding a tiny blanket-wrapped infant on his shoulder. Beside Colton Werner was his petite and pretty wife, holding a delicious-looking cake. Marlys greeted Beatrix in German, and the woman smiled her pleasure.

"I'm so glad you could make it," Leah said. "The parlor has been set aside for the children."

"Hannah Johnson will be there to get the baby settled," Marlys told them.

Beatrix set her cake at the back of the table, and exited with her husband to find the parlor where cradles lined the walls. The committee had asked older children to watch the younger ones, with adults taking turns supervising.

The food smelled so good, Marlys's stomach rumbled. She'd spent so much time preparing her dish and getting ready, she hadn't eaten.

Will approached her, his ever-present silver-handled cane in hand, and with him was Grace Burgess, who had headed the committee, and a man she'd never seen before. "Have you two met?" Will asked.

"We have not," she answered.

"Dr. Boyd, this is my good friend Noah Burgess. Noah, this is the new lady doctor."

Noah extended a hand. "Sorry I haven't made it into town, doctor. I'm not much for socializing, but Grace wouldn't let me miss this celebration."

"Your Grace kept the committee on their toes," Marlys told him.

He smiled at his new wife. Marlys had learned they were newlyweds.

"You will meet the girls, too," Grace told her, referring to her twin daughters from a previous marriage. "I believe they're taking a turn in the baby room."

What Pippa magnanimously referred to as the orchestra warmed up, silencing the crowd momentarily, and then the musicians played a few songs.

Will, Noah and Daniel moved to the stage, where they got everyone's attention. "We're excited to celebrate this day with our fellow countrymen," Will said in a loud, clear voice. "In the words of our president, Mr. Andrew Johnson, 'The annual period of rest, which we have reached in health and tranquillity, and which is crowned with so many blessings, is by universal consent a convenient and suitable one for cultivating personal piety and practicing public devotion.'"

Applause broke out, and the crowd cheered.

Sensing a presence at her side, Marlys turned to find

Sam, dressed in a handsome black suit and white shirt. From beside him August gave her a smile. His hair was slicked into place, and he wore a shirt and tie with a smartly embroidered vest.

She gave them both smiles as around them people clapped and cheered.

After several minutes Daniel raised his hand, quieting the people. "Today is Thursday, the twenty-sixth day of November, and all the people of the United States have set this day aside as a day for public praise, as President Johnson decreed. 'For thanksgiving, and prayer to the Almighty Creator and Divine Ruler of the Universe, by whose ever-watchful, merciful, and gracious providence alone states and nations, no less than families and individual men, do live and move and have their being.'"

At the warm touch of Sam's hand engulfing hers, a tingle went up her arm, and her heart fluttered. She didn't look aside, but she returned the grasp and held his hand during this important and moving moment. For the first time she truly felt like a part of a community, as though she'd been guided to this place for this moment and for the time to come. Right then and there the future became less daunting, less of an obstacle and more of a promise.

"And in light of that purpose," Daniel continued, "Reverend Taggart will lead us in a prayer to set the tone for our gathering."

Reverend Taggart climbed the stairs, and in a strong respectful voice, gave God thanks and praise for the rebuilding of the nation, asked for comfort and peace for the people who had lost so much, and asked God's blessing on the hardworking, God-fearing people of Cowboy Creek and Webster County.

Marlys doubted there was a dry eye in the ballroom when he'd finished. She clung to Sam's hand and turned to look up into his dark eyes, glistening with the same emotion she experienced.

"And now I'll say a prayer for our meal, and we'll form two lines and share this bountiful banquet," Will announced. "After dinner, we have a special performance from our very own Pippa Kendricks, who will sing a selection of songs written by Septimus Winner." People lowered their heads, and he prayed a blessing over their meal. A chorus of joyful "Amens," rose from the crowd.

"Will you do us the honor of sitting with us?" Sam asked.

"Thank you, yes," she said to Sam and then repeated it to August in Chinese.

He grinned and said it back to her perfectly.

The banquet tables were laden with food. They stood in line, filled their plates, and carried them to where Sam had located empty seats.

This newest development was as confusing as all the other encounters with Samuel Woods Mason. Had he held her hand before? She didn't think so, but had she been too self-involved to remember?

Had he always been this kind?

There was a commotion at the food tables, but she couldn't see anything around the crowd. "What happened?" she asked when Sam returned.

"Beatrix Werner's cake was overturned on the floor, and it looked like Will was talking her husband down from going after that Eugene kid from Booker & Son. Colton looked fit to be tied, and his wife was near tears."

"You think Eugene had something to do with her cake being ruined?"

"Overheard some of the men saying he's gotten into a bad crowd, so who's to say?"

"Poor Beatrix."

"He'll take care of her. He's a good man."

It took quite a while for everyone to eat and return their plates and settle down for the performance. Pippa's "orchestra" was a surprisingly talented ensemble including a pianist, a bass player, a flutist and two violinists. She swept on stage in a striking blue satin dress that shone under the chandeliers.

"Tonight we will perform for you songs by Septimus Winner. This talented songwriter was inspired by the Book of Hebrews and the message of hope to write this first song."

The musicians led into the song with a lilting introduction. Pippa took her place, feet planted in a ballerina's pose, hands loosely together at her waist…and sang.

"Soft as the voice of an angel, breathing a lesson unheard
Hope with a gentle persuasion, whispers her comforting word
Wait till the darkness is over, wait till the tempest is done
Hope for the sunshine tomorrow, after the darkness is gone
Whispering hope, oh, how welcome thy voice
Making my heart in its sorrow rejoice."

Marlys listened, barely breathing, to Pippa's clear exquisite voice and the heart-touching words. The musician played the bridge and she waited for Pippa to continue.

"If in the dusk of the twilight, dim be the region afar
Will not the deepening darkness brighten the glimmering star?

Then when the night is upon us, why should the
heart sink away?
When the dark midnight is over, watch for the break-
ing of day
Whispering hope, oh, how welcome thy voice
Making my heart in its sorrow rejoice."

The song ended, the last violin died away in the enormous ballroom, and the crowd sat in silence, a few snif-
fles the only sound for the longest time. At last someone
clapped, and the sound prompted others out of their reverie, and applause filled the room.

"Did you know she could sing like that?" Sam asked
from beside her.

"She comes to my office twice every week, and I had
no idea," she answered.

They looked at each other and broke into gleeful smiles.

Pippa's other selections included "How Sweet Are the
Roses," "I Set My Heart Upon a Flower" and she ended
with the upbeat "Listen to the Mockingbird," during which
a hundred bad whistlers joined in. When she had finished,
the crowd cheered and whistled some more. Pippa took her
bows and left the stage.

Marlys clapped along with all the others and glanced at
the empty spot beside Sam. She'd been so engrossed with
Pippa's singing, she hadn't noticed him leaving. "Where's
August?"

"He took another turn in the baby room. Seems Cowboy Creek is bursting with babies."

"More brides, more babies," she agreed.

The evening wound down and she collected her now-
clean baking dish from the buffet table. Sam and August
walked her home.

Sam retied August's knitted neck scarf. "Four more

days, and it will be December. I have a feeling we haven't even begun to experience winter in Kansas yet."

"And then it will be Christmas, won't it, Papa?"

"That it will."

"Can we go sledding?"

"Next time it snows," Sam promised.

"Want to come sled with us, Dr. Boyd?"

She blinked into the darkening sky. "Well." She looked back at the boy's eager expression. "I have never gone sledding before, so I guess if you want to teach me, I will do my best."

"You're teaching me Chinese. I can teach you sledding." His tone was matter-of-fact, but she had to hold back an amused laugh.

"It sounds like an ideal exchange." She unlocked her door. "Good night."

They wished her a good night, and she went into her office, but she stood at the front window and watched father and son trudge through the twilight toward Eden Street. She relived the moment Sam had taken her hand and held it while the sentiment and emotion of the event encompassed them.

Why had she never felt those emotions in the past? Why now, after all this time had elapsed? They had both continued with their separate lives and followed their dreams. The war had knocked everyone's lives out of balance, and they were all picking up the pieces and starting over.

Starting over.

She'd begun a new life here in Cowboy Creek. She'd thought her practice was all she'd ever wanted. She'd been so sure. But now she was doubting whether the goals that had meant everything to her for as long as she could remember would be enough to make her feel truly fulfilled.

She still wanted to help people, to be the best doctor she could be.

But now another aspiration had revealed itself, a yearning she'd never anticipated. Never wanted. Whatever this confusing glimpse into another realm of possibility meant, she was intrigued. She'd made friends. She, Marlys Boyd, the peculiar outsider, had made friends. And in those friends' lives she'd begun to recognize the fulfillment of love and relationships. What it meant for her, she had no idea. The possibility was a little frightening, a lot puzzling. But Marlys liked a challenge.

Chapter Nine

It was the first week of December, and Sam left Israel in charge for the morning to visit businesses, the land office and the town clerk to take stock of recent happenings and note properties being sold. Weather had slowed construction, but the train still arrived daily, bringing visitors, new residents and the occasional bride. The citizens took pride in reading about the continual influx and growth of their community, so along with the national and local news, advice about agriculture, housekeeping and everyday living, Sam had developed a popular weekly column he'd titled *Boom Town Bulletin*.

It was time to write another installment of Marlys's story, so midmorning he arrived at her office. She hurried from the back room, wiping her hands on toweling. The interior smelled strongly of a combination of eucalyptus, cedar, jasmine and other scents he couldn't identify. Her forehead was etched with concern. "Are you all right?"

"I'm perfectly fine. I thought I'd see if you had a few minutes to continue an interview."

"Yes, of course. But if you don't mind, I'll continue working while we talk." She gestured for him to follow her. He'd previously been inside the front waiting room and as far as her office, but this venture intrigued him. She used a key to open an enormous storage closet. Three walls of shelves held woven baskets, glass jars, pottery containers of all sizes, all labeled, all in precise rows. Dried herbs and all manner of leaves and roots hung from the ceiling. The powerful smells reminded him of the pleasant scent that always clung to her. She took a pair of shears and snipped a few unidentifiable leaves.

"What do you want to know?"

"Tell me about the jobs you worked and the woman you took care of while you were putting yourself through school."

"My tasks were not all that interesting."

"Trust me with that part."

She led him out and locked the storage closet. He followed her to a long counter in another small room. She used a granite mortar and pestle to grind the leaves to a powder, then set out a bowl and added the powder and a few tablespoons of boiling water. He watched in fascination until she covered the bowl with a chipped plate.

As she worked, she answered questions. "Excuse me for a moment."

She disappeared behind one of the closed bathing room doors, and while he couldn't make out their words, he could tell she was speaking with another woman. She returned, and a gust of warm scented air followed her. "Where were we? Oh, yes."

"I didn't realize you have a patient."

"I get more as the ladies discover the joys of soft, moisturized skin this time of year. I can't actually refer to them as patients, because dry winter skin isn't an illness or injury, but they are paying clients." She picked up where she'd left off with her history.

He was fascinated by her matter-of-fact recitation of

jobs and duties. Anyone else would have worked themselves to exhaustion or given up, but her dogged determination had driven her to succeed at everything she lifted her hands to do.

"You're an amazing woman, Marlys."

She seemed to lose her train of thought, standing in her work room, the sun slanting through the panes of glass to set fire to her hair. It had grown out since she'd been here, and she now tucked one side behind her ear before lifting her gaze to meet his eyes. "Not so amazing," she said barely above a whisper.

"Completely extraordinary," he corrected. "You see yourself differently than I see you. I see someone who sacrificed and worked hard to achieve a dream. I see a woman whose dream is also sacrificial, wanting to heal others because she genuinely cares about all humanity."

"My father said I was selfish. He told me I was spoiled for putting my own dreams ahead of what he wanted for me." She rested her fingertips on the counter. "He made me feel guilty for wanting to become a doctor."

"No one thinks twice about a man wanting to become a doctor," Sam replied.

"And in addition, I chose a different path than the commonly accepted studies and treatments."

"All the great people who came before us chose different paths. Blaise Pascal, Louis Braille, Isaac Newton."

She cast him a cynical glance. "Your opinion of me is highly inflated to list me in their company."

"Who's to say? You're young. You could still find a cure for consumption."

"I'm not a scientist."

"You work with medical science every day. Some inventions are quite by accident."

She didn't argue with that, but she had managed to twist the topic.

"My opinion that you're amazing and extraordinary remains."

"You confuse me, Sam."

"I don't mean to."

"I know you don't. But everything was settled." She gestured with a hand in the air. "My life was on a path. I knew exactly what I wanted." Her hand fluttered back to the counter. "I've always set my expectations high, and I've refused to be disappointed. I came here to build a better future—for myself. For this land."

"And you are."

"And then I walked into your newspaper, and everything changed. I'm not certain of myself anymore, and I don't like the feeling."

He set down his pad and pencil and took the few steps toward her, reaching out to bracket her shoulders. Her scent reached him, and yearning curled inside. "And I'm probably a fool for entertaining the idea that you might feel something in return. We've been down this road once, and it didn't turn out well for me. But I can't help what I feel."

Her breath touched his chin as she looked up at him. "What do you feel?"

"I've always admired you, your determination, your intelligence, your fervor. You're a visionary. I understand what you want, what you're trying to do here. I even want to help you. Somewhere along the line I think you got the idea that you would have to give up your dreams to be loved. I'm not asking you to change. I think you're perfect just the way you are. I just wish you'd let me in. Let me be part of that better future you want."

Her lips parted as though she wanted to say something, but no words came out.

He took the moment to lean forward and touch his lips gently to hers.

She grasped the front of his shirt and kissed him back.

They clung together that way, and his pulse hammered mercilessly. She had to feel it. Her painful honesty was contagious and inspired him to tell her his feelings. Was it too soon to call it love? Maybe, but his heart certainly seemed to be headed that way.

A bell rang, and she took a step back.

The bell rang again. She blinked. "I have to tend to my patient."

Turning, he watched her hurry from the room and stood collecting his thoughts, gathering his composure.

He took a seat and made a few notes. The two women's voices came from the other room, and it didn't sound as though they were speaking English. Abruptly the clanging bell over her door rang.

"Doc! Doc Boyd!"

Marlys left her client to dress and rushed to see who'd called out.

A man in a bulky fur coat hobbled across the waiting room. "Stepped on a nail, I did. Thing went clean through my foot and hurts like the very blazes."

She moved behind him and helped him shrug out of his heavy coat.

"What can I do?" Sam appeared from her office, and she avoided eye contact.

"Hey, Sam."

"Owen."

"Don't know how I did such a fool thing," he said with a grimace. "Nail went clean through the sole of my boot."

"How did you get here?" Sam asked.

"Hobbled to the doorway and hollered till Irving heard

me over at the furniture store," the older man explained. "He borrowed someone's horse from behind the hotel, and I rode. He's taken the animal back now."

"Owen Ewing is the undertaker," Sam explained to Marlys. "Cabinets, too, I understand."

"We met the day of thanksgiving celebration." Marlys gestured. "Can you make it back to an examination room?"

"Here, lean on me," Sam offered.

Owen took him up on the offer and the three of them moved to the back. She prepared an area with clean toweling and helped him get situated on the exam table so she could remove his boot. Blood still pooled from a wound on the top of his foot and another on the bottom.

Sam cringed but asked, "Mind if I stay and watch? I'm doing a piece on the doctor."

"Stay if you like, as long as somebody puts out the fire in my foot." The man bared his teeth in pain.

"I am going to see my last patient out and put on more water to heat. Put your foot up on the table." She left and returned minutes later to offer Owen a cup of tea. "Drink all of it."

He made another face after tasting it, but obeyed.

"All right, now lie back, and we'll keep this foot elevated to be certain the bleeding has stopped."

She propped the foot on rolled towels and stood applying pressure to both of the punctures.

"I can't afford to be laid up," Owen said. "Because it's winter I have a lot of jobs for interior building lined up. Houses are going up all along the street east of Lincoln Boulevard. The town council is deciding on names for a couple more streets."

"I don't believe this will be a lengthy recovery," Marlys assured him. "I once treated a man with a larger wound to his foot, and he was working two weeks later."

"Two weeks is a lot of money I'd be losing."

"If the healing time stretches out, maybe some of the rest of us can help you," Sam offered. "I'm not much with a saw or hammer, but I can take directions and fetch for you."

"That's real generous of you, Samuel."

"Yes, very generous, Mr. Mason." She gave Sam an approving glance, and he almost puffed out his chest.

"We're going to soak your foot first," Marlys told Owen. "To make sure it's clean before I treat it." She left and returned with an oblong pail of water that smelled of one of her mineral concoctions. "Let's get your foot in here."

Owen gingerly let down his foot into the warm water and hissed.

The water turned red with his blood.

"That's mostly from the blood already covering your foot," she told him. "The wounds have pretty much stopped bleeding. I added an anesthetic property to the water that should help when I treat it."

Owen nodded his understanding.

"I'm going to scrub your foot in fresh water now," she said. "The tea should help with pain, too. I won't directly touch the wound just yet."

She did as she'd explained, using a soft brush and a grayish pungent mixture. She'd been right about the bleeding. It had all but stopped. When he removed his foot from the pail, she dried it gently and examined the puncture marks. "All right. It's clean, and now I'm going to apply dressing and wrap it."

"What about stitches?"

"I don't think you need stitches. As long as you keep that foot up the rest of today, the wounds are going to close up nicely on their own."

She returned with a dish of bruised leaves. "The Gardners' housekeeper is named Ewing, as well," she mentioned. "Are you family?"

"Valentine is my sister," he said. "She was bored with only me to look after. Caring for the Gardners isn't work to her. She took to Leah right off when the poor gal was laid up before the baby. Daniel is one of the finest men I've ever had the pleasure to know. And now with Little Evie—well, my sister is as happy as a hog in a sweet potato patch. She has a gentleman friend who calls and comes for dinner or takes her out. I suspect he's asked her to marry him, but she's not agreed for fear of leaving me alone."

"What are those leaves you're applying?" Sam asked.

"Peach leaves," she answered. "Prevents lockjaw and promotes swift healing. I think Owen will be amazed how quickly the pain is relieved and new skin grows. Reportedly this remedy works on horses with hoof injuries, as well."

"Did you learn this from your Chinese studies or is this an Indian remedy?"

"Neither," she answered. "I learned it from one of the German-speaking families."

Sam shook his head. "You're a force to be reckoned with, Dr. Boyd."

She looked to Owen. "Where's your place, Mr. Ewing?"

"Valentine and I share a house on Grant Street, just across from my shop to the west."

"Sam, do you have time to get a horse or a friend to escort Mr. Ewing home? I'd prefer he stay completely off that foot until tomorrow."

"Happy to oblige."

"Thank you. I'll walk over to the Gardners' house and let Valentine know what happened, and that you'll be at home resting."

Sam got his coat and hat and headed out, the bell over

the door clanging behind him. She mixed a powder with a small amount of water and handed the corked bottle to her patient. "Take this in a cup of tea to help you sleep tonight."

"Thanks, Doc. How much do I owe?"

She gave Owen a price, and he paid her in coins. "That Mason fellow is nice. Puts out a fine newspaper. He's smart, but not conceited smart, if you know what I mean."

"I do."

"You're mighty smart yourself. Calm. Efficient. Not hard on the eyes." He chuckled.

She grinned. "Thank you for trusting me with your care."

While they waited, she cleaned up the mess, rinsed and bundled the towels. When Sam returned with a wagon, she got Owen's coat and helped Sam assist him up to the seat. After tugging on her boots and shrugging into her coat, she walked through a light-falling snow to the Gardners' home, where she gave Leah the message for Valentine.

"I'm so glad you knew how to help him," Leah told her.

"So am I."

She walked back feeling as though she'd accomplished something positive with her day. It was a good feeling. Underneath the satisfaction, however, was the confusion of Sam's kiss and her unsettling feelings for him. She'd never been afraid of change—or so she'd thought— but somehow this particular change frightened her. She prayed for wisdom and took comfort that God had granted Solomon much more than he'd asked for because he'd desired wisdom. Back in her rooms, she took her Bible from her bureau drawer and thumbed through the pages until she found what she searched for in the First Book of Kings. *And God gave Solomon wisdom and understanding exceeding much, and largeness of heart, even as the sand that is on the sea shore.* "Thank You, Lord, for wisdom and understanding and largeness of heart."

On Saturday she was awakened to pounding on the rear door. Patients never arrived in the back; in fact no one had ever knocked on that door. She pulled on her dressing gown and slippers and stood at the door. "Who is it?"

"It's me, Dr. Boyd!" came a familiar childish voice from the other side. "It snowed all night!"

She pushed open the door to find August and Sam had already scraped snow off her stoop. The space between her building and the back of the laundry was sparkling white with fresh new snow.

"Get dressed," Sam told her. "You promised August a morning of sledding."

August set a warm covered bowl in her hands. "It's oatmeal."

"All right. Give me a few minutes. I have to dig in my trunk for leggings and warm clothing. Go around to the front, and I'll let you in so you can wait inside." She hurried to unlock the front door and scurried back to prepare, pausing for bites of the tasty maple-sweetened oatmeal.

"Which one of you knows how to cook such delicious oatmeal?"

"Neither," Sam replied. "We smelled Aunt Mae's cooking next door when we woke up and invited ourselves over to eat with the boarders. She never minds. I asked for something easy to bring to you, and she scooped oatmeal into a bowl."

She joined them, dressed in her warmest garments and a red knitted cap and sat to pull on her boots. Sam helped her into her coat, she left a note on the chalkboard that hung in the window, and they set off.

A new wooden sled with red-painted runners waited at

the edge of the street, and the tracks showed they'd pulled it all the way from Eden Street.

"Which way?" she asked.

Sam wore his revolver in a holster tethered to his right thigh. It was winter, and there were wild animals nearby. His precaution made her feel safe. "The land to the west, where it slopes toward Cowboy Creek, should be the best hill nearby. A good slope, and only a few trees."

As they plunged through the snow, Sam identified the tracks of several woodland animals for August. They saw a shaggy coyote slink away, and winter-white rabbits froze in place as they passed.

"Someone finally came to apply for the assistant position yesterday," she told Sam.

"Have you reached a place with business where hiring someone is feasible?"

"I think so. He's young and has no medical experience, but I need help with heating water, cleaning, transporting the laundry, errands and the like. I mentioned I might only need him to work a few hours a day for now, and he agreed to that."

They approached a bank and trudged to reach the top, where they stood in a row and looked down.

"This is perfect!" August squealed.

"Looks like the ideal spot," Sam agreed.

Marlys's stomach plunged, and her oatmeal felt like lead now. The long steep hill took her breath away. She'd never done anything like this before. The ideal spot?

At her silence, they both turned to look at her, and she managed a weak smile.

"Don't you like it?" August asked.

"It's a marvelous hill. Now we're going to get on the sled and ride down?"

"Yep! Let's show her how it's done, Papa!"

"Sitting up or lying down?" Sam asked.

"Face first, o'course!" August replied.

Sam made sure his woolen hat was secure, then lay stomach down on the sled. August scrambled to lay atop him in the same head forward position. He wrapped his arms around his father.

"What if there's a rock or a limb under the snow that we can't see?" Marlys asked.

"We'll hit it and fall off," Sam replied, using his arms and hands to propel the sled forward. He rocked it back and forth a couple of times and then shoved with a grunt of exertion.

Marlys's heart leaped into her chest as she watched them shoot down the snowy hill with August's high-pitched cry of excitement reverberating around the white-blanketed countryside. Holding her breath, she covered her face with her mittened hands as the duo neared the bottom, but immediately pulled her hands back down, lest the twosome crash and bleed and need her assistance.

At the bottom, the sled skidded sideways, and they tumbled off into the snow. Laughing, they got to their feet.

"That was great!" August cried and reached for the rope to help his dad pull their sled back up the hill.

Near the top, Sam said, "After about a dozen times, this is the hard part."

"Your turn, Dr. Boyd!" August said gleefully.

"You should probably start calling me Marlys," she said.

"Yes'm. You wanna ride down with me or with Papa?"

She opened her eyes wide. "I don't want to be the responsible one."

"It's not that difficult," Sam assured her. "But I'll come with you so you can see what's it's like this first time. And we'll sit up—less overwhelming for a beginner." He promptly seated himself on the wooden sled. "You can't steer well, so you have to use your weight, leaning one way or the other."

Marlys looked at August. He waved his mittened hand in impatience. "Go! Go!"

She made sure her hat was secure, then lowered herself in her bulky fur coat behind Sam.

"Ready?" he asked.

As she'd ever be. "Yes."

Her heart pounded when he rocked the sled back and forward, then propelled it forward with the strength of his arms. Bits of snow hit her cheeks and the hillside blurred as they picked up speed. She buried her face in the back of Sam's coat.

"Ahhhhhhhhh!" she screamed as loud as August had, and in front of her Sam laughed. She dared look again. The bottom sped quickly up to meet them, and the sled spun at the same spot it had previously and dumped them unceremoniously into the snow. They rolled, and she ended up lying on her back facing the cloudless blue sky and panting as though she'd run a race. Laughter burst from her, and she rolled away.

Sam's laughter joined hers, and they sat on the frozen ground gasping for breath.

"That was fun!" she managed finally. "I can't believe I just did that."

"I can't believe you've never been sledding. There's always several feet of winter snow in Pennsylvania."

She pushed herself to her feet and brushed her coat and mittens clean. She reached down for Sam. "I can't believe I haven't, either."

He took her hand, and rose to stand in front of her, leaving her shockingly aware of how close he was. And how handsome. Her heart zigzagged in her chest, and she spent an inordinate amount of time studying him. Under well-shaped black brows his deep blue eyes held amusement and promise. His full nicely-shaped lips wore an unfamiliar mischievous smile. He had a straight nose, symmetrical bone structure, and he hadn't shaved that morning, so a dark shadow highlighted his jaw and chin. She couldn't remember ever taking such pleasure in looking at a person.

"What are we doing?" she asked, truly perplexed about her exaggerated fascination.

"I'm not sure," he answered. "But I'm willing to spend as long as it takes to find out."

Chapter Ten

She tore her gaze from his, his words echoing in her mind. She wanted to explore the growing feelings between them, but she felt so out of her depth. Attraction to another person was what perpetuated the human race...but she'd always assumed she was immune. She didn't want to fall in love and behave irrationally. She was sensible and levelheaded.

She hurried ahead, leaving him to pull the sled himself.

At the crest, August beamed. "You were brave, Marlys!"

She had been, hadn't she? She'd faced every obstacle and challenge in her life head-on. She'd never backed down, never taken no for an answer. "I was, wasn't I?" She pointed to the sled. "You and I this time, August."

If love always felt the way she'd felt with Sam lately, she was ready to face her fears and consider it. She turned and looked over her shoulder at Sam. "There's a first time for everything, and I'm not going to be afraid anymore."

He met her gaze with a nod, and understanding passed between them.

"Push us, Papa!"

She and August both hollered all the way down.

* * *

A month had passed since Marlys had visited the Cheyenne, so she arranged a traveling party, packed supplies, and purchased jars of mincemeat and jelly to bring as gifts. Once again Sam and James accompanied her, and this time Sam allowed August to join them. The boy enjoyed the adventure, took in every detail, and learned as many Cheyenne words as he could in a day.

They traveled home in the late afternoon before dark, and Sam invited Marlys to join them for dinner at the hotel. Though they were all weary, it was an enjoyable evening. August showed off his new skills and spoke Chinese to one of the women who carried their dishes away. The woman smiled in surprise and held a brief conversation with Marlys before returning to her duties.

Sam was thankful Marlys had been able to make a strong connection with his son. August had visibly bloomed in her company and under her tutelage. He'd become more open with Sam, more content with their new home. Sam listened to the two of them speaking in Chinese and understood more than either were probably aware. His uncanny memory extended to remembering foreign words and phrases.

"Are you able to wife my father?" August asked in Chinese.

"Marry," she corrected.

"Are you able to marry my father?"

"He has not asked me."

"What if he will?"

"I might say yes."

"Would you be our mother?"

"My mother," she corrected.

"Would you be my mother?"

"Would you want me to be your mother?"

"Yes."

They both looked at Sam. He gave them an innocent smile, but his heart swelled at the same time a tremor of trepidation passed up his spine. He'd proposed to her once before.

She'd accepted.

He'd counted his blessings.

And then she'd called it off.

This was different, he assured himself. She'd already attended university and earned her degree, so that was behind her. She'd come here to start over. But, then again, maybe there was more she wanted to do that didn't include a husband or child.

Nothing worthwhile ever came easily, his mother had told him often as a boy, and he'd taken her words to heart and lived by them. Making oneself vulnerable was one of the most difficult things he could imagine. And he'd imagined it plenty. He'd even had confusing dreams of asking her to marry him. He'd turned over every scenario in his mind. But unless he made the effort, he would never know if they had a chance for future happiness together.

To be reasonable, he always asked himself what was the worst that could happen? In this situation the worst that could happen was that she'd say no, take offense and no longer want his friendship or want to spend time with August.

That would be the worst result. However he would simply be back where he'd started before she'd walked into his newspaper office, and he'd lived through it once. He could survive, though he didn't want August to lose his only friend.

And so he hesitated, castigating himself for his cowardliness.

And he prayed. *Lord, show me Your perfect plan for us. Help me to be humble and honest. Help me protect my son and make the best possible life for him.*

They walked her home and wished her a good night.

"Thank you again for accompanying me this morning," she said.

"August enjoyed every minute of the trip, so it was our pleasure."

"Well. Good night."

"Papa, you said we were going to ask Marlys about Christmas trees."

"Oh, yes."

"What about Christmas trees?" she asked.

"Papa and I are going to cut a tree to decorate. You can come cut a tree, too. We can help you decorate it."

"It's still almost two weeks until Christmas," Sam told him. "It's too soon this week, but if Marlys wants a tree, we can go next week."

"You have to have a tree," August said with a serious expression.

"I could put one in the waiting room here so my patients can enjoy it," she said.

August grinned. "See, we have a plan."

Sam nodded. "Good night, Marlys."

He avoided her for a week, seeing her only at church. On Wednesday she came by the *Webster County Daily News* to thank him for the second article on her. He stood to greet her. "I had two new patients yesterday," she told him. "Both had read the article."

"It's your story," he said. "I just wrote about it."

"Well, thank you." As though she sensed his withdrawal, she hesitated, standing beside him in front of his desk. "You've been busy yourself lately."

"Yes." He glanced at the stacks of papers.

Marlys had never been good at interpreting social cues, but she sensed them now. Sam had been quiet the last couple of times she'd seen him. "I've never in my life thought about this or imagined I'd ever ask a person, but have I done something to offend you?"

"No." He met her gaze briefly and glanced away. "You haven't."

His reply and expression didn't dispel her concern, but she didn't know what else she could say. She was too socially inept to understand this friction. "All right." Feeling completely inadequate, she turned toward the door. "I'll be going then."

"Wait."

At his voice, she stopped and turned back to face him.

He took the pencil from behind his ear and tossed it on the desk, then came to stand directly in front of her. "I have to admit to you I've been confused because of our history."

She looked up at him, his dark penetrating expression sending a shiver across her shoulders. "You mean our brief engagement."

"Yes."

She pursed her lips in thought. "I've pondered that, too. I've questioned my choices. I don't believe I was at a place where I could recognize or appreciate anything beyond my single-minded focus."

"Which is what makes you the great doctor you are."

She shook her head. "I don't know."

"I do. You're a good doctor. You're focused and confident and open to new strategies and theories. You've made a difference already—I don't think Little Deer would have survived without you. At that time you didn't have time or energy for anything other than your studies. I admired your drive."

"But I embarrassed you." She lifted her eyebrows in question. "Or hurt you?"

"Perhaps my pride was wounded. And my heart."

"I'm sorry for that."

"It's in the past. But it does make me hesitant to suggest anything more now."

"More?"

"Yes. Are you satisfied with things the way they are or are you able to entertain the possibility of a future together?"

She could appreciate Sam's logical approach. Still, his question caught her off guard because she'd been questioning so many things herself. "I've been doing a lot of thinking. You're different from others, because you don't think my goals are selfish."

"Everyone should get to choose their own future."

"That sounds like a fine statement for a political leader. Maybe you should run for office."

He shook his head. "No. I have no interest in that arena. Journalism is how I choose to affect the world. And besides, Will Canfield is going to be the forerunner for governor." He grimaced. "How did we get on that subject?"

"What is the subject?"

He put a hand on each hip and took a breath. "I'm not going to ask you to marry me today. I don't want to make you uncomfortable or pressure you, and I sure don't want to get turned down. But I do want to get these feelings between us out in the open."

Her heart rate picked up. She became aware of her hands feeling cold. Recognizing all the physical signs didn't make the unfamiliar panic any easier.

"If you should feel that you might be willing to consider a proposal of marriage, will you tell me? And if you're sure you wouldn't consider it I want to know that, too."

His convoluted approach to what wasn't truly a proposal made Marlys laugh. The sound erupted from her lips, and the more she thought about it, the more humorous it became. She pressed a palm to her midriff and let out her amusement.

"Stop it," he said.

"Sam, it's funny. You just proposed that I let you know if I'd consider a proposal."

"That's not funny. It's absurd and...well, humiliating."

She reached and took both of his hands in hers. His were large and warm, and she ran her thumbs over the soft hairs at his wrists. "I didn't know if you would still have feelings for me or trust me."

"I do."

Summoning her courage, she admitted, "I do, as well. I may not have an answer for you just yet, but I can tell you without a wait that, yes, I will entertain a marriage proposal. From you. Right now."

He glanced over his shoulder. The office had been quiet, but now she wondered if Israel was nearby. Changing their grasp so he was holding on to her hands, Sam lowered himself to one knee. Her heart fluttered. "Marlys Boyd, will you consider marrying me?"

Her throat felt thick with emotion. Nerves made her tremble. "I will have a reply by Christmas."

He got to his feet, enfolded her in a gentle embrace and kissed her. She didn't feel suffocated or devalued. Sam didn't want to limit her or hold her back. He gave her freedom to be herself, which made her want to be his all the more. She drew inches away to say, "I need to know if you would ever ask me to make a choice between being your wife and being a doctor."

"Marlys, I would never ask that of you. I admire your independent spirit and your individuality—and I appreciate all you do as a doctor. I am proposing marriage so that you and August and I can be family, so you and I can be partners."

"Don't be aloof anymore."

"I apologize. Open and honest, that's our policy."

"I like it."

He smiled that devastating smile that made her want to hug him, so she did. He slid his fingers into her hair and cupped her jaw. "We could be a family, the three of us."

"Will you tell August what we're thinking?"

"Not yet. I don't want him to be disappointed if…if you chose another plan."

If she said no. "I don't want him disappointed, either." She frowned. "I have no idea how to be a mother. I can barely remember mine."

"He's never had one, so he'll have no comparison."

"I wouldn't want to be ineffective."

Sam grinned. "I can't imagine you being ineffective at anything, but no one can do everything well."

"Being a mother is pretty important."

"He would probably give you pointers as to what he expected. He did me."

"I appreciate that he knows what he wants."

"You already get along like two peas in a pod."

He ran his knuckles along her jaw and across her lips. His gentle loving touch showed her all she'd miss out on if they didn't find a way to be together. The scripture verses about marriage had never made much sense to her. All she'd been shown and told in her past made it seem as though the woman had to set aside her life to be a wife. But if it could be different with Sam, then was that what she wanted after all?

Her hand trembled when she raised it to his cheek, but she rested her palm there against the warmth of his skin. When he smiled at her, she felt the movement beneath her palm as well as the responsive tug at her heart. She didn't want to be moved by emotion. She'd prayed for wisdom.

Loving Sam would be easy. Doing the wise thing would be less simple and far more confusing.

Did she love him?

In the week that followed they had dinner together at the hotel. Aunt Mae invited them to join her gathering at the boardinghouse for a Saturday morning breakfast, and they sat side by side in church the following day. On Tuesday, with Christmas three days away, they bundled up after school was out and selected two fine trees from a ridge near where they'd sledded. In the woods August pointed out plants with oval-shaped leaves and red berries growing in the branches of conifers. "What are these?"

"Pick me a pocketful of those, August. They're from the botanical genus *phoradendron.* The plant is related to sandalwood. The seeds are spread by birds and grow in host trees."

"That's mistletoe, son, and its best use is for hanging in doorways at Christmastime. Pick me a fistful, too."

"Why would you hang it in a doorway?" August asked.

"Because when a girl stands in the doorway under a sprig of mistletoe, a boy gets to kiss her."

August wrinkled his nose. "I'm not kissing any girls."

"Oh, me, neither," Sam teased with a wink at Marlys.

They loaded the sled with their trees and pulled them home. Sam made a base for one that he placed in the open area at the *Daily* office and another for Marlys's waiting room. Neither of them owned any decorations, and rather than buy glass ornaments, Sam popped corn, Marlys brought out the bag of cranberries she'd ordered, and August made paper chains, the rings linked together with flour-and-water paste. Sam and Marlys stood back in her office and watched August adjusting the last chain on the branches.

"I thought he was going to miss his grandmother," he said in a whisper. "But now it seems this is going to be one of his best Christmases ever." He wrapped an arm around her shoulder and gave her a fond hug. "Thanks to you."

She looked up at him. "I promised you would have an answer by Christmas," she said. "I know you're praying about it, too. I've been searching the Word for answers, and last night I read instruction in Ephesians for every man to love his wife as he loves himself and for each wife to reverence her husband. It seems that if a man loves his wife as himself, he will care about the things she cares about and not discourage her goals or dreams. Because he'd care as much for her dreams as his own."

"That sounds right to me."

"And you've shown that already. When I want to visit the Cheyenne or talk about my practice, you encourage me."

"I wasn't too sure about either one at first," he agreed. "I still didn't understand the scope of your ability or the way your compassion shows people your true heart. But I want you to be able to follow your dreams."

She wanted to take his hand but glanced to discover August watching them. He caught her gaze and pointed to the chain. "Do you like it?"

She left Sam's side and knelt beside the boy to gaze up at the tree. "I think it's perfect. It's the most beautiful Christmas tree I've ever seen."

"'Cause we did it together?" he asked.

"Because we did it together."

He turned and wrapped his narrow arms around her waist. She knelt and wrapped her arms around him in turn. He smelled like the glue they'd made and the cinnamon from their hot cocoa. She glanced over his shoulder and caught the glimmer of a tear in Sam's eye. Sam busied himself picking up bits of string and paper from the wood floor.

There was a knock, and the door opened, jangling the brass bell. Eugene closed the door behind him and took a few steps. "Ma'am. Mr. Mason."

Marlys released August and got to her feet. "Hello, Eugene. How can I help you?"

"Mr. Booker closed the store for the evening, but he sent me out to bring you this. He said it might be important." Eugene extended a long envelope.

Marlys stepped forward to take it. "That was nice of you. Thank you."

"You're welcome, ma'am."

"Have a good night."

"You too, ma'am."

"My, how his attitude has changed," Sam commented.

She agreed. "I don't know that he likes me any better than he did before. I suspect he just wants to keep his job."

She looked at the Philadelphia postmark and turned the envelope over, recognizing the university's seal and flipped it back.

"Let's finish cleaning up," Sam said to August, and the two of them busied themselves.

In her fastidious fashion, Marlys went for a letter opener and slit open the top of the envelope. Unfolding the piece of heavy vellum, the official stationery caught her off guard. Who at the American College of Medicine in Pennsylvania would send her a letter? She dropped her gaze to the signature. James McClintock had been the dean at the Philadelphia School of Eclectic Medicine. She read through the missive quickly, checked the envelope to make certain it was indeed addressed to her, and then read it through again. Her heart raced with excitement. She flattened her hand over her chest.

"What is it, Marlys?" Sam asked. "Bad news?"

"No." She read the words again. A smile broke out on her face. "Dr. McClintock from the university where I graduated is starting a new medical school. I can hardly believe this!"

"What? What can't you believe?"

"They've asked me to come teach at the American College of Medicine. The salary is, well, it's staggering, but the honor. Oh, my, I can hardly catch my breath. Me! They've asked me to teach at their college!"

Chapter Eleven

"I'm sure you're quite a catch," Sam commented. "I know you're honored to have been asked, but they're the ones who would be fortunate to have you. That's quite a distinction, Marlys. I'm very proud of you."

"Thank you." In her excitement, she flung herself into his arms, the hand with the letter behind his head. August came up behind Sam and took the letter from her fingers.

"This says the new college is on Fourth, between Race and Cherry Streets, and that housing is provided. These streets aren't in Cowboy Creek. Is the college in Philadelphia?"

Marlys released Sam's neck and backed away. "I... Yes." She looked at August's stricken face and back at Sam's atypically placid expression. The hair on her neck prickled.

"You're leaving?" August asked.

The moment stretched out, silence reverberating between the three of them. "I haven't accepted, of course," she said finally. "I've only just read the offer."

Sam's expression didn't waver. "It sounds like a good one. You'd be respected, paid well. Have the opportunity to teach students like yourself, mold them and send them out to practice in communities like this one."

Her numb gaze took in her name on the window, the glow of the lights in the waiting room as evening grew dark, and she glanced toward the back. She'd only just established herself here. Only now connected with Sam and August.

August handed the letter back to her, and she took it, unfolding it and reading the words again.

"It's getting late, August." Sam headed for their coats on the hooks. "We'd better get home and read a few chapters before bedtime."

"Is she leaving Cowboy Creek?" August asked, not to be ignored.

"Marlys has a lot to think about." He gestured for August to put his arms in the sleeves of his coat.

"But what about us?"

"That's enough, August." His tone was more harsh than she'd ever heard it. "We're not going to influence her decision. It's hers to make."

Crestfallen, August buttoned his coat and pulled on his hat. Bunches of mistletoe springs fell from his pockets when he retrieved his hat. He piled them on a chair. "Night, Marlys."

She didn't know what to say and didn't want to expose her muddled feelings or disorientation in front of the child. "Sam, I…"

He stopped and looked at her.

She shrugged.

"We'll talk later," he said and ushered his boy out the door.

The next day while there were no patients, she left her new assistant, Darius, with instructions to come for her if there was an emergency, and walked to the *Webster County Daily News* where the smells of ink and paper permeated the building. The presses were running, and both Sam and Israel were working to stack the printed pages that rolled from the press. He looked up to see her, signaled to Israel, and stopped the steam engine. The noisy machine halted, leaving her ears ringing.

"I didn't mean to interrupt your work."

"That's all right. No one dies if I leave the press for a few minutes. What can I do for you?"

"Can we talk?"

He wiped his hands. "Sure. Back here."

He led her to a small storage room and closed the door. The confined space was dark, save the light from the transom over the door.

"Sorry, my office is out there."

"This is all right. I just wanted to talk to you. We didn't have any privacy last night."

"We do now."

"Yes, well." She took off her mittens and shoved them in her pockets.

"I'm sorry. Would you like to take off your coat?"

"No, I'm fine, thanks. That letter was such a shock, Sam. I didn't know what to think. I still don't."

"Understandable. It's a lot to take in. A big decision."

She nodded. "Of course you understand."

"I do, Marlys. They've offered you the respect and recognition you've always wanted. That you earned. That's mighty flattering—and well deserved."

He hadn't been able to think of anything else since the previous evening. Her dream had come true. A prestigious university wanted her to come work for them, to share her knowledge, teach young doctors. She could make a difference for medicine. For women in the field. The last thing he wanted to do was hold her back. Well, next to last thing.

The last thing he'd wanted was for her to choose her career over him again.

He swallowed hard against his turbulent emotions. He loved this woman. But he would not be the one to keep her from becoming all she could possibly be. One man couldn't hold back a river or he'd drown trying.

He wasn't that drowning man. He'd taken yet another chance, knowing the risks, knowing her passion and drive, but it didn't look as though he was destined to have this woman in his life.

He regretted getting August involved only to have him disappointed. That hadn't been a good choice on his part. The boy had already been through enough. But that wasn't Marlys's concern or her responsibility; it was his.

"You should take the position," he told her. "It's a once-in-a-lifetime opportunity."

"Do you believe that?"

"I do. You can make a difference in medicine, in the lives of those students, and the results would be far-reaching. A much broader reach than you can make here in Cowboy Creek. I don't know anyone who would hold it against you for going."

"Not even you?"

"Certainly not me. I know you." His heart ached with every genuine word from his lips. "I believe in you."

In the dim interior, she studied his face as though searching for the truth, searching for answers, for permission.

"The last thing I ever wanted was to hurt you," she said.

"I know."

She moved to his left, and he stepped out of her way, so she could open the door. He blinked into the light and watched her disappear down the hallway. The outer door opened and closed. He leaned his forehead against the wall, his hand fisted on the wood and took deep breaths.

He'd taken a risk. He'd done it fully aware. He would never regret going after the woman he wanted. He had a business and a career he enjoyed. He had an amazing son. He would move on without her. He'd watched her spread her wings, and he would always know he hadn't held her back.

Marlys finished her day barren of any excitement she would've expected to feel. The offer was everything Sam said it was. It was all the respect and recognition she'd ever wanted. But every time she pictured her life if she moved back to Philadelphia she felt sick and empty inside.

Not seeing August for one day, and knowing he was unhappy and probably bewildered by the thought of her leaving, cut into any pleasure she could hope to experience. Sam was no doubt keeping them away so as not to influence her decision or make her feel bad.

She felt bad anyway.

She remembered every moment they'd spent together, privately, with August, with friends. Anticipating her future in Cowboy Creek had been exhilarating. She'd gone so far as to imagine them buying a home together. She'd struggled with feelings of inadequacy because she didn't know how to cook or run a household, and she realized now those insecurities had risen from her desire to please a husband, to make a family, to become more than only a doctor, but a wife and mother, as well.

Sam had encouraged her to take the teaching position. He believed it was an excellent opportunity, and it was. But the opportunities that waited for her here were enticing, too...

It was impossible to sleep with the burden of this decision on her mind. She woke exhausted at dawn on the day before Christmas and prepared herself a mineral bath. She didn't often allow herself the time for this luxury, but she needed to lift her spirits. She soaked and prayed. Washed her hair and dried it in front of the stove. There was a service that evening, so she took time to select a dress from the new ones Hannah had sewn and hung it on the door of her cupboard.

She dressed and heated more water. By noon she had treated blisters, a burn, a stomachache and been asked if she could make hair grow on a sixteen-year-old boy's chest.

He looked a mite puny to her. She imagined he worried he wasn't manly enough to interest someone of the fairer sex. She made him a tonic with iron and castor oil, and advised him to take it daily.

"Will hair grow on my chest?" His voice had already changed, and it was only a matter of time until his wish came true.

"It may take a while," she told him, "but if you eat well and get fresh air and exercise, you can be sure that hair will grow."

He extended a coin to pay her.

She raised her palm. "Not today. It's Christmas Eve. My gift to you."

"Thank you, Doctor."

Darius added wood to the stove. "Couldn't help overhearing, Dr. Boyd. That boy is going to grow chest hair on his own."

"You know that, and I know that, but he didn't know that. He wouldn't have believed me if I'd told him and might have even sent for one of those harebrained concoctions available in the catalogs. What I gave him was safe and will actually do him good."

Smiling, her assistant clanged the stove door shut.

"Mrs. Kendricks won't be here until eleven," she reminded him as she prepared to depart. "I'm going out. If there's an emergency you can reach me at the Gardner home on Lincoln Boulevard."

Darius nodded. "Yes, Doctor."

She bundled up and walked the short distance. As soon as Leah opened the door, tears rolled down Marlys's cheeks.

"Whatever is it? Come in."

Once settled on her settee, Evie in the bassinet nearby, Leah said, "Out with it."

Marlys told her the whole story, stumbling over her words, explaining with flushed cheeks how Sam had asked her to marry him and how she'd promised him an answer by tomorrow. "And then the letter changed everything."

"What did it change?" Leah asked. "Did it change how you feel about Sam?"

"No. That's why I'm so perplexed."

"Did it change how Sam feels about you?"

"I don't think so. I know he's proud of me. He believes it's a golden opportunity."

"Which it is."

"Yes. He thinks I should accept the position."

"Why do you think he said that?"

"Because he doesn't want to hold me back. Because he doesn't want to…stop me."

When she glanced up, Leah had one brow raised.

"He didn't tell me to stay."

"Why do you suppose not?"

Marlys shook her head. "It took a lot of courage for him to propose a second time. Last time I backed out."

"But he *did* propose."

"Yes, because I wanted him to."

"Because…"

"Because I love him." She blinked at Leah. "I wasn't even sure before, but I do love him."

"Has he told you he loves you?"

"No." And before the other woman could ask, she added, "Because he's afraid."

"I'd guess you're right. He was afraid you'd choose your career over him again. And now you truly have to make that choice."

She mopped her eyes with her handkerchief. "What am I going to do?"

"No one can tell you that. You're going to have to look into your heart for that answer."

On the way home, Darius met her at a run. "You have a patient. Thinks his arm is busted and Doc Foster was nowhere to be found."

The rest of her day was filled with patients and ladies coming for their mineral baths. She barely had time to eat a quick meal and dress for the evening service. At a loud knock at the front office door, she discovered Daniel Gardner. "Leah says you're riding with us."

"Pardon me for nosing in on your business," Leah Gardner said to Sam that evening as he glanced around the crowded church for a seat. He'd wanted to slip in at the last minute to avoid Marlys, but August had to be there early to prepare for his part in the program. "But it's come to my attention that you must have rocks in your head."

"Excuse me?" Sam frowned at the woman.

"Dr. Boyd might have an easier time making a decision if you'd just tell her you love her."

Sam's collar felt tighter and warmer than it had minutes ago. He ran a finger under it, and his gaze landed on Marlys taking a seat beside James Johnson and reaching to procure the baby.

"That's all I have to say." Leah took her leave and joined her husband, who held their baby wrapped in a white blanket.

Sam found a place several rows behind Marlys, deliberately not beside anyone he knew. Marlys had probably spoken to Leah in confidence as a friend, and he doubted Leah would share their personal business, but still he felt uncomfortable.

And annoyed. Did Leah Gardner really think it was that easy to put his heart out there for Marlys to trample over again?

The children's choir sang a selection of Christmas songs, and Hannah Johnson directed them in a play about the birth of the Christ child. August was a shepherd, and he beamed at Sam. When he recited his verse that Sam had helped him memorize, Sam's throat got tight with emotion. During the rest of the service, his thoughts wandered to what Leah had said. If Marlys was having a hard time deciding, she must not want to stay very badly. The lure of this opportunity had to be stronger than the idea of staying here. If she truly wanted to stay, she would make that choice. Nothing he said would change that.

Would it?

He was afraid. He was proud. He didn't want to be hurt, so he was being defensive. Telling her to go had been self-protective. If he told her he loved her, the choice to leave would be a deliberate rejection of that love. Hiding his personal loss and pain was a character flaw; it wasn't strength. Who had he fooled?

The program ended with the children carrying lit candles along the aisle to the rear of the building.

"Mr. and Mrs. Canfield have provided refreshments at their home," Reverend Taggart announced. "Please, join us."

"How did I do, Papa?" August asked.

"You were undoubtedly the best shepherd I've ever seen," Sam replied with a forced smile.

August grinned. One of his incisors was loose, making the tooth charmingly crooked, but not yet loose enough to pull. Sam loved his boy so much. Was August secure in his love? "Do you know how much I love you, son?"

"I love you, too, Papa. We're going to be just fine, so don't worry."

Was his agitation so obvious that an eight-year-old was compelled to encourage him? He helped his son remove his costume and fold it. August reached for his hand, and they got their coats and followed the crowd across the yards in the dark toward the well-lit house behind. Will Canfield had built a home suitable for a man with his eye on the governorship. They found refreshments set out on a sideboard in the elaborate dining room, then carried plates to a large reception area.

A boy who'd been a wise man in the play invited August to sit with several children at a low table surrounded by short stools. "Go ahead," Sam told him. "Have fun."

Sam visited with James, who held little Ava. A doting father, he bounced the infant on one arm and gave her exaggerated smiles that made her grin and drool. Sam even laughed at that.

August tugged the sleeve of his jacket and drew him to a doorway which led to an enormous entry. Leah led Marlys to the same spot, and he recognized the second Marlys spotted Sam. She gave him a weak smile.

"This is sure a nice house, isn't it, Papa?"

"Yes. It's nice." He glanced from Marlys down at August.

August pointed upward.

Sam looked up.

A sprig of mistletoe hung over Marlys's head. She noticed where they were looking and glanced up. Her gaze shot back to Sam's, and color flooded her face.

It became obvious that several guests were watching the scenario unfold as well, smiling expectantly.

"Others have been kissing under the mistletoe just like you said, Papa. I saw 'em." August gave his father a gentle shove.

As Sam approached Marlys, her eyes widened in surprise. She wore a pretty blue dress he'd never seen before. Her glowing cheeks flushed in embarrassment. She had no idea how beautiful he found her. Perhaps because he'd never told her. Her confidence was in her knowledge and ability, not in her femininity. But she was feminine...and exotic in a way that lured him to her like a sweet mystery.

"You're beautiful, Marlys."

Her eyes widened. Her lips parted, but she said nothing.

"I've told you how smart you are, what a good doctor you are, but I've never told you how beautiful you are. How pretty your hair is in the sunlight. How I like the way your eyes sparkle when you're pleased or flash when you're aggravated. I've never told you a lot of things because I was a coward.

"Even if you decide to take that teaching job and leave, I still want you to know this one thing. I love you."

Tears welled in her eyes, and she blinked.

"I loved you a dozen years ago when I asked you to marry me the first time. I loved you the second time I asked you to marry me. And I love you right now."

"Sam." His name came out on a distressing sob, but she stepped toward him and placed her hand on his shirt front. "I love you, too. I do. I wasn't even sure...have never been sure what love is. But I know now. And I know it's what I feel for you. I don't want to leave you or August and go to Philadelphia. I don't need the acceptance or respect I once believed was so important. Nothing could ever be as satisfying as loving you. You love and respect me for who I am."

"I do."

He wrapped his arms around her and drew her closer. Nothing else existed except this moment in time, except her smile and the hitch in her breathing when he lowered his face. He kissed her as tenderly and sweetly as he'd wanted to since he'd seen her standing here. He kissed her like he wanted to for the rest of their lives.

A smattering of applause caught his attention, and he drew back to look at her. Her cheeks were bright red now. He glanced aside at the same time she did to see their friends and fellow townspeople, including August, Leah, Hannah and James, all grinning from ear to ear.

"That mistletoe really works!" At August's exclamation, laughter broke out.

August darted forward and wrapped his arms around Marlys's waist. "You're not leaving?"

"Never. I'm staying right here and marrying your father."

"And you'll be my mother?" he asked in more-than-adequate Chinese that Sam understood.

"If you want me to be your mother, I'll be proud to have that title, and the hugs that come with it."

"I do," he said in English.

"Then I do, too." She bent and kissed his forehead.

"I think we're going to be hearing more 'I do's very soon." Reverend Taggart's grin split his face.

"This calls for a song!" Pippa exclaimed. "What would you like to hear?"

"I'd like to hear our song," Sam said.

Marlys looked up at him. "*Our* song?"

"It's a love song, but not the love song one expects."

Marlys gave him a broad grin. "From the thanksgiving celebration."

"I know now," Pippa said. She took a pitch pipe from a concealed pocket of her full skirt, provoking a few chuckles, and blew into it, creating a note in the key she'd chosen.

"O worship the King, all glorious above, o gratefully sing His power and His love; our shield and defender, the Ancient of Days, pavilioned in splendor and girded with praise."

Others joined in on the second verse. Sam held Marlys's hand the way he had that evening in the ballroom, and they looked into each other's eyes. The Lord had answered all of their prayers. Against all odds they'd found each other again after all these years, searched their hearts and discovered a broader and a deeper love than either had ever imagined.

"We have so much to be thankful for," Marlys said near his ear.

"Like finding each other again after all this time," he agreed.

"And making a family together."

He smiled. "I could never have anticipated a reunion under the mistletoe."

"There will plenty of Christmases," she assured him.

"And plenty of kisses."

"O tell of His might, o sing of His grace, whose robe is the light, whose canopy space. His chariots of wrath the deep thunderclouds form, and dark is His path on the wings of the storm."

* * * * *

Dear Reader,

I enjoyed heading back to Cowboy Creek, Kansas, to re-visit the characters from my book, *Want Ad Wedding*, as well as those from *Special Delivery Baby* (Sherri Shackelford) and *Bride By Arrangement* (Karen Kirst). Once a setting as interesting and vivid as Cowboy Creek has been created, it's a shame not to keep it alive and populated.

I adored the character of Dr. Marlys Boyd, an innovative and determined young woman ahead of her time. She came into focus on the pages when I read *The Doctor Wore Petticoats*, a book about early women doctors that my friend Julie Steele sent me. It's shocking now to imagine, but in the 1800s miners, trappers, drovers and emigrants chose to suffer and die rather than be treated by a female doctor. Those women's strength of spirit and determination forged paths equal to those fighting for the vote.

Author and journalist Sam Mason has already had his feathers singed by the ambitious lady doctor, so when he encounters her in the town where he's only recently started a newspaper, he's not likely to fool himself into thinking she might take a shine to being a wife and mother. Her headstrong ways bring out his protective instincts, however, so it was fun to discover all the ways Marlys made him crazy—and crazy in love with her.

I can't wait to hear what you think of Sam and Marlys's story. Email me at SaintJohn@aol.com.

Cheryl St. John

MISTLETOE BRIDE

Sherri Shackelford

To Barb. I miss you.

Thou wilt shew me the path of life:
in thy presence is fulness of joy;
at thy right hand there are pleasures for evermore.
—*Psalms* 16:11

Chapter One

Kansas, late October 1868

Colton Werner knew death. He'd survived the War Between the States. He'd seen enough men perish to recognize mortality was rapidly overtaking the woman in front of him. She was heavily pregnant, her stomach full and round beneath the blankets.

The promise of a new life contrasted sharply with her ashen face and glazed eyes. Kerosene lamps scattered throughout the doctor's examination room offered wan circles of illumination. The flames seemed to battle the darkness, as though sorrow was sapping their glow on its way to claim the woman. The mingled scents of alcohol, laudanum and chloroform sent his stomach churning.

Sweat slicked the woman's skin and plastered her dark hair against her forehead. Propped into a half-sitting position on the bed, her head lolled against the stacked pillows. She was young and might have been pretty. He couldn't really tell under the circumstances.

Catching the woman's desperate gaze, Colton sucked in a breath.

"Bitte," the woman spoke weakly. *"Hilf mir."*

Please, help me.

The foreign words echoed deep in the recesses of his brain, clicking into life the rusted gears of a language he hadn't used in over a decade.

"*Wo ist Quincy Davis?*" the woman asked, her voice barely more than a whisper.

Where is Quincy Davis?

Colton's chest seized, and he caught sight of Leah Gardner near the foot of the bed. Leah was married to his friend Daniel and also served as the town midwife.

Leah beckoned him nearer. "Thank the stars you're here. She's gone into labor. She was speaking some English before, but she's delirious, and she's slipped into speaking only German. I think she understands what we're saying, but I can't be sure."

Colton backed away, bumping into the doorjamb. "I can't."

He was done. Done with death. Done with the dying. Done. He wanted his own peace.

Leah crossed the narrow space in two strides. Catching his sleeve, she urged him through the door and into the narrow corridor of the doctor's offices. Always calm and efficient, Leah wore her blond hair in a neat roll at the base of her neck, and a white apron covered her elegant yellow dress. She'd clearly come from a formal engagement—a dinner at the Cattleman Hotel with her husband or a trip to the local opera house.

"You're the only one who can help her," she asserted, her voice low and urgent. "You speak German, don't you?"

"As a youngster. With my grandparents. That was years ago."

"You're the best we have under the circumstances." Sorrow glistened in Leah's cornflower-blue eyes. "She doesn't have much time."

Not much time. A euphemism. Refusing to say the words didn't hold the reaper at bay. "What's wrong with her?"

"I'll spare you a lengthy medical explanation, but I will say I've only seen a few cases during my time as a midwife, and I've never had a mother or baby survive." The midwife's expression grew pleading. "I've also never seen the illness this late in the pregnancy. She's already in labor. I might be able to save the baby."

Colton flinched away from her optimism. "What about the doctor? Can't he help?" Even as he asked, he feared he already knew the answer.

His gaze slid over the pregnant woman, and he shied away from the gravity of the situation. It seemed the woman recognized she was combating death. He'd caught the torment in her dark eyes. A death prolonged in the young was all the more tragic. That's what his brother Joseph had taught him. That's what the war had soldered into his soul. First there was shock, then the inevitable 'why.' *Why me? Why now?*

Leah's mouth tightened into a thin line. "The doctor has gone to fetch Reverend Taggart."

"I see."

If she'd sent for a clergyman, Leah was not as optimistic as she'd have Colton believe.

"I need your help." The midwife splayed her hands. "The only clue we've discovered is a name."

"Quincy Davis?"

"Yes. I'm afraid so."

Whatever the pregnant woman wanted from Quincy Davis, he wasn't coming. Rubbing the back of his neck, Colton stared down the darkened corridor. Quincy, the former town sheriff, had been killed by the Murdoch Gang the previous spring.

"Where did she come from?" Colton asked, unable to contain his morbid curiosity. "Why is she here?"

"She arrived on the evening train. We need your help to find out the rest."

"I shouldn't be here." He wrestled with his honor, wanting only to push through the front doors and run as far and as fast as his feet would take him. "What about the Schuylers? They speak German. A woman would be better."

"You were the closest. She doesn't have time for us to fetch someone else."

A muffled cry interrupted Leah's next words. With a last beseeching look, she hurried past him and into the examination room once more.

Colton braced his hands against the opposite wall and rested his forehead against the rough plaster. He'd served in the war with Leah's husband, Daniel. The life of a soldier consisted of long days of boredom punctuated by hours of sheer terror. The hazardous conditions had forged unbreakable bonds of friendship. The thought of refusing to help his friend's wife went against the grain.

Before the war, Colton had apprenticed as a blacksmith beneath his grandfather's tutelage. After the war he'd moved to Cowboy Creek at the invitation of three men he'd known in the war—including Daniel. His fellow soldiers had founded the town, and they'd needed a farrier.

The years peeled away, and he was boy again thrust into an unknown situation. Though his father was fluent in German, his parents had spoken only English when he was a child. For the first few months after being sent to live with his grandparents, the language barrier had left him completely and utterly isolated in their home.

There was no greater loneliness than being surrounded by people, yet trapped behind an invisible wall of words. He'd remained quarantined in his own misery until he'd finally managed to grasp a few phrases. The poor woman in the other room was dying, which was terrifying enough. He couldn't leave her alone, divided from the people trying to help her by the lack of a common language.

After a long moment, he pushed off and joined Leah by the woman's bedside.

"*Ich bin Colton Werner*," he said. "*Wie heissen sie?*"

"Beatrix," she replied. The startled relief on her face shamed him for hesitating. "Beatrix Haas."

Her next words tumbled over each other in frantic succession, and he struggled to comprehend. His German was eroded, buried beneath years of disuse. She'd traveled from Austria, and her accent was unfamiliar, as well. He knew little of the country beyond what he'd recently read in the papers. Following the Austro-Prussian War, Austria had been unseated as the head of the German Confederation. But that was the extent of his knowledge.

He held up his hands. "*Bitte langsamer*," he urged her. *Speak slower.*

Her face screwed up, and she hunched forward.

Leah put her hand on a blanket covering the woman's bent knees. "Breathe through the pains."

Colton translated the words. He must have spoken passably well, because Beatrix nodded and followed the instructions. Long seconds passed before she collapsed against the pillows once more.

For the next hour, between the contractions, he pieced together her story. When Beatrix completed her tragic tale, Colton relayed her story to Leah. "Her name is Beatrix Haas. The father of the baby refused to marry her. To keep them apart, his parents arranged his marriage to someone more suitable."

Beatrix clutched his hand, panting and moaning amid torrents of rushed speech. With each agonized groan, with each tragic piece of her story, his heart ached for her. He'd never been able to separate himself from the suffering of others.

"Good," he said in German, the words weak and insufficient. "You're doing well."

He was out of his depth in a sickroom.

Metalwork had always made more sense to him than people. Following the war, he'd immersed himself in his calling. He understood the personality of each ore—the melting points, the yielding points. He was a farrier like his grandfather before him, but he also excelled at other forms of metalwork. He found the mechanisms involved in crafting locks especially fascinating.

"The poor thing." Leah rinsed a cloth in the basin at her feet and extended her arm. "I have a feeling I know how this story ends."

Colton draped the material over the woman's forehead. The sound of her own language soothed her, and she turned her forehead into the palm of his hand.

Beatrix was stronger than he'd first supposed. This was not a woman who'd slip away quietly without a struggle.

"Her father shunned her." Colton quietly relayed the final piece of her story. "The pastor of her village arranged her marriage to a distant cousin of his, Quincy Davis, but her would-be groom never sent the tickets for her travels. She sold most of her belongings and gathered enough money to make the trip."

"I was afraid of that," Leah said. "We must tell her."

"She's already weak," Colton said. "What if she's not strong enough for the truth?"

"If the baby lives, we'll need to make arrangements. She must know the truth."

Colton gathered himself and spoke in his halting German. Beatrix's eyes welled, and she blinked rapidly. Though he was only relaying the news, a sense of disgrace filled him, as though he was the one who'd shattered her hopes and dreams, and not simply the messenger.

When she finally spoke, her words were faltering, and he interpreted as best he could.

"She doesn't want her baby born illegitimate," he said, his chest tightening. He understood her sense of shame. He'd disgraced his own family. More than dishonor, he'd brought death. His brother Joseph's death. "She doesn't want more shame on her family."

Beatrix clutched his hand. "*Bitte*."

Please.

"The shame is not hers to bear." Grim but sympathetic, Leah wiped her brow with the back of her hand. "This is no time for a lecture on the responsibilities of men in the making of children. I'm afraid it's too late. This baby is not waiting."

"How much time?"

"An hour. Maybe less."

Beatrix invoked a protective instinct within him. Spurred by a remarkably strong emotion, Colton made his decision. All his life he'd been atoning for Joseph's death. This was another penance, though a weak penance. He couldn't save Beatrix—but Leah was correct, the shame did not rest with her. If giving her baby a name provided the dying woman with a modicum of peace, then his path was simple.

He was not meant to be happy, and there was no joy in this occasion.

"When Reverend Taggart arrives," Colton said, "I'll marry her."

Beatrix started. The next pain hit with a force that sucked the breath from her lungs. She panted and squeezed her eyes shut, stifling a moan. For an eternity she could focus on nothing but her body, on the all-consuming need to push her child into the world. When the pain subsided, she crumpled against the pillows.

At least she had the man's halting German. Speaking English required concentration, and she was exhausted. Colton Werner, he'd called himself. A German name. He spoke with a German accent. Her father would hate him. As an Austrian, since the war, her father loathed the Germans.

Colton was a giant compared to the men in her family. Dark-haired and handsome, without a hint of callowness in his bold features. The skin on his face was tanned and weathered, with a slight stubble of shaven whiskers casting a dark shadow over his jaw. He adjusted the pillow behind her head with work-roughened hands.

Numerous nicks and burns covered his fingers, and a raised scar slashed the back of his hand, disappearing beneath his cuff. His shoulders were broad, and his biceps stretched the fabric of his ready-made canvas shirt. The only softness to his fierce visage were his eyes, a curious shade of bottle green surrounded by a lighter hue of brown that was almost golden.

"Do not let my baby suffer for my mistakes." Beatrix spoke slowly, flattening her accent, willing him to understand.

She was too weak to mitigate her sordid tale, too tired to care what these people thought of her. They may judge her, but her child was not to blame. She didn't regret her baby, only the foolish person she'd been.

"There are no judges here." Colton pressed a hand against his chest. "Only here."

The anguish in his eyes mirrored her own remorse. This was a man who understood shame. The sure knowledge of his kinship in suffering created a bond between them. His ability to speak her language only drew her tighter into the sense of familiarity and comfort he provided. How long since anything had been familiar? Everything was unfamiliar: the sights, the sounds, the smells.

"Talk to me," she begged.

"I understand the words better than I speak them," he replied sadly.

"Do you know a song? A poem? Anything."

Her insistence provoked a frustrated sigh, and she was immediately remorseful. "Never mind."

He crooked his finger and reverently touched the side of her cheek. An instant later he jerked away, a flush of hot color washing over his weathered cheeks. "I will try."

He spoke a few words of a childhood poem, his pronunciation thick, his forehead creased in concentration over each syllable.

Despite his awkward phrasing, she took a desperate comfort in the sound of his voice. She fought the tug of sleep, certain that if she gave in, she would never wake. But staying alert was so difficult. She'd exhausted the last of her strength on the journey. A journey that never should have been.

Peter had promised her marriage, but when his father had arranged his courtship to another girl, he'd turned his back on her. He'd turned his back on their child. She pressed the heel of her hand against her throbbing forehead. Marriage to Peter would have been a misery, but at least her child would have had a home, a family.

Her father thought women were weak, yet she doubted he could withstand the pain she was suffering. Her father thought women were weak, and yet his eight girls had survived into adulthood, and her three brothers had not lived past infancy. He thought women were weak, and yet

Peter was the weak one. He had not been strong enough to face his family. He had not been strong enough to face her father.

She wanted to shout against the injustice. He had not been strong enough to face her.

For the whole of her life she'd been told that women were the weaker sex, yet women were the ones left to bear the burden when men turned feeble.

She placed a limp hand on Colton's sleeve, halting his torturous recitation with a grateful smile. "*Danke schön*."

"You're welcome."

"I know a little English," she spoke haltingly. "But my English requires much thought."

He smiled, softening the harsh lines of his face. "Then I will speak my poor German."

How long had it been since she'd smiled herself? Nothing had turned out as she'd planned.

When the pastor had arranged her marriage to Quincy Davis, she'd been certain of his strength. He was a sheriff. He'd survived the War Between the States. There'd been no love between them, no promise of future love, only a simple partnership against a harsh land. He'd chosen to marry her and care for her baby even when Peter had chosen another and her father had shunned her.

Quincy Davis had been her last hope. But now he was gone. There was no one left to count on but herself.

Moments later another pain struck. The agony bloomed from her spine around her middle, sending her head throbbing with bone-crushing pressure. She'd had a backache since early that morning, but she'd been traveling for weeks; of course her back ached. As for the rest of her discomforts, she'd thought the traveling had made the swelling worse. Her headache had been from the meal she'd skipped. She hadn't wanted to believe that anything could be truly wrong. She'd been so very close, and now everything was slipping away.

She caught Colton's hand and forced him to look at her. "My baby?" she asked in her native tongue. "Will my baby survive?"

His gaze flickered for a moment, the barest second, and her hope drained.

"*Ja,*" he said. "*Dein Baby ist stark.*"

Your baby is strong.

Her English was lacking, but she wasn't a fool. She'd seen the sad shake of the doctor's head; she'd noticed how the midwife's brow had furrowed. After attending the births of numerous nieces and nephews, she understood full well that what she was experiencing wasn't normal. The next pain tortured her bones. The agony intensified until she feared she would split in two. She fumbled for Colton's fingers once more, craving the reassurance of human touch. Even as her life slipped away, he was vital and alive. Strong. She clutched him as though she could tap his power for her own.

Closing her eyes, she pictured the mountains of her homeland. She'd left Austria behind forever.

Another voice spoke, and her eyes flew open. A man stood in the threshold of the room. Older than Colton, he was shorter and stouter, with light brown hair and a neatly trimmed beard. His face was set in a grim line, and his eyes were filled with sympathy. The collar of his neat shirt marked him as clergy.

"*Nein!*" Beatrix called. "No."

Chapter Two

～❦～

She wasn't dying. Her baby wasn't dying. She wanted to see her child's eyes and touch the tips of her baby's tiny fingers. She wasn't leaving this world without a fight.

With his heavy enunciation, Colton spoke, "The reverend will marry us."

The offer took Beatrix aback. "You have no wife?"

A grim smile lifted one corner of his mouth. "*Nein.*"

Certainly he'd been married before. He was handsome and kind. Not old, but not young, either. Surely that sort of man had been married by now? A widower, perhaps.

"*Warum ich?*" she asked.

Why me? Why had he offered? She was nothing to him.

"I will give your baby a name." He clasped his hands and rested his elbows on his knees. "If that is your wish."

Some of her confusion eased. He was offering her a name, not a life together. Though no one had said the words aloud, they were all avoiding the same truth. Her life was slipping away. If she lost her struggle, her child would be an orphan. An orphan at the mercy of these strangers. But that prospect was not so frightening when she thought of the mercy already shown by this gentle giant of a man.

Her time was running short. Decisions must be made.

She didn't know Colton Werner, but she hadn't known Quincy Davis, either. At least with the sheriff, she had the word of his cousin. This man was unfamiliar to her. Through her pain and misery, she sensed a contradiction in Colton. He was offering the marriage as much as a kindness as a sacrifice.

What had he done in his life that required a sacrifice?

Leah, the midwife, spoke, and Colton translated.

"She says that I am a good man." His face flushed. "She says that your baby will always have a home. *You* will always have a home."

Despite their charity, a part of Beatrix held back. Tears leaked from the corners of her eyes. The kindness of these people, strangers, was almost too much to bear. Dare she trust in their generosity? Colton brushed the tear from her cheek. "What about your family? How can we reach them?"

"No. No family."

Let her sisters believe she was settled and content, as she had planned to be. Let her father believe whatever he chose. Though weak in body, her consciousness had not diminished, only narrowed, and she battled with herself. Her hope in the future warred with the experiences of her past.

Another labor pain struck, and the urge to push temporarily robbed her of any rational thought. Leah voiced instructions, and Colton translated.

"Very soon," Leah said, her eyes kind. "You'll meet your baby soon."

Colton Werner would give her a baby a name. A strong, German name her father would loathe.

"There are better men," Colton's voice grew thick. "But there's no time."

His admission flooded her with reckless gratitude. Her

grandfather had said that only the blessed could see beautiful things in humble places. Colton was a humble man.

Beatrix studied her unexpected savior. "You served in the war?"

"Yes. Four years."

He was hearty and fit. She'd read about the War Between the States, and she'd seen the faces of the boys at home who'd served in the Battle of Königgrätz during the Austro-Prussian War. Colton Werner had the same haunted look in his eyes. He was a survivor. From the train window she'd seen the endless stretches of merciless prairie punctuated by the occasional lonely town or solitary outpost. Only a strong man would seek to build a life here. He'd be the defender that her child needed in this stark and unforgiving land.

The nearer she came to death, the more focused she became on life. There was an odd kind of power in accepting the inevitable. She knew with a certainty born of suffering that everything she did in this moment changed the next. Not just for her, but also for the life she'd cradled within her.

Allowing herself only a moment to grieve for the future she'd never see, Beatrix touched Colton's sleeve. "Yes. Yes, I will marry you."

Her rushed gratitude sent Colton's stomach folding. He wasn't worthy of her admiration. He was a fraud, and if she looked into his past, she'd see the proof. His intervention was no more substantial than a false storefront. Leah had already assured him that if the baby survived, she and Daniel would raise the child along with their own baby—Colton had done nothing, save answer the call for a translator.

The reverend cleared his throat. "These are very unusual circumstances." Before Colton could voice his justification, the reverend held up his hand. "I've grown accustomed to unusual circumstances around Cowboy Creek."

Leah snapped her fingers, drawing their attention. "You've got about four minutes to perform the ceremony before the next contraction arrives. The baby isn't far behind."

Her urgency spurred them into action.

"Duly noted." The reverend adjusted a pair of spectacles over his nose and opened his Bible in the palm of his hand. "Please, join hands."

Colton took Beatrix's tiny hand, sensing the tension in her trembling fingers. Without stopping to think, he dropped a kiss on her flushed cheek and brushed the damp hair from her forehead.

Her eyes glistened. "*Danke schön.*"

The reverend scooted nearer the kerosene lamp and bent his head. "A wedding is the celebration of the marvel of love. Colton Werner and Beatrix Haas, today, in the presence of God, we celebrate this wonder of your lives."

Colton started to translate, but Beatrix held two fingers against his lips. "This I understand in my heart."

The reverend dabbed at his forehead with his handkerchief. "Do you, Colton Werner, take this woman, to live together in marriage; will you love her, comfort her, honor and keep her, in health and in sickness, in prosperity and in adversity; and forsaking all others, be faithful to her, so long as you shall live?"

"I do," Colton replied, his throat tight.

The reverend repeated the words for Beatrix, and Colton interpreted the sentiment as best he could.

"*Ja,*" Beatrix replied. "I do."

"Since my arrival in Cowboy Creek," Reverend Taggart said. "I have come to admire a passage from an Indian ceremony." He closed his Bible and held the book before him. "'Now you will feel no rain, for each of you will be shelter for the other. Now you will feel no cold, for each of you will be warmth for the other. Now there will be no loneliness, for each of you will be companion to the other. Now you are two persons, but there are three lives before you; His life, Her life and Your life together.' Soon there will be a child to complete your family. Amen."

"Amen," Beatrix and Colton spoke in unison.

The word fittingly translated into both languages.

"In accordance with the laws of the state of Kansas, with the authority of God's Word, and with great joy, I now pronounce you husband and wife." Reverend Taggart leaned closer to Colton's ear and spoke low. "I'll file the paperwork with the town clerk tomorrow. Tonight you're married in the eyes of God, and that's what matters."

Beatrix nodded, and her eyes fluttered and closed.

Fighting back his panic, Colton's heart hammered in his chest. He'd stepped into this commitment knowing the grave nature of the situation, fully aware of what he was undertaking. With the moment nearing, he raged against the inevitable.

"I'll leave you," the revered murmured, his face somber. "The doctor is on his way from the apothecary. There's a candlelight prayer service for Beatrix and her child at the church."

The pressure behind Colton's eyes built. "Thank you."

The reverend rested a heavy hand on Colton's shoulder. "You've done a good thing here today, son."

His words sent a flush of heat over Colton's face. "I did nothing."

He'd given her nothing. None of them had. Everyone had broken their promises to Beatrix: her own father, the father of her baby, Quincy Davis, even her own body. They'd all made promises they hadn't kept.

"You gave her peace in a time of need," the reverend replied quietly. "Who will give you peace, Mr. Werner? We'll be waiting at the church when there's news."

Colton didn't trust himself to speak, answering only with a curt nod. There was no peace for him, not with the guilt he would carry to his dying day.

Leah glanced up with a frown. "Where is that doctor? I need another set of hands."

"I can fetch him," Colton offered.

"Don't you dare leave me alone," she said sharply.

A hot wave of anxiety slipped along his spine. Leah never lost her temper. At least not in the time he'd known her. The midwife was frightened, and he took a firm grip on his brittle emotions. There'd be time enough to break down later. Leah needed him strong. Beatrix needed both of them at their best.

Another wave of contractions struck, and Beatrix weakly squeezed his hand.

"Almost there," Leah soothed. "Another push and you'll have your baby."

Beatrix screamed. The sound reverberated through Colton's chest, shaking him to the core.

"It's a boy," Leah exclaimed. "You've given birth to a boy."

Beatrix had gone slack. Colton touched her cheek, but her eyes drifted closed, and her breathing was shallow. Needles of alarm punctured his feigned calm.

"Help," he begged Leah. "You've got to help her."

"The baby first. I can't help her without finishing up with the baby."

Colton half stood and cupped Beatrix's cold cheeks. "You have a baby boy. Be strong. Be strong for your son."

Her eyes fluttered, and tears pooled on her lashes. "I'm tired."

"I know. I know you're tired." He'd given up on so much in his life; he wasn't giving up on this. "Fight for your baby."

Her eyes slid shut. While Leah dealt with the baby, he rubbed warmth into her chilled fingers.

An eternity seemed to pass.

"What's taking so long?" Colton demanded.

Leah stood, her face a mask of sorrow, she shook her head. "He's not reviving. I've tried everything I know, and a few things that aren't in the books. I'm afraid I can't help him." She stood and crossed toward Colton, then gently handed up the bundle into his outstretched arms. Speaking quietly, she said, "I'll try and save Beatrix. She mustn't know about the baby's condition, or she'll never fight. Clean him up and wrap him in a blanket. Once the doctor arrives, I'll assist you."

Nausea pitched in Colton's stomach. The bundle was smaller than a sack of flour and painfully light. He'd seen death in so many forms, but never one this small and helpless. He had to grow beyond himself, to be tougher than he'd ever been before to even deal with the thought of it.

Fearful of dropping his precious burden, Colton followed the corridor and discovered the kitchen. The fastidious doctor kept the space meticulously neat and tidy. Jars were arranged by height along the counter, and the enormous cast iron stove gleamed as though it had never been used.

Tucking the baby into the crook of his arm, Colton ladled water from the stove well into a pan he'd discovered hanging beneath the sink.

His hands full, he bent and snagged a towel from the

side of the washbasin with his teeth, then crossed to the butcher-block table in the center of the room.

He gently rested the child in the center and forced himself to peel back the edge of the enveloping blanket. Though an unnatural shade of purplish blue, the tiny face was wrinkled and discolored and absurdly perfect. Colton's eyes burned even as impotent rage flared in his chest. Where was God for Beatrix Haas and her baby?

Colton's hand dwarfed the tiny head. Keeping his fingers cupped protectively around the infant's body, he dipped the rag in the warmed water and pressed the wetted material against the baby's still rib cage.

The infant startled. Tiny arms splayed. Colton stumbled back a step, then frantically reached for the infant once more. He rested his hand on the tiny chest and felt the vigorous beating of a miniscule heart. The baby's first raucous cries sparked a jolt of pure joy through him. He scooped the bundle against his chest and wept with utter gratitude, his mumbled prayers and words of thanks pressed against the downy tuft of dark hair on the baby's head.

"You keep crying," Colton ordered. "You keep crying and fighting."

Reaching for a second clean towel, he snuggly wrapped the baby, then tucked the angry, howling infant into the hollow of his neck.

He caught the sound of a second voice echoing through the corridor. Giddy with relief, he returned to the sickroom. Leah and the doctor leaned over the bed in solemn examination.

The doctor held Beatrix's wrist and ducked his head. "Thready. She's very weak, but she's a fighter."

Leah caught sight of Colton. "What's the matter? What's happened?"

The crying that had resembled a thousand clanging bells in the kitchen was muffled against the blanket.

"He's alive." Colton declared. "He's a fighter."

"Oh, my word." Leah clutched her throat and lunged forward. "What? How?"

"I don't know. I was cleaning him, and he startled."

"This night has been full of surprises." Leah flipped back the blanket, her joyous expression at odds with the tears streaming down her cheeks. "His mother is struggling." She stood, swiped at the moisture, and reached for the baby. "I'll take this angry little fellow. We should leave the doctor to his work."

"No." Colton moved nearer the bed. "We're not leaving. Either of us."

Leah stilled. "I know you want to help. We all do. But the doctor is in charge now. There's nothing more for you to do."

"I don't believe we're helpless."

"Leah is right." The doctor glanced over his shoulder. "There's nothing you can do here."

Colton widened his stance and braced for battle. "I'm not leaving."

Chapter Three

Leah held up her hands in supplication and glanced at the doctor. "His presence certainly can't hurt."

"I won't be in the way." Colton tensed his jaw for a fight. "Beatrix needs her child."

With two fingers the doctor pushed up his glasses and pinched the bridge of his nose. "She doesn't even know he's here. She doesn't know any of us are here. There's little use in the infant remaining."

"She knows." Colton avoided confrontation at all costs. Because of his size, he was often seen as a challenge by other men. They'd pick a fight against him as a way to prove their manhood. He'd learned long ago to hold his tongue and keep his peace. Not today. Not now. He knew in his heart what needed to be done. "This child stays with his mother."

Sensing his implacable stance, Leah softened. "Let me at least examine the baby. I've got some supplies."

"As long as he doesn't leave the room."

"I promise." Leah gestured for the baby. "The child won't leave his mother's side."

Colton didn't know why, and there was no time for

searching his feelings, he only knew that Beatrix and the child needed each other desperately.

"He should have a name," Leah said. "You're his father in the eyes of the law. What name do you choose?"

Colton's chest tightened. *You're his father.* He'd married Beatrix. This was his child in the letter of the law. As the blue-black eyes blinked, he accepted the deeper truth. This child was his responsibility—not Leah's, not Daniel's. Watching the tiny warrior enter the world, seeing the little fighter struggle for his first breath, this was his son in every way that mattered.

Emotion clogged Colton's throat. His life had been inexorably shaped by his superior strength and size. He'd always had to be the toughest, because he was the one the others challenged. Right then he feared he might weep like the infant in his arms.

"Joseph." He glanced at Beatrix's pale face. None of this was fair. She should be laughing and crying with him, celebrating the life she'd brought into this world. She should be naming her son for someone who was important to her. Yet they knew nothing of her family beyond the few clues she'd provided. She'd given them little information, leaving him bound and helpless. Since she couldn't give her child a name, Colton chose the one name that meant the most to him, his brother's name. "We'll call him Joseph."

He prayed that Beatrix would understand and bless the choice he'd made for her.

Leah gave a somber nod, and Colton reluctantly released his cherished burden. Beneath his watchful gaze, she spent the next half an hour cleaning up the child and coaxing Joseph to suckle. When she'd wrapped the baby in swaddling, she returned him to Colton. Once in his arms, Joseph's eyes drifted closed.

"You've had a tough day," Colton crooned. "You deserve a rest."

The doctor had finished cleaning up the evidence of his birth. Beatrix lay beneath a sheet pulled up to her shoulders. Her ashen face blended with the white pillow beneath her head. Her lips were parted, and her breath came in shallow gasps. Leah had lovingly brushed the snarls from her dark hair and fanned the tresses over her shoulders.

With her features softened in slumber, Colton admired the soft curve of her cheeks and the gentle sweep of her brows. She couldn't be more than twenty, far too young to die. He recalled her eyes in the pale lamplight, a radiant shade of brown. The color of afternoon sunlight reflected through a russet bottle. Free from pain, in peaceful slumber, her beauty shone through once more. Not the delicate prettiness of filigree work, but the strong, tested beauty of tempered steel.

Taking a seat near the head of the bed, Colton brushed the hair from her shoulder and tucked Joseph against her bare skin.

Leah slumped against the wall, her stance mirroring his exhaustion. "You don't have to stay. You've already done more than most."

"I'm certain."

"This night will not go easy."

"I'm staying."

The doctor straightened the tools he'd arranged on the side table. "We can bleed her. There's little else we can do for her condition."

"No," Colton spoke brusquely. "She's suffered enough."

Colton had expected the doctor to be indignant at the presumption, but instead he seemed almost deferential.

"You're the husband," the doctor replied. "You make the decisions."

The weight of his responsibility humbled Colton. He wasn't a doctor, he didn't know medicine, but he'd seen plenty of men die. That knowledge gave him some sense of his duty. The time had come to wait and pray.

Daniel, Leah's husband, arrived a short while later. He wore the rough canvas pants and boots that had become his uniform around the stockyards he owned. His hair was brown, and his eyes were an intense green. Though not overly tall, he was a man to be reckoned with in a physical fight or a mental challenge.

The Gardners clearly adored one another. Daniel quickly took in the solemn event and wrapped his arm around his wife's shoulder, folding her into his embrace. She burrowed her head against his chest and circled her arms around his back.

"If only I could have done more," she said, her voice muffled into his shirt.

"You did everything you could, my love." He glanced at the squirming infant nestled against his mother's shoulder. "You saved the baby."

"That was Colton's doing. He wouldn't give up on his son."

Daniel jerked back. "His son?"

"It's a long story. I'll tell you everything once we're home, and I've put up my feet with a cup of tea in hand."

"You should be resting," Daniel said, exquisitely concerned for his wife. "My curiosity will wait at least that long."

After the two broke apart, Daniel placed his hand on Colton's shoulder. "I'm sorry, my friend. I had no idea what I was getting you into. Leah needed a translator, and I knew you spoke German."

"It's all right," Colton said, unbearably weary. "Take your wife home and let her get some shut-eye. I'm staying."

"I'll catch a few hours of sleep and return." Leah stifled a yawn behind her elegant fingers. "That baby will wake hungry. I'll show you how to prepare the pap and feed him."

The doctor stretched and rubbed his eyes. "I'm sorry, Mr. Werner. There's nothing to do now but wait. I'll be in the next room. Morning will come too soon."

Daniel frowned. "Colton shouldn't be alone—"

"He's fine." Leah pressed the backs of her fingers against her husband's cheek. "The doctor's room is right next door. Colton can call out if he needs anything, if anything changes…" Her throat worked. "If anything changes, if the baby fusses, send for me immediately. I'll be back in a few hours either way."

Once the three of them were alone again, Colton knelt beside the bed and rested his elbows on the edge of the mattress. Joseph nestled his tiny nose against the frail pulse at his mother's neck. Colton had given up praying a long time ago. Today was different. Today he prayed.

He pressed his thumb and forefinger against his eyes, stemming the flood of tears. He'd never had God's ear before, and he feared today was no different.

For the next few days Beatrix floated in and out of consciousness. She dreamed of Austria, she dreamed of her sisters and of her nieces and nephews. She dreamed of babies crying and babies feeding.

A sense of familiarity gradually surrounded the voices inhabiting her imaginings. There were two distinct male voices. One deep and calming, one higher-pitched and frail. There was a female voice as well, alternatively soothing and cajoling. As the days passed, her sensations of time and place were fluid until one morning her reality shifted, and she sensed a change. Beatrix fought toward the surface of her swirling dreams.

Her whole body ached. A sound caught her attention.

She forced open her weighted lids and took stock of her surroundings. Chilling panic infused her body, and she struggled upright. She didn't recognize anything. Where was she? What had happened?

"Easy, there." A firm hand rested on her shoulder. "You'll hurt yourself."

"Where am I?"

"What's the last thing you remember?"

"I arrived in Cowboy Creek. I wasn't feeling well."

The man sucked in a breath. "You don't think you're in Austria?"

"No. I traveled to America."

She blinked a few times, clearing her vision. Her eyes were watery, and she made out the form of a taller-than-average man.

"Don't try and move," he said. "I'll fetch the doctor."

The male voice disappeared, and the next instant another voice joined him. Beatrix focused on the face of a whip-thin man with graying hair and round spectacles. Instead of the German the other man had spoken to her, he spoke in English.

"I'm Doc Fletcher," the man said. "You are one amazing woman, Mrs. Werner."

The doctor was the polar opposite of the giant who'd spoken first. He was small and wiry thin. Balding on top, a gray fringe of hair showed around his ears. Laugh lines framed his gray eyes, softening the advancing years evident on his clean-shaven face.

Beatrix frowned. Her English must be worse than she'd thought. "Who is Mrs. Werner?"

"Oh, dear." The doctor shook his head. "This complicates matters."

Beatrix studied the enormous man hovering in the corner of the room, his arms cradling a bundle of blankets, and her memories of that first evening in Cowboy Creek came flooding back. These were the two male voices drifting through her slumber.

"We married!"

She'd married Colton Werner. The man with the strong German name her father would loathe.

"This isn't a dream?" she demanded.

The doctor chuckled. "You surprised us all, Mrs. Werner. I've been a doctor for more years than you've been alive, and I've never seen a recovery like yours. Your husband sat with you day and night. Wouldn't let us take the baby out of the room."

The tall man translated the words, and at one in particular, her heart nearly leaped from her chest.

"My baby! Where's my baby?"

Her dreams took shape, the cry of an infant, the feel of nursing the tiny life.

The giant—she still couldn't quite think of him as her husband—stepped forward and revealed a bundle with only a tiny mop of dark hair peeking through a mass of enveloping blankets. "You had a boy."

"Let me hold him."

She reached for the child, but a wave of nausea overwhelmed her. Quick on his feet, the doctor retrieved a bucket and settled her back once more.

"You've lost a lot of blood, Mrs. Werner. You've hardly been lucid for days. We nearly lost you. No sudden moves."

"Let me sit up at least."

The frantic need to hold her baby superseded all her other aches and pains.

The doctor arranged the pillows behind her head, and she fought against another wave of nausea. The small effort exhausted her, and she panted, catching her breath. Colton took the seat nearest the head of the bed and wrapped his arm around her shoulder, tucking the baby into the crook of her neck.

Despite his size, her new husband was surprisingly gentle. *Her husband.* She didn't know what to make of him. Everything had happened so suddenly that first evening, she'd made the decision to wed solely in order to give her child a name. She'd wanted her baby to have a father—she hadn't really thought of what it would mean for her to have a husband. Now she was alive and married to a stranger. She couldn't quite comprehend the sudden turn of events.

The baby mewled, a gentle coo, and the sound tugged at her heartstrings.

There'd be time enough to worry about her husband later. She studied her baby, filled with a sense of awe and wonder unlike anything she'd ever known. He was perfect, from the tiny lashes surrounding his blue-black eyes to the perfect bow of his lips. Those tiny lips opened and closed, seeking. A sense of complete an utter love blanketed her spirit.

She reached to pull her baby closer, but her arms were feeble and uncooperative.

"You're still weak," Colton said. "Little Joseph likes to nuzzle the spot right at the hollow of your neck."

"Little Joseph?"

Colton's face flushed. "We didn't know what name you would… We weren't certain… My brother's name was Joseph."

"Joseph," she said, testing the name on her tongue.

The changing of tenses wasn't lost on her. His brother was gone.

She'd put off thinking about names until after she was married and the child was born. She'd assumed she'd make the decision with her new husband—except her new husband was not the man she'd expected.

Though her mind temporarily rebelled at having the choice snatched from her, the flash of sorrow in Colton's eyes gave her pause. Joseph was a strong name. Joseph's brothers had sold him into slavery, but he'd become an important man. Beloved by his father...

She studied the tiny fingers of the infant. "Joseph is a fine name."

The doctor left, and a woman entered the room. She held a bowl of porridge with a glass of milk. "You should try and eat something," the woman said. "You need your strength. For the baby."

"I know this voice," Beatrix exclaimed.

The blonde woman perched on the side of the bed. "I'm Leah Gardner, midwife for Cowboy Creek. You've given us all quite a fright."

Beatrix automatically turned to Colton, and he translated. She struggled for the words in English.

"Thank you," she managed, "for looking after me."

Leah grinned. "Thank me by taking care of yourself. Please, eat."

The aroma sent Beatrix's stomach rumbling. She couldn't recall the last time she'd eaten.

Taking a sip of the milk, she grimaced. "This is different than the milk in Austria."

The midwife patted her arm. "I added some heavy cream. You need the weight. You have a big, strong boy to raise. I'll be back in a half an hour. Joseph will be hungry, too, by then."

She quietly exited the room.

"I recognize this tone," Beatrix glanced at Colton. "This tone means I should not argue."

"*Ja*," he teased. "I never argue with Mrs. Gardner when she takes that tone."

Though her hunger pains intensified, Beatrix was unwilling to let go of Joseph, even for a moment. She'd carried this precious life near her heart for nine months; she'd waited an eternity for this moment. As though sensing her difficulty, Colton arranged the tray on the other side of the bed.

She flashed a grateful smile, and he looked away. Her smile faded. She didn't know what to make of this man, Colton Werner. *Her husband*. She'd come to America to marry a stranger, an act she'd considered with trepidation. Men weren't always to be relied upon.

At least Quincy Davis had desired a companion. Though they'd only exchanged a few letters, they had each wanted the same thing: a partner. Nothing more.

She doubted Colton had wanted a wife. He'd married her because he thought she was dying and that her child would need a parent. She could release him from his bargain this instant, yet a part of her held back. He'd been so extravagantly kind that she wanted to do something for him in return. She had so little to give, only nurturing, yet she sensed nurturing was what he needed most.

There was a sorrow about Colton Werner. This gentle giant of a man seemed so alone—he needed care as much as anyone else in her life.

She turned her head toward Joseph and pressed a kiss against his downy cheek, then met Colton's gaze.

"Can you hold him?" she asked, speaking slowly in deference to her accent. "While I finish eating?"

Colton gently lifted the baby into his arms. His hands nearly enveloped the tiny form. She doubted he even realized what he was about, but he crooned, swaying back and forth.

Beatrix plucked at the blankets. "Thank you."

"For what?"

She blushed. "For marrying me."

Chapter Four

"I'm sorry you weren't able to marry the man you intended." Colton jostled baby Joseph. "You didn't come all this way to settle for me."

Beatrix's fears softened at his modest words. "I didn't even know Quincy. He was the second cousin of the pastor in my village. He'd left for America as a boy. I only knew him from his letters, and he wasn't much for writing."

"I didn't know Quincy well, either. None of us were aware that he sent for a bride."

She glanced away. "He knew I was expecting a baby. Maybe that's why he didn't tell anyone. Maybe he was ashamed."

Colton took a step nearer. "Never be ashamed of this beautiful life."

"You're not..." Her heart filled with a tenuous hope. "You're not embarrassed of me? Of Joseph?"

"I gave you my name. I gave Joseph my name. You should be proud of the life you've brought into this world."

She'd been living as a pariah for so long, his simple acceptance of her and her baby lifted a crushing weight from her shoulders. Even her sisters had been forced to turn their backs on her. Once her father had shunned her, the men in their family had followed suit. Her sisters would not go against their husbands.

Was Colton the exception? Would others in Cowboy Creek be as welcoming?

"I am proud of Joseph," she replied. "I know this isn't the bargain you intended."

"You survived, Beatrix. That's what I prayed for."

"Danke schön." He'd prayed for her. He'd stayed with her, and he'd prayed for her. He'd kept Joseph by her side. In the moments she'd felt herself slipping away, she'd clung to the gentle whisper of Joseph's breath against her neck. She owed Colton Werner her life. "Your German is better than before."

"I've been practicing. Reading old letters from my grandparents."

"Your grandparents are German? That's how you learned the language?"

"Yes. When I was younger, my brother died. I was sent to live with my grandparents. They spoke mostly German, although they learned English over the years."

The grief in his eyes was raw. "This brother was Joseph?"

"Yes."

She recalled her three brothers who hadn't survived past infancy and reached for baby Joseph, touching his tiny fingers. "How did your brother die?"

"An accident," Colton replied tersely. "It was a long time ago."

Why had she asked such a foolish question? That had always been a flaw of hers—she asked too much of people. She and her husband could start with at least a little common ground. Colton knew suffering, and she knew suffering. First, from the loss of her mother, and then, from the loss of her dreams. The youngest girl in the family, her father had expected she'd remain home and care for him once his wife passed away.

She'd craved something different. She'd seen the love her sisters shared with their husbands and their children, and she'd wanted that love for herself. She'd hoped to escape her father's plans with Peter, but she'd been foolish in thinking Peter could set her free. Holding Joseph, feeling the pure adoration in her heart, she was determined not to make the same mistakes. A life without love was better than a lifetime of one-sided love.

Colton noted when she'd finished eating and rested Joseph in the crook of her arm. "You'll want to be alone for a while." He rubbed the back of his neck. "You don't have to make any decisions just yet. No one will hold you to the choice you made before."

She locked gazes with his striking, exotic eyes, so beautiful and so at odds with the brutal nicks and scars from his profession that covered his hands and arms. When everyone else in her life had abandoned her, this stranger, this man, had stayed. He seemed so very alone and so very lonely. Was it wrong to hope she could bring some warmth into his life?

Yet something had brought this humble man into her life in her time of need. Whether it was God or fate or simple chance, she needed her suffering to have some meaning.

She swallowed back her nerves and gathered her courage. "I can make a good home for us."

Colton paused, his enormous hand braced on the doorframe, his eyes downcast.

An unconscious shiver rippled through her. Growing up, her father had not been opposed to using his hands to strike her. When he'd discovered her pregnancy, he'd used his fist. Colton was a giant compared to her father, capable of doing much more damage.

Yet she'd seen how the others treated Colton. During the journey to America, lacking the benefit of language, she'd become attuned at reading other signs of intent. The doctor, the midwife, the reverend—they all treated Colton with respect and deference. When people spoke to her father, they tensed, as though preparing for battle. No one grew tense when they spoke with Colton.

He lifted his gaze. "You don't have to make any permanent decisions. Everyone understands the circumstances. You have…other possibilities. Someone else may suit you better."

She sensed that he truly cared about what was best for her, and hope blossomed in her chest. This man she'd only known for a day cared more for her fate than others who should have cared the most. His consideration was more than she'd ever known. That was enough to build a life on.

"What about you?" she asked. "Do you have other possibilities? Is there someone who suits you?"

A self-deprecating grin lifted the corner of his mouth. "No."

Relief flowed through her. While she doubted he'd have married her had he been courting someone else, there must be some reason he hadn't married before now. Perhaps he was simply shy. There was only one last barrier she needed to cross.

"You named the baby Joseph," she said. "Can you love him? Care for him?"

"Yes." Colton gazed at the infant, his approval evident. Though he hid his feelings well otherwise, he didn't hide them now. "Any man would be lucky to have such a fine son."

His affection for Joseph was the foundation on which she'd build. While she didn't doubt her abilities to raise her child alone, she'd experienced the intolerance in the world and hoped to shield Joseph from it.

Peter's actions had dissuaded her of foolish dreams

of romantic love. She wanted only kindness and respect. A peaceful home in which to raise her child. They were united for Joseph.

"Rest," Colton ordered gruffly. "You've had a harrowing journey. I'll come back tomorrow. If you still feel the same, we can talk of the future."

His tone was deceptively neutral. Clearly he assumed she'd change her mind.

"*Morgen*," she said. "Tomorrow."

He leaned forward and brushed the pad of his thumb over the fluff of hair on Joseph's tiny head. "*Morgen*."

She'd give him a reprieve, a chance to recognize they were well-matched before she pushed her suit.

Once Colton exited the room, Beatrix propped Joseph on her bent knees. "I choose you, Colton Werner. I must convince you to choose us."

She had little faith in her own abilities to win Colton, especially considering the bleakness behind his eyes. He was mourning a deeper loss, a loss she didn't understand. But she'd seen the way he cared for Joseph, and that was one thing they had in common.

Her vision clouded.

What if Joseph wasn't enough?

Colton had heard rumors about the new lady doctor in town, Marlys Boyd. People said she practiced an odd form of medicine, something that drew from Chinese remedies and Indian herbs rather than the tonics and purgatives that traditional doctors used. He'd never put much stock in rumors, but after seeing the odd assortment of bathing tubs and potions in her office, he was inclined to pay more attention in the future. He turned his concentration back to the task at hand—installing a new door latch and lock on her storage room.

Kneeling on the floor before the door, he maneuvered the locking mechanism he was currently installing while he cast a surreptitious glance at the doctor's exotic dispensary. The pantry-like space held baskets of herbs as well as numerous glass bottles and jars. None of the items reminded him of anything he'd seen in the doc's office. She must consider her unusual potions valuable, though, because she'd requested a sturdy lock on the door.

After securing the metal box, he brushed the wood shavings from his trousers. Satisfied the mechanism was level, he screwed on the cover and added the handle.

Once he'd tested the lock a few times, he stood and extended his hand, presenting Dr. Boyd with the key. "This will give you all the security you need."

Dr. Boyd sported wavy chestnut brown hair that had been cut short and hung around her ears in an absent-minded, although not unpleasant, disarray. She was exotic-looking more than pretty, with intelligent brown eyes. Her gray dress was serviceable, without any added adornment or frippery. Everything about her struck him as smart, logical and straightforward. He admired her no-nonsense attitude, though he found her intense watchfulness slightly unsettling.

She tested the lock a few times, turning the key smoothly.

"This does appear secure," she said. "How is your wife? I admit I'm fascinated by her recovery. I've heard of similar cases, and the outcome is rarely positive."

"Beatrix is a fighter."

"She sounds remarkable. I'm looking forward to meeting her. Reverend Taggart revealed the whole tale when he organized the vigil for her. Of course, we all assumed she was dying. You believed that as well, I presume. I should warn you, there's been some gossip."

Colton ground his back teeth together. "I shouldn't be surprised."

"From what I've been told, a lot of people are expecting you to annul the marriage and leave town. Mostly folks are wondering why Quincy Davis didn't tell anyone she was arriving."

Dr. Boyd's forthright and dogged recitation of the situation had Colton unnerved. Then again, she was only repeating what other folks were thinking. Everyone was curious. Nothing unusual with that. He'd had his own bouts of curiosity in the past.

After the arrival of the first "bride train," organized by the town leaders to bring mail-order brides to Cowboy Creek, he'd been shocked by his friend Daniel's immediate marriage to Leah. Only later he'd discovered they'd been childhood friends. The hasty marriage had made more sense once he'd gathered all the pieces.

Colton smoothed a splinter near the recently installed locked. "Maybe no one asked Quincy Davis about his plans. He was a private man. With the Murdoch Gang on the loose, he didn't have much time for gossip."

Colton was tired of discussing Quincy in the same breath as his wife. The man was dead. While Colton mourned his loss as he would any other human being, all this talk wasn't bringing the man back or changing the facts. Colton had married Beatrix in his stead, and that's all anyone needed to know.

"You seem annoyed." Dr. Boyd blinked. "I shouldn't have pried."

"You're no different than anyone else. Everyone is curious. I'll give you some advice, though. Don't wager any money." Colton replaced his tools in his bag. "I'm not going anywhere."

"I don't gamble. There's no logic in gambling, and I don't believe in luck."

Colton wasn't a fool; he'd accepted his hasty marriage would inspire curiosity and gossip in equal measures. Acceptance of the inevitable didn't make him any less uncomfortable.

"I have to go," he said. "Let me know if you have any trouble with the lock."

"I've made you uncomfortable, Mr. Werner. My apologies. I've never understood social niceties. I prefer plain speaking to trivial small talk." Turning away, she straightened a sheaf of papers on a tall counter holding a microscope. "I've done some reading on the condition Leah described. A doctor in Europe proposed using a tincture of magnesium on the patient. Dr. Fletcher should have informed me of the woman's troubles sooner. The chance for experimentation is rare."

For one black moment, Colton was tempted to use an oath before a lady. "Beatrix is a person, not an experiment."

"When the alternative is death, drastic measures must be taken." Dr. Boyd crossed her arms. "When there is nothing to lose, there is everything to be gained. And any new information we gather can be used to save lives in the future."

"I have another lock to install."

Colton understood the need to look ahead to future patients, but Beatrix was a flesh-and-blood person, not an opportunity for a medical breakthrough. He sure hoped the doctor didn't need anything more anytime soon. While he admired her intelligence, he'd recently discovered an affinity for trivial small talk as opposed to plain speaking.

"My interest lies with healing." Dr. Boyd plucked a small square tin from a low shelf. "Thank you for the lock, and congratulations on your marriage—and on your son. Oh, and I have a salve for those scars, if you'd like."

At the considerate gesture, Colton's annoyance dissipated like steam vapor. She wasn't being deliberately insensitive; she was a doctor who considered all the possibilities, even the most desperate procedures. He should have known better than to take offense. In the war, there'd been a great many breakthroughs out of sheer desperation.

He was edgy because he honestly didn't know what to do about his marriage. Beatrix hadn't been lucid for days. While she hadn't appeared horrified at the prospect of being his wife when they'd spoken this morning, the chance for rumination might have changed her thinking. She'd nearly died, only to wake up married to a stranger.

He was exhausted and not thinking straight himself. He'd only kept his appointment with Dr. Boyd to keep his mind off his circumstances. So much for that idea.

"Beatrix has said she wants to stay married." Colton set his bag on the counter with more force than he'd intended, rattling the glass plates on Dr. Boyd's microscope. "But she hasn't met anyone else. That'll be one dollar for the lock."

He shied away from thinking about Beatrix courting another man.

"She'll have an abundance of choices. According to my research on the town, there are plenty of men in the area looking for a wife. Then again, she *is* an immigrant. There's the language barrier to consider." Dr. Boyd slipped the key he'd provided into her pocket. "She could easily be taken advantage of."

"No one is going to take advantage of her."

"The baby is also a drawback. Men tend to prefer their own progeny. Most likely a result of biology."

The back of Colton's neck heated, and he placed both hands on the counter. "I'll send you a bill."

He had no one to blame but himself for wading into such

an uncomfortable topic. He was still sorting out his feelings on the matter. Feelings which were surprisingly strong.

"Someone needs to look out for the best interests of Beatrix and her child," Dr. Boyd's tone was gentle, but firm. "You seem fond of them both, and I sincerely hope she chooses to stay with you. One would hate to see the child raised by a neglectful father."

Colton suddenly felt as though all the warmth had been leached from the room. From the moment he'd seen Joseph take his first, shuddering breath, he'd felt responsibility for the infant. The mere idea of someone else raising the child sent his blood alternately freezing and boiling.

His gaze clashed with Dr. Boyd and saw true concern in her eyes. He raked his hands through his hair and pulled in a deep, calming breath. Whether Dr. Boyd had meant to or not, she'd forced him to consider a situation he'd been avoiding.

Beatrix had been gazing at him with something akin to hero worship this morning, but he was a fraud. If she ever discovered the truth, he'd never see that look again. He'd accepted long ago that he wasn't meant to live the same sort of life as everyone else. Since his brother's death, his rare chances at happiness had always slipped away, and he'd given up trying for more.

"Thank you for your business, Dr. Boyd." Though somewhat uncertain of the new doctor, Colton had to admit she was a formidable presence. He paused at the doorway and reached for his hat. "I wish you well with your practice."

"I'll need the encouragement. People can be very closed-minded." She extended the tin she'd retrieved earlier. "Don't forget your salve."

Colton accepted her offering. "You might try a less forthright approach."

"I am a doctor. If people are only comforted by empty platitudes, they may fail to hear my message."

"Suit yourself." He might as well try the concoction. He glanced at the scars covering his hands. Did women find those scars repulsive? Was that why Dr. Boyd had offered him the ointment? Best not to dwell on the subject. "Good day, Dr. Boyd."

"Good day, Mr. Werner."

Colton stood on the slatted boardwalk for several minutes, lost in thought until someone brushed past him, pulling him from his reverie. He paused before the livery and set his bag inside the door. When he returned outside, Gus and Old Horace, the two town gossips, appeared behind him.

Old Horace was in his seventies, and his long gray hair hung down his back. Gus Russell had a white beard and loose jowls that shook when he laughed. The two of them sat on a bench outside the mercantile on sunny days—except for in warm weather, when they busied themselves by playing horseshoes. Together they kept track of all the comings and goings of the Cowboy Creek residents. Though they spent endless hours rehashing age-old arguments, their friendship was obvious.

Colton passed the saddle shop and admired the elaborate stitching on a saddle in the window. When he glanced behind him, he noted Walter Frye, his assistant at the livery, had joined Gus and Horace. A few steps later he passed Aunt Mae's boardinghouse, and a movement caught the corner of his eye. Aunt Mae, a short round woman with an easy smile, shuffled down the stairs and joined the three men trailing behind him.

Colton groaned. Yep. Word had sure gotten around town about the events of the previous week. He might as well give them something more to gossip about.

By the time he crossed the street, a parade of people

had formed behind him. Keeping his gaze fixed forward, he ignored the gathering crowd. Upon reaching the town clerk's office, he pushed open the door and winced at the loud clang of the overhead bell.

The crowd followed him inside, jostling and muttering for a better view of the proceedings. Mr. Howe, a banker, had clearly leaped from his work behind the counter. He wasn't wearing his jacket, and he still sported his visor and sleeve protectors.

If Colton delayed the inevitable any longer, he'd have the entire town crowded into the small space. He skirted past the horseshoe of chairs surrounding the pot-bellied stove and leaned over the counter. The door to the back room was closed, and he rang the bell on the desk since the alert from the front door hadn't summoned assistance.

A short, thin man in his late fifties wearing a dark suit and polishing a pair of spectacles stepped into the room. Colton recognized him as Gerald "Cookie" Kuckelman, the county clerk. According to the newspapers, Cowboy Creek was growing fast enough they'd soon need a deputy clerk, as well.

Cookie set his glances on his nose and glanced up, his magnified eyes growing even wider at the sight of such a large crowd. "May I help…one of you?"

Nothing annoyed Colton more than being the center of attention, but there was no escaping the inevitable.

He'd made a vow before God to a certain dark-haired beauty with eyes the color of molasses. If he couldn't have happiness himself, maybe he could bring a modicum of happiness to someone else.

Colton braced his hands on the counter, and the crowd behind him hushed, waiting to hear what he would say.

"I need to file for a marriage license."

Chapter Five

In the second week following her traumatic arrival in Cowboy Creek, Beatrix found her strength slowly returning. She'd managed to sit up by herself that morning, a vast improvement from the days before. The doctor had warned her that it might be a while before she could walk on her own, and she'd accepted that she must rest and recuperate.

They'd settled Joseph into a bassinet beside her bed, where he slept soundly.

The clock on her bedside table ticked, and she plucked at a loose thread on the counterpane. Breakfast had come and gone, and soon there'd be a lunch tray.

There'd been no sign of Colton. He'd promised to come this morning.

As reality settled in with each passing minute, she slumped against the pillow. The more time passed, the more she feared she'd frightened him off with her bold offer. She'd botched her future yet again. Perhaps if she'd waited a few days and let him warm to the idea, he might have come around.

It was too late now. Of course he'd bolted from the albatross of an instant wife and child. She'd meant to present their union as a partnership, but she'd gone about her explanations all wrong, and she'd lost her chance.

Leah had advised her to sleep when the baby slept, but her thoughts were too disarrayed for rest. She needed to discover another solution. She was alone, and she had a child to care for with no ways and means of her own.

She glanced at the large case in the corner. She'd sell her armonica. The last thing she owned of any value. The instrument had been passed down to her from her grandfather, and she'd carefully accompanied the glass pieces along land and ocean. The money from the sale would buy her some time. Though her heart ached at the loss, grandfather must understand her choice. She'd need the money to build a life for herself and for Joseph. While the money wouldn't last forever, she was certain something would come up. There were more opportunities for women in America than in Austria, and she'd always been resourceful.

A soft knock sounded on the door, and her stomach rumbled in anticipation.

"Come in," she called, eager for the lunch tray.

She hadn't been able to eat much yesterday, and today she was famished. Though it went against her nature to be waited upon, there was little other choice. She'd find a way to repay the doctor and Leah for all their nursing when she'd finished convalescing.

She turned to find Colton filling the doorway. A rush of emotion stole her breath. He wore a somber gray suit with a crisp white shirt and black string tie. In one hand he held his hat. In the other, a small, wrapped box. The corner of his mouth quirked into a sardonic smile, and he gestured toward the clock.

"*Guten Morgen*," he said in German. "Have you changed your mind yet?"

To her complete and utter horror, Beatrix burst into tears.

The color immediately leeched from Colton's face, and he was at her side in an instant.

"What's the matter?" he demanded, his voice charmingly gruff. "What did I do?"

"N-nothing," she hiccuped. "You wore a suit."

The bed dipped beneath his weight, and he cupped the back of her head with his enormous hand. "Don't cry. I can't stand a woman's tears."

She bit her lip, but the tears leaked out. "I'll s-stop. Just give me a m-moment."

He wrapped his arm around her shoulder, and she crushed her face against the rough wool of his suit until she'd collected herself enough to sit back and look at him. Her senses filled with the details of his appearance. The smoothly shaved chin and his neatly trimmed hair. He'd made an effort for her.

She caught the faint hint of cologne and choked back another sob. "You're late."

What a foolish thing to say, but she couldn't think of anything else.

He ran the backs of his neatly clipped nails along his smooth cheek. "I had to stop at the barber. It's not every day a man gives a woman a ring."

"You l-look very nice."

He looked charming, dashing, handsome, and she was a complete and utter mess of tangled hair and tears. This hadn't gone at all as she'd planned. Having a baby had released the floodgates of her emotions, and she couldn't stem the tide.

He released his hold and stepped away. "I'll come again. Later. I didn't mean to upset you."

She swiped at her face with the heels of her hands. If she didn't get a hold of herself, he'd be fleeing into the streets fearing he'd married a madwoman. "You didn't upset me. I'm happy."

"If this is happy, I don't ever want to see you sad."

His quip earned a watery smile, and she fought her traitorous emotions. "Thank you. For coming."

"You're welcome." He set the wrapped box on the table. "That's for you."

In an instant, she sensed his ambivalence, his hesitation. A shuttered expression came over his face. She couldn't force him into something he didn't want, yet she sensed their union was for the best. How could anything that felt this right be wrong to hope for? She forced back her tears and plucked the strings from the box.

A simple gold ring nestled inside, tied to the velvet backing with a blue satin ribbon.

"It's lovely."

She slid the ring on her finger, where the gold circled loosely over her knuckle.

"The ring is too large," he said, reaching for the box. "I can have it sized."

"I'll keep it." She tucked away her hand. "It's perfect. *Danke schön.*"

She had an unnatural fear that if he took the ring back, she'd never see him again. The idea was ridiculous, but she couldn't manage to push it away. Taking a deep, tremulous breath, she covered the ring with her opposite hand. She'd thrust herself into a foreign country, and she barely comprehended the language. If she was feeling a little shaken and fragile, she'd soon recover her wits.

Colton leaned over the bassinet and peered at Joseph. "How is he today?"

"Doing well. Would you like to hold him?"

"I have a short break." He gathered Joseph into his arms. "Then it's back to work. I, uh, I started the paperwork with the town clerk. We need a marriage license filed with the county. I'll send over the paperwork this afternoon. Let me know if you have any trouble filling out the form. Everything is all legal and set."

"Thank you. That was very thoughtful of you."

She hadn't even thought about a marriage license. At least Colton had remedied the oversight.

Minutes later, as she watched him leave, a warm, wistful ache settled in her chest. She crossed to the window and followed his progress on the street below. As though sensing her scrutiny, he tipped back his head and smiled. She pressed her palm against the chill window in return. She must be very careful with her heart around the blacksmith. She'd lost herself once to a man who didn't return her affections, and once was enough.

Colton ran his hands down the horse's fetlock until the animal bent the joint. He cradled the hoof in his lap. Using his buffer iron, he bent each of the clinches outward, loosening the metal. He pulled the old nails free with his pincers, then worked the horseshoe loose, starting with the heel.

The horse snuffled, and he muttered soothing words. By now he knew the personality of almost each and every horse in Cowboy Creek. Though Walter Fry, who oversaw the livery, was slowly taking over more and more of the farrier jobs, freeing Colton for other forms of metalwork, he still enjoyed the simple satisfaction of working with animals.

The door to the livery opened, and Colton glanced up.

"Will," he called out his friend's name. "I didn't expect you this soon. I'm not finished."

"Take your time," Will replied. "I had to escape the house."

Will Canfield had been Colton's commander the final two years of the war. He was tall and distinguished with dark hair and eyes. He always dressed impeccably and carried a silver-tipped cane in deference to a war wound he'd suffered. During those battle-hardened days, Colton had come to admire the man's intelligence and integrity. When Will had approached him to serve as blacksmith in Cowboy Creek, Colton had been more than eager to comply.

He pulled the metal shoe free, released the horse and stepped back a pace. "Since you married, Will, I've never known you to escape your home for any reason."

"Tomasina is nesting, and she's driving me mad."

Tomasina, Will's wife, was a local legend. She'd arrived in town with a cattle drive, and ran the local rodeo and sharpshooting contests. Petite and pretty with fiery red hair, the free-spirited cowgirl known as Texas Tom had seemed as different as possible from the urbane, refined Will, who everyone expected to run for governor one day. And yet Will had fallen hard for his wife. They were expecting a baby soon.

"You're lying," Colton said.

Will was looking out for him. Old habits died hard.

"You could always tell when I was lying." Will chuckled. "I thought you might want to talk."

"Not particularly."

"Your choice." Will hitched his trousers over his knees and sat on a nearby hay bale. He stretched his legs before him and rested his cane by his side. "Cold weather we're having."

"I've seen worse."

Will rubbed his leg where a piece of shrapnel remained lodged. "We're in for more snow. The old wound is aching."

"Maybe."

Pushing off, Will limped toward his horse. Colton raised his eyebrows. Will rarely let anyone see him walk without his cane. A town leader, he took great pride in his reputation and appearance. His friend ran his hand along the roan's haunches.

"I never got used to losing the horses during the war," Will said. "When the wounded were cleared after the battle, and the horses remained, I'd sit and weep in solitude for them. The grieving seemed easier, more manageable that way."

"I never knew."

"Funny, isn't it? You serve with a man, and you think you know everything there is to know about him. You know how he rolls his socks in neat little balls and stuffs them in the bottom of his rucksack. You know you can't say two words to him before he's had his first cup of coffee in the morning. You know about the time he and his brother stole apples from the neighbor next door. You know he learned German from his grandparents and that he doesn't like parsnips. You think you know everything about a man after serving with him in battle, but you never know how he grieves."

Colton rested the horseshoe on his gavel and pounded out the edges. "I never could tolerate parsnips."

"You should be prepared. The ladies in town are putting together an archive of the soldiers who served in the war. The project is for a one-hundred-year time capsule. They'll want to talk with you."

"Why would anyone want to do a fool thing like writing about the war?"

"The new editor of the newspaper, Sam Mason, was a soldier, too, and he wrote a book about the war. He even had a journal about his experiences in the newspaper." Will shrugged. "People are interested for history, I suppose. Sam's success is what inspired the ladies. They want something that's specific to the town. For the children and grandchildren of Cowboy Creek."

"I don't see why."

"Oh, come now. Tell me you weren't riveted by the passages about the American Revolution during history class."

Colton heaved a breath. "War is nothing like it says in the books."

"No. Nothing ever is, I suppose." Will limped back to his hay bale. "You were one of my bravest men." He extended his thumb. "You gave me a callus pinning all those medals on your uniform."

"I did what I was told. You were a good commander."

"I was only ever as good as men I led. And they always gave me everything I asked for and more. Sometimes I wondered what you were atoning for."

Colton straightened. He wasn't getting roped into this conversation. "You should probably be getting home. What with Tomasina expecting and all."

"You always volunteered for the most dangerous assignments, yet you hated the recognition. You never wore your medals. A man has to wonder. Why would someone put himself in harm's way, over and over again, and not care a whit for the glory?"

"You'd have to ask that man."

"I *am* asking that man."

Colton pressed hands into the small of his back and arched his cramped muscles. "I married Beatrix because she needed to know someone was looking out for the baby. None of us thought she'd live til morning. Now she wants to stay married. I honor my vows."

"That's not what I asked."

"It's what you wanted to know."

"I already know why you married her. You've always been the one to sacrifice."

A scorch of anger surprised Colton. "Why does everyone see this marriage as some great sacrifice? Any man would be fortunate to have Beatrix as a wife. And the baby, Joseph, he's a wonder."

"Don't get your back up." Will rested his elbows on his knees and clasped his hands before him. "After word got around about what happened, Tomasina was asking about you. She got me thinking. What do I know about you? I know your brother died. I know you went to live with your grandparents after that. I know both of your parents have passed away."

"That sums up my life."

His terse answer drew a dry chuckle. "We're friends, Colton. I had to ask. I had to try."

Colton stared at the horseshoe in his hand. What did hiding matter anymore? He and Will had shared more together than most men. They'd seen enough blood and death together to bind them for life. They shared a bond unique to a select group of soldiers.

"Joseph and I were twins," Colton began. "He was younger than me by a minute, but I always looked up to him. He was everything I wasn't—adventurous and fearless. He was smaller than me, and the other kids picked on him sometimes. But not when I was around."

"What happened to him?"

"We'd stolen some apples from the neighbor, an irascible old fellow, and he started a feud. Little things at first. A broken fence, a few lost chickens. Joseph and I took to retaliating. Harmless pranks our parents didn't know about. A fish in the hay bales to stink up the barn."

"Sounds like you were two normal boys."

"Then word got out there were Indians in the area.

Nothing scared the settlers more than Indians. We got this idea to dress up and ride our horses past the old man's place. Figured we'd scare him." Colton's vision dimmed, and he stared down a long tunnel into the dark past. "We scared him all right. He shot at us. A bullet hit Joseph."

"I'm sorry, Colton. I didn't know."

"Joseph survived for a month. Worse thing I ever experienced. It was like watching someone die by bits and pieces. You'd try and hold those pieces together, but they just kept breaking apart."

"That's why you fought so recklessly? Because you blamed yourself?"

"Can you really blame me?" Colton tipped back his head and stared at a spider web clinging between the dusty rafters. "And it wasn't just Joseph, it was like we tore apart the whole town. Even though everyone knew it was an accident, that old man couldn't live with himself and passed away within the year. My ma stopped talking to my pa. She stopped talking to me. No one invited us to supper anymore. My parents eventually sent me to live with my grandparents."

Will remained silent while Colton fought against the lump in his throat.

"You know how when a tree gets struck by lightning, sometimes one half dies while the other half lives? That's how it felt. I didn't know how to be a whole person without him. When Joseph died, a part of me died, too. After that, I just thought of what he'd do, and that's what I'd do. It was like I was trying to live his life and mine, too. Till one day I couldn't tell who I was anymore. That's why I took all those assignments during the war, because that's what Joseph would have done."

Inexplicably exhausted, Colton bent and resumed hammering out the horseshoe.

After several minutes, Will stood and reached for his cane. He braced both hands on the silver tip. "I didn't serve in the war with Joseph, I served with you. I know the man I served with, and I know that man well. You're a good man. You deserve to live your own life—to find happiness for yourself."

"I've tried for happiness a few times since then, but something always stands in the way. I don't think I was meant for a life like yours."

"You make your own fate, Colton. Maybe you don't think you deserve the life you seek."

Colton kept his head bent. "I'll bring the horse by later."

"I can fetch him."

"I'll bring him by."

Will heaved a gusty breath. "Promise you'll stop in and say hello to Tomasina."

"Promise she won't ask me any questions?"

"I never make promises for Tomasina. You know that."

Will tipped his hat and turned.

When the door closed behind him, Colton scrubbed a hand down his face. Talking about Joseph brought up the same old feelings. The guilt, the shame, the sorrow.

If he allowed himself to know joy, true joy, then all that suffering was nothing. His mother's, Joseph's, everyone's suffering meant nothing.

And if he couldn't go backward, how could he move forward? He wasn't the hero Beatrix thought him to be, and he couldn't stand the idea of her turning away from him if she found out who he really was.

Chapter Six

Beatrix checked her hair in the gilded mirror hanging in the parlor of the Cattleman Hotel one last time. "I look nice, *ja*?"

"You look lovely," Leah replied.

Shortly after Joseph's birth, Beatrix had moved to the Cattleman Hotel for the remainder of her recuperation. Apparently there was a boardinghouse in town as well, but a friend of Colton's owned the hotel and had insisted she stay there. The hotel was lovely, but her recuperation had gone on far too long. She was anxious for some fresh air and new faces. Leah and Colton had been her two faithful, and only, visitors. Fearful of her health, the doctor had strictly limited her company. She'd spent the solitude practicing her English relentlessly. She'd pored over books and magazines, and forced herself to speak only English with strangers.

Though she was still most comfortable speaking with Colton in German, she was making progress.

With Leah's guidance, she'd also developed a routine feeding and sleeping schedule for Joseph, and Colton always timed his visits while the baby was awake. Colton clearly enjoyed holding Joseph, and he appeared to be developing a genuine affection for the infant.

He would stay for precisely forty-five minutes. Never a minute more or a minute less.

He often brought along a gift for Joseph, a carved wooden figure of an animal or an intricate metal puzzle piece that was far too advanced for the baby's tiny, pudgy fingers. Sometimes the gifts were for her, instead, like the metal clothes iron with an elaborately twisted handle.

Leah had teased him for bringing such a domestic item, and to her chagrin, his gifts to her had ceased. No matter how many times she praised the workmanship of the iron, his ears only turned red and he changed the subject.

After begging and pleading, Colton and the doctor had finally agreed to allow her a brief turn around the town in a covered buggy. Since this was their first official outing as husband and wife, she wanted to look her best.

"Thank you for the dress." Beatrix adjusted the lace collar. "The color is pretty."

The dress was a deep periwinkle-blue with jet-black piping crisscrossing the fitted bodice. The skirts were modestly full, with only a slight ruffle at the hem. None of the dresses she'd brought from Austria were nearly this pretty—nor did they fit well since Joseph's arrival.

"Keep the dress," Leah insisted. "Consider it a gift."

Though Beatrix had grown adept at understanding many English words, she still struggled with her own speech. She couldn't recall the English word for expensive.

"*Nein*," Beatrix said, "It's…a…*teuer*."

"It may be expensive, but she can afford the price," a familiar voice spoke in German from the doorway.

Beatrix started and blushed. "*Guten Morgen*."

"*Guten Morgen*," Colton replied.

He kept one enormous shoulder propped against the

doorjamb, nearly taking up the entire space. She some-times forgot the sheer enormity of his size and strength. Today he wore a tan suede coat with sheepskin lining showing at the collar.

There was something lighter about him today, a hint of a smile in his eyes that she rarely noticed. His buoyant mood lent him an almost rakish look. She was keenly aware of his bold maleness, and her blood warmed.

"You look lovely," he said. "Do you have a warm coat?"

For an instant she felt as giddy as one of the schoolgirls on the playground when a boy cast a look in their direction. "Leah has lent me her cloak."

She gestured toward the matching periwinkle fabric draped over a chair. She crossed the room, but Colton reached the spot first. He arranged the material over her shoulders and gathered the ties near her throat.

They stood so close, their breaths mingled.

"This color suits you," he said, his voice gliding over her like a caress.

She was instantly aware of him, and her mouth grew dry. His unique eyes glittered in the light shafting through the open drapes, that curious shade of brown circling the evergreen center. He smiled at her, softening his face into a tenderness that was as unexpected as it was heady.

Leah plucked baby Joseph from his bassinet. "I'll leave you two alone."

Colton immediately moved away, leaving Beatrix oddly bereft.

"Not without a hello from my number-one fellow," he said.

Colton grasped the tiny bundle and held the baby close. Over the weeks he'd shown a fatherly interest and pride in Joseph.

"I've just fed him," Beatrix said. "Sometimes I think that boy is hollow from his toes to his fingertips."

Intent on the infant, Colton gave a distracted nod at her joke. Beatrix quashed the tiny surge of loneliness. She was blessed. She'd married a man who adored her child. If she occasionally felt superfluous, that was a small price to pay for the obvious affection Colton harbored for Joseph.

Today, though, once they left on their outing she would have her husband all to herself, and she intended to make the most of her time. This was her first real chance to see the town and have some time alone with Colton. A fragile bond had begun to build between them in the quiet moments they spent together with Joseph.

Though Colton didn't appear to regret his hasty proposal, they were both still getting to know one another. They were both still learning the rules of their hurried marriage and unfamiliar relationship.

As he cooed over Joseph, she waited patiently by the door. As much as she was anxious for a breath of fresh air, she couldn't interrupt the two. Eventually sensing her eagerness to be on their way, he handed the baby to Leah.

He carefully extracted his fingers from Joseph's chubby grip. "Strong as an ox, this boy."

Once outside, Colton gestured. "Booker & Son is just across the street. I have something I need to pick up there before the buggy ride. Can you walk that far?"

"I'm not an invalid. I can walk."

"You nearly died." He wrapped his arm around her shoulder. "And the wind is biting today."

"But I didn't die." She shivered and pressed herself closer to his warmth. "And I will take your shelter from the wind."

He took her hand as she traversed a rough patch, and she quietly refused to let go.

Glancing down, he asked, "You're certain you're warm enough?"

"Yes."

"And you're okay leaving Joseph with Leah for the next hour?"

"Yes." Beatrix rolled her eyes. She adored Joseph, but she'd been cooped up for far too long. The baby would be fine without her for an hour or two. "Leah has been a wonderful help to me. I don't know what I would have done without her."

As they made their way along the boardwalk, Beatrix soon realized the two of them were something of a curiosity. There were points and whispers, and even a few outright stares. Colton tensed beside her.

He tucked her hand into the crook of his elbow. "We're something of a novelty."

"Surely their curiosity will wear off quickly."

A muscle ticked along his jaw. "I sincerely hope so."

Beatrix shivered. Though she truly believed Peter had been genuinely fond of her in the beginning of the relationship, she'd soon come to realize that he was ashamed of his affection for her, especially when they were in public together. Though their families were both working class, Peter traced his lineage back to royalty. She'd imagined things were different in America. There was no royalty to trace, no lineages to compare. Since she'd arrived, though, she'd learned that class systems existed in all forms. She'd also discovered not everyone was welcoming of immigrants. There were probably many single girls in town who thought the handsome blacksmith could do better than an immigrant with broken English and the burden of a child.

A discouraging thought sank its teeth into her joy. Was Colton ashamed of her?

There was little time to ponder the disquieting reflection. Colton pushed open the door of the mercantile, and she was immediately assailed with a myriad of sights and smells. Booker & Son was an absolute delight. More than twice the size of the store in her village, and full of exotic labels and colorful packages. Freed from the prison of her sickroom, she skipped from one display to another.

Colton indulged her enthusiasm, trailing behind her through the store and translating when necessary. She laughingly donned hats, and whipped a fur-lined scarf around her neck with a saucy grin. Though she hadn't the coin to purchase any of the extravagant items, playacting was enough to entertain her.

When she'd circled the mercantile twice, he excused himself to check the post office for any correspondence. Beatrix spent the time perusing the store. She couldn't get enough of all the goods for sale. With her fingers threaded behind her back, she approached the counter and stared at an enormous jar filled with hardboiled eggs in some sort of liquid.

The young, pimpled clerk, no more than eighteen or nineteen years old, stood behind the counter.

He lifted his head from polishing the glass countertop, and she pointed at the jar.

"*Was ist dass*?" she asked, the words blurting out in German in her excitement.

The man sneered. "Speak English, you dunce." He chuckled. "You don't even understand that, do you? I just called you a dunce."

Beatrix gasped. While she didn't understand all the words, she was fairly certain of the sentiment. Her cheeks burning with shame, she backed away from the counter and bumped into another gentleman.

He was tall and distinguished with jet-black hair. His dark suit was precisely tailored, and he leaned heavily on a silver-handled cane. "Mrs. Werner, I presume. I'm Will Canfield. *Wie geht es euch?*"

A rush of relief weakened her knees. "*Sehr gut, danke schön.*"

"I'm afraid I've exhausted my knowledge of German." Mr. Canfield nodded in the direction of the store clerk. "Is young Eugene bothering you?"

Beatrix shook her head. "*Nein.* No."

She didn't want to complain or make a scene that might cause her husband to be embarrassed by her. She'd simply have to work harder on her English.

The clerk's expression had altered at the sight of Mr. Canfield, and he offered the man a friendly greeting. "Always nice to see you, sir. Is there anything I can get for you from behind the counter?"

"I believe the lady was asking about the jar of pickled eggs, Eugene."

"Pickled eggs?" Beatrix annunciated the words carefully. "Good?"

Mr. Canfield wrinkled his nose. "More of an acquired taste."

Colton joined the two of them surreptitiously and set his purchases on the counter. She spied the fur from a muff she'd admired earlier under a red tartan blanket, and her joy grew. Was he purchasing the item for her? Probably she should refuse the gift, but what was the harm? It wasn't as though she'd asked for anything. If Colton wanted to buy her something, surely there was no fault in accepting.

He spoke a few words to the clerk. Eugene pulled a set of rings for sizing from beneath the jewelry counter and shoved them in her direction.

"See. Which. One. Fits," Eugene spoke loudly and slowly.

Colton frowned.

Mr. Canfield set his jaw. "Mr. Booker holds a high standard for his store. I'm sure he wouldn't want to hear that one of his clerks has been rude to a paying customer."

Colton expression turned thunderous. "Was this boy treating you rudely?"

"*Nein.*" Beatrix's heart thumped heavily against her ribs "No. He does—he did—nothing."

The two men exchanged a glance. She sincerely hoped Mr. Canfield hadn't heard the clerk's offensive comment earlier. She'd simply avoid Eugene in the future. At least until her English improved.

She hastily tried several of the rings and found one that fit perfectly. "This one."

She spoke the words in her best English.

Colton covered the ring sizers with his enormous hand. "I can size the ring myself if you let me borrow these."

"Can't do that," the clerk replied with a smirk. "Store rules."

The pimpled clerk made a point of writing down the number, and Beatrix reluctantly handed over her ring for sizing.

She slanted a glance at Colton. "Will you wear a ring?"

"It's not safe to wear rings in my line of work."

"Of course," she said, though his answer only increased her trepidation.

Men rarely wore wedding rings. Only Colton's immediate dismissal of her question had her worrying that he was ashamed to publically acknowledge their relationship. She'd noticed rings on several of the married men in town, and she'd assumed Colton would follow suit. Except his explanation about his work made perfect sense. He handled molten hot metal. Not exactly conducive to a piece of gold jewelry.

She glanced at the wide gold band on Mr. Canfield's hand. Probably he had a different job. He appeared to be a businessman.

Mr. Canfield tipped his head a in a polite bow. "It was a pleasure meeting you, Mrs. Werner. Now that the doctor has lifted the restrictions on your visitors, my wife would like to meet you."

"Yes," Beatrix eagerly replied. She was anxious to expand her circle of friends and practice her English. "I would like to meet her, as well."

"We're having a baby soon." Pride twinkled in Mr. Canfield's eyes. "She'll want to visit your little one."

"I would enjoy that."

Even the promise of having visitors stirred her excitement. She couldn't help the burst of pride at her pronunciation. There were certain phrases she'd practiced to exhaustion.

After saying their polite goodbyes, Colton took her elbow, and together they stepped outside once more. While Beatrix was delighted with her purchases and with Colton's thoughtfulness, her unease over the clerk at the mercantile lingered. Had Mr. Canfield heard more than he'd revealed? Would he tell Colton that her lack of proper English had caused her to be mocked? More than anything she wanted him to be proud of her.

They reached a smart, black covered buggy pulled by a beautiful white horse, and Beatrix stopped short. "She is lovely."

Colton ran his gloved hand along the animal's haunches. "*She* is a *he*. His name is Gabriel."

"Gabriel is beautiful."

A biting wind lifted the hair off Beatrix's neck and sent her shivering. Colton's breath puffed vapor into the air. Though Austrian winters were cold, there was something harsh about the temperature in Cowboy Creek. As though the air was sharper in America.

Colton rubbed the horse's ear between his thumb and

forefinger, and the creature bumped its muzzle against his chest. Clearly he was good with animals. A man who was good with animals and children would surely be good to his wife.

Colton tossed the extra packages up and assisted her into the wagon before settling beside her. She scooted nearer his warmth. He unfurled the tartan blanket over their knees, and she tucked the edge beneath her hip.

"Where are we going?" she asked.

"Daniel Gardner, Leah's husband, owns several houses in town that are newly built and available for purchase."

"There is so much here that is new. This is much different than in Europe."

Everything in America, especially in Cowboy Creek, was new. There was no sense of history or the past; everything stretched forward toward the future. The idea was both exciting and unnerving.

"Then we must buy a new house?" Beatrix asked.

"Yes."

"We cannot live in your house?"

"It's too small."

"A small space is good for me."

"Not for me." He presented her with a brown-paper wrapped package tied with twine. "I saw you admiring these in the store."

"Thank you." Beatrix removed the brown wrapping and exclaimed over the delightful gifts. He'd purchased the muff and the matching fur-lined hat, as well. She tucked her nose into the soft pelt and rubbed the hat against her cheek. "You should not have. They are expensive."

She recalled the word he'd used earlier.

"I wanted to," he said. "And I knew you'd like them."

Her heart warmed. "I do like the gifts, but I liked the clothes iron even better."

She spoke in German because she had more words to make him understand.

His cheeks reddened. "Leah said I should never give a lady a gift that's for chores."

"I loved the iron because you made it. This makes the gift special. I like having something special when I do chores."

He concentrated on driving the horse, his hands threaded through the reins. "You should have warmer boots, too."

His voice was hoarse, and she looked at him uncertainly, then smothered an indulgent smile. Judging by the pleased expression on his face, she'd finally made him understand that she was happy with his first gift.

"Opal Godwin and her husband own a boot shop," he continued. "I crafted some shoe forms for his shop, and he owes me a new pair of boots. There's a dress store next door. Hannah Johnson is the proprietress. I don't know much about ladies' clothing, but the other women in town admire her work."

A warm sense of peace rippled over her. She couldn't recall the last time someone had been considerate enough to look out for her needs. She'd meant to take care of Colton, and the opposite was happening. She must do a better job of seeing to his concerns. Certainly the task would prove easier once they were living under the same roof. She'd have a better idea of what he needed.

Colton tucked the blankets tighter around her legs and placed a warming brick beneath her feet. Her new husband was a study in contradictions. He was kind and considerate, yet there was also the underlying sorrow she sensed in him. The shadow over his eyes that never quite seemed to lift. Even today, when he was happy, she sensed he held himself at a distance. Whatever burden he carried, he carried in the space between them, and she wondered if she'd ever breach the chasm.

After a few minutes of driving, he paused before an enormous two-story home with a wraparound porch and twin round cupolas flanking the second floor.

Beatrix anchored her new fur hat with one hand and tipped back her head. "Are all the houses this large?"

Perhaps this colossal home explained his distant mood. She wouldn't be a burden to him. She'd find them a suitable house that wasn't this large or expensive.

He turned his quizzical gaze on her. "You don't like this one?"

"We should keep looking."

They drove past two more houses that Beatrix discounted. They were far too large and extravagant. Instead of pleasing Colton, her refusal of the houses only seemed to make him more frustrated. Uneasy, she decided on a change of scenery.

"Where is your shop?" she asked.

"This way. Would you like to see it?"

Beneath his curious regard, she grew flustered. "*Ja.*"

They turned down a street toward one of the more established sections of town. Because of the heat and noise, the smithy was located a distance behind the livery.

The outside of the brick building was covered in soot and ash, with a chimney rising from the far side. Colton held open the door, and she stepped into his work space. Though most of the brick was blackened from the smelting fire, his tools were hung in neat order along a slotted board attached to the wall. The smells were familiar as well: coal and iron ore along with the mingled scents of hard work and toil.

Closing her eyes, she inhaled with an almost giddy laugh.

"This is the most familiar place I have been in America," she said.

"How do you mean?"

She recalled visiting the local blacksmith with her father. "All of the tools are similar. The smells are the same. So many things are done differently here in America, but this is just as I'd expect it to be. It's like a bit of home."

His eyes revealed a flash of vulnerability. "Do you miss your home?"

She pictured her sisters and her nieces and nephews, and her own eyes burned. She missed them terribly, and yet not one of them had come to see her off. They would not go against her father's word. Just once in her life she wanted someone to choose her above all else. Peter had chosen to follow his family's wishes; her sisters had followed her father's decree.

Colton had not chosen her. He'd been a kind man doing a good deed, and he'd been saddled with an unwanted bride as payment for his good heart. There was so little that was fair in this life.

"I miss mountains," she said. "I find the endless horizon frightening. It's strange, how far one can see."

"I never thought of the prairie that way. I always felt trapped by the mountains."

"We crave what we know."

"Yes." His voice sounded a little off, tighter than usual. He pulled a letter from his pocket. He studied the missive intently, as though divining the words through the paper envelope. "This arrived today."

She stilled at the heightened tension in his voice. "What is it?"

"I wrote to my grandparents about you." He paused. "They'd like to visit."

His uneasy attitude left her perplexed. "This is nice, yes? You miss them?"

"I do miss them." There was genuine emotion in those four words, and she sensed his loneliness for them, his obvious affection. "I haven't seen them in a long time. Too long."

She missed her own grandparents. Her grandmother had died when she was young, but her grandfather had always been a commanding presence in their lives. She missed the comforting warmth of his love. He'd have been disappointed in her, because of Joseph, but he'd have stood by her and would not have allowed her father to throw her out of the family. He'd cared for her unconditionally, and she mourned the sanctuary of his absolute love.

Surely by the sound of his voice, Colton had known that sort of affection. And yet the longer he stood there, the letter in hand, the greater her worry. She sensed his regret, his sadness, and a sudden burst of frustration caught fire in her heart. He piled his sorrow like bricks between them, blocking her out. He was lonely, and she feared she was the wrong person to bring him comfort. She was the wrong person, and yet she'd come too far to turn back now.

Colton avoided her questioning smile. "I'm going to put them off for a while," he said.

A great dread crushed her chest. She swallowed back a wave of trepidation, and forged ahead. "Because they will be ashamed of me?"

Chapter Seven

Colton's heart constricted painfully. "Why would you think that?"

"Because of…because of…"

"No. Not at all." He caught her hands, regretting his clumsy words. "Never think that. They're not that sort of people."

"How do you know?"

An avalanche of self-recriminations pounded over him. He'd doused her enjoyment of the day. "I know."

"But you do not want them to visit."

He scrubbed a hand down his face. The words backed up in his throat. "You're a new wife. A new mother. I'm still training Walter Frye to run the livery. He's not ready to take over just yet. I won't be home much until he's able to take over more work. I'd rather have them visit when I can be around the house more."

"I understand this."

The relief on her lovely face more than made up for the small lie. He couldn't bring himself to tell Beatrix that it was not her that brought shame, but rather himself.

His grandparents had never blamed Colton for what happened with his brother. Moreover, Colton trusted his grandparents; they wouldn't reveal his secret. Yet having them here would be a constant reminder of his past. A constant reminder that he wasn't the man Beatrix thought him to be.

He recalled his new wife's delight at the mercantile. Seeing the store through her eyes had brought him a torrent of childish pleasure. The only hitch in her enjoyment had been the clerk's rude behavior. He'd speak with Mr. Booker about Eugene. The clerk had recently struck up a friendship with the Schuyler boys, which didn't bode well. The Schuyler boys were drawn toward trouble, and Eugene seemed like the type to give in easily to a bad influence.

Beatrix ran her gloved fingertip over the metal anvil in the middle of the room. "I miss my grandparents. I miss the way they loved me."

"Do you miss Peter?" he asked, instantly shocked by his own audacity.

What right did he have to question her about her past, when he was unwilling to share his own?

The question had come from nowhere, and yet, somehow, from everywhere. He was curious about the sort of man who'd marry another woman and abandon both his lover and his child. He was curious about the sort of man who'd let Beatrix travel halfway around the world to wed a stranger. He was curious about the sort of man who'd failed her already.

He was jealous of the man she'd loved.

Beatrix went rigid. "No. I do not miss Peter."

There was a wealth of emotion in that first word. In an instant he felt her pain, her betrayal. He sensed her resolve. She'd traveled halfway around the world to marry a stranger because she wanted a better life for her baby. She'd fought death itself for her child.

"I could forgive Peter for abandoning me," she said,

her voice quivering with emotion. "But he left our child. I cannot love a man who does this."

Colton caught her against him, embracing her and inhaling her rosewater scent. "I shouldn't have asked."

"No. You have every right. Someday I'll tell you more. But not today. Today I want to be happy."

A new fear settled in his heart. Though happiness had eluded him, he mustn't let his own sorrow crush her buoyant spirit.

"We have a lifetime together." He held her away from him. "I'll wait."

From that very first evening, he'd admired her stark honesty. She'd never shied away from the truth. If she wasn't ready to talk about all of her past, he'd practice his patience.

But there was one place where his patience had run thin. They needed a place to live, and he was heartily confused by her refusal of all the choices he'd shown her. "I know you didn't like any of the houses, but I was rather partial to the first one. The white house with the large porch. Would you be willing to look again?"

A band of emotion tightened around his chest. There was only one obvious explanation for her reticence. She was reluctant to leave the safety of the Cattleman Hotel for the uncertainty of marriage with him. He'd done nothing to put her at ease, because he didn't know how.

She placed her hand on his chest, and the contact was electric.

"I admire that house," she said. "But it's so grand, so fancy."

He trembled like a schoolboy, and breathing became a tiresome chore. "It's not so grand."

"Joseph is very small. He does not need much space."

Perhaps her hesitation was for the better. Having her

near muddled his thoughts. "There will be room for Joseph to grow."

A knock sounded, evaporating the misty enchantment of the moment. He and Beatrix broke apart.

Colton turned, forcing breath back into his lungs. He tugged on the collar of his coat, letting the cool air drift over his skin.

Turning toward the door, he caught a glimpse of Beatrix's equally flustered countenance, and a surge of pure masculine pride rushed through him. Neither of them had been unaffected.

He swung open the door and quickly masked a grimace. Though not exactly the people he wanted to see just then, he kept his expression neutral.

"Mr. Schuyler, Eric and Dirk," Colton greeted the man and his two sons. "This is a pleasant surprise." He turned his body and spread his arm. "Mr. Schuyler, this is my wife, Beatrix."

Mr. Schuyler touched the brim of his hat in greeting. "Pleasure, Mrs. Werner. I've heard a lot about you."

Rumors and gossip.

Colton's gaze shot to the man's face, but he read no malice in the words.

His shoulders relaxed a notch. He moved nearer to Beatrix. "Mr. Schuyler owns a salt mine outside of town. These are his sons, Dirk and Eric. I confess I have trouble telling the two apart."

"As do I." Mr. Schuyler slapped one of the boys on the shoulder. "They're a year apart in age, and rarely without each other."

The Schuylers were all blond-haired, blue-eyed, sturdy replicas of one another. The family was hardworking and had provided Colton with several lucrative jobs since he'd arrived in Cowboy Creek. Though Mr. Schuyler was occasionally difficult in his dealings, he and Colton had come to an understanding of sorts.

The Schuyler boys were another story. The sheriff in town had had more than one run-in with those two. They were fifteen and sixteen respectively, and known for stirring up trouble and instigating fights with the other boys in town. Mr. Schuyler took an odd sort of pride in his boys' shenanigans, as though their rowdiness gave him a sense of satisfaction. Colton avoided the pair whenever he could. With Eugene a part of the group now, he'd be doubly cautious.

Mr. Schuyler leaned against the wall and folded his arms. "You are *Österreicher*, Frau Werner?"

"*Ja.*"

She took a step nearer to Colton.

Mr. Schuyler had only inquired if Beatrix was Austrian, and yet the tone of his voice raised the tiny hairs on the back of Colton's neck. The way she'd placed herself nearer his side had him grappling between satisfaction and alarm. He was relieved she felt comfortable with him, while worried about the tension between her and Mr. Schuyler.

He rested his arm over her shoulder.

The two exchanged a few civil phrases in German, and his tension dropped a notch. Perhaps he'd read too much into the initial exchange.

Colton eased his hand around her waist and rested his fingers on the gentle swell of her hip. Mr. Schuyler's gaze flicked toward the affectionate gesture and back to Colton's face.

"Congratulations," Mr. Schuyler declared in English. "On your marriage. Come by the house next Friday for dinner. We can discuss the new drill bits for the mine. I'll have my wife prepare something that will remind Beatrix of home."

Beatrix tensed, and Colton flashed her a concerned look. She smiled brightly. "*Ja.* I would like that."

The difference between her cheerful words and her obvious anxiety left him uneasy. Following the odd incident at the mercantile, he was wary of the undertone. Though Beatrix had denied any problem, he'd seen the derision on the clerk's face. He made a note to speak with Will at the first opportunity. Perhaps his friend had heard more of the exchange. Until Beatrix trusted him, there was little else he could do.

Colton flashed what he hoped was an apologetic smile. "We'd better put off the dinner for a couple of weeks. We're moving, and I'm sure Beatrix will want to get settled."

"Moving?" Mr. Schuyler exclaimed. "Congratulations again. I'll send over my boys to help."

"There's no need."

"I insist."

"If you insist." Colton buried his annoyance. There was little he could say to that without appearing rude. "Thank you."

After more small talk, the Schuylers departed. The two men shook hands, and Colton quietly closed the door behind them. Beatrix crossed her arms and rubbed her shoulders.

Colton took her hand; her fingers were ice cold. "Are you certain you don't mind having dinner with the Schuylers one day?"

"Why would I mind?" she asked, her eyes downcast.

He recalled Mr. Schuyler's tone when he'd inquired if Beatrix was Austrian. Certainly her hesitancy had nothing to do with events that had transpired in Europe? The idea was ridiculous. They were thousands of miles away from the Austro-Prussian conflict. There was no reason for any animosity between immigrants. Then again, there were all sorts of prejudices in the world he didn't understand.

He could tell that she *did* mind having dinner with Mr.

Schuyler, but he didn't know why. One way or another, he was determined to find out.

"Beatrix," Colton called out in exasperation. "I thought we discussed this."

A cloud of dust dissipated, revealing the crouched figure of his wife sweeping out the hearth.

"I am not working," she replied over a delicate cough. "I am sweeping the hearth."

"Sweeping the hearth is most definitely work."

Since Beatrix had repeatedly declined the larger houses he'd initially considered, they'd settled on a smaller cottage two blocks north of the livery. Her choice had fewer rooms, but the spaces were well divided. The ground floor featured a bedroom, parlor and kitchen, with three decent-sized bedrooms on the second floor.

"Not very hard work," she grumbled. "You said no hard work."

"Sit, please." He yanked a chair from its tucked location beneath the kitchen table and strode into the parlor. "Sitting in a chair is not working."

Meek now, she slumped onto the chair, her knees pressed together and her heels splayed. "I can't simply sit like a...like a stone. Certainly there's something useful I can accomplish."

She'd slipped into German, a sure sign of her annoyance.

"You can ease my worrying by not lifting, dusting or scrubbing," he declared, refusing to be swayed by her pleading. "I would find that extremely helpful."

His own mood was rapidly souring. Though neither he nor Beatrix had much in the way of belongings, simply crossing town was a misery. Colton yanked off his hat and slapped it against his thigh, clearing the moisture from the brim. Icy flakes had peppered his cheeks and burrowed into the space between his gloves and coat sleeves.

The snow was more a mixture of sleet and ice. An odd temperate day amongst the frigid chill had softened the previous layer. The slushy mess had turned the streets to sludge, sucking at the wagon wheels and splattering mud on the horses. He'd loaded most of his belongings into the wagon bed and thrown a tarp over the top to keep the worst of the weather at bay. With the howling wind, he'd spent the short trip battling to keep the tarp in place.

He'd ordered Beatrix to sit more than once, but she'd defied his well-meaning orders at every turn. Between watching the weather, organizing the transfer of furniture, and ensuring Beatrix didn't overextend herself, his temper was running thin.

Colton mentally dug in his heels. "I have to finish unloading the wagon. Remember—no work."

He'd also had to face the galling truth of a flaw in his own personality. He didn't like change. Though content with the choices he'd made, having his living situation thrown into an uproar had him off balance. Frustrated by his own shortcoming, he struggled against his rapidly decaying mood. The Schuyler boys had him on edge, as well. He'd be happy when the two were all finished and would go home.

"No work," she muttered.

At least the chaos suited Beatrix. She'd wound a handkerchief around her hair, but her curls had escaped in charming confusion. She wore a white apron tied over her tan wool dress, and her old brown boots peeked from beneath her skirts. She huffed, levitating a ringlet from her damp forehead.

"No work," he ordered once more, punctuating his command with a pointed finger.

She lifted her eyes heavenward. "*Ja.*"

Ten minutes later, Colton pushed through the backdoor into the kitchen and rested a box on the table, then glanced at the vacant room on his left. They'd decided to leave the first floor bedroom empty in anticipation of his grandparents' eventual visit.

A sound caught his attention.

Beatrix balanced on a chair, whisking a feather duster around the high shelves. She'd rolled up the sleeves of her tan wool dress and stretched up on her tiptoes. Taking one look at her precarious balance on the chair, he didn't waste time with words.

Striding the distance, he swooped her into his arms. She startled and cried out.

"What are you doing?" he demanded. "Where is Joseph? Shouldn't he be keeping you occupied?"

"He's sleeping." She playfully slapped at his arms. "You gave me a fright."

He set her on her feet. She held the feather duster between them. Colton sneezed.

His pulse picked up rhythm. He removed the cleaning implement from her hand and set the duster aside. His free hand lingered on her waist. Not for the first time he noticed how delicate her wrists and hands where. She wasn't fragile, but she was still distinctly feminine in a way that made him want to cherish her, protect her.

He'd never had this heart-pounding reaction with another woman. Not that he'd had much experience with the fairer sex. During the war, ladies had occasionally assembled dances for the soldiers, but he'd rarely participated. Following his move to Cowboy Creek, he'd spent his time working and growing his business. As the only blacksmith in town, he'd kept busy. Though Will and Daniel had invited him to various town celebrations, he'd always declined.

At first, Noah Burgess—the third soldier from their unit who had helped to found Cowboy Creek—had been on Colton's side. Both confirmed bachelors content with their solitude, they'd banded together against Will and Daniel's meddling attempts to make the pair of them be more sociable. But since Noah had gotten married—to a mail-order bride arranged behind his back by Daniel and Will—Colton had been pushed to attend far too many social occasions. He'd held stubbornly to his refusal. Perhaps that had been a mistake. Maybe he would be a better husband, better able to make his wife happy, if he was more accustomed to interacting with women.

Beatrix tilted her head. "What are you thinking?"

"Nothing."

"Hmm, you are making faces as though you are thinking about something."

A gust of wind outside caught one of the shutters and slammed it against the house. Her startled jump brought her even closer. Circling his waist with her arms, she leaned into him. Taller than average, her head rested just beneath his chin. She fit against him as though she belonged there. He closed his hands around her waist and pulled her even closer. Her soft sigh whispered against his neck.

He recalled the sight of her balanced on the chair, and a rampant protectiveness surged through him. "No more dusting the shelves."

Her glorious hair tickled his chin. Tendrils escaped the knotted handkerchief, fluttering in abandon around her face.

She chuckled. "You nearly toppled me by grabbing me so suddenly."

"I saved your life. Besides, I'm the one who should be terrified." He pressed his lips against the smudge of dirt on her forehead. "Seeing you teetering on that chair scared the life out of me. I thought we agreed. You are only here to give directions and dictate the placement of furniture."

He leaned back enough to see the hint of a pout in her expression.

"I'm not an invalid," she said. "I'm accustomed to hard work. You needn't coddle me."

He smoothed a stray lock of hair from her forehead and dropped another light kiss against the smudge. "I know."

And yet he very much did want to coddle her. She'd been through so much over the past months. That first day, she'd seemed appallingly isolated and alone. While he mustn't pursue this untenable attraction, there was no reason he couldn't care for his wife, show her concern and take away some of her burden. There was no reason she couldn't find a modicum of happiness.

She touched the collar of his coat, smoothing it down. His breathing hitched in his throat, and he stared at her hands. Her fingers were bare, her wedding ring still with Mr. Booker for sizing, and he made a note to check on the progress. He might even buy a wedding ring for himself. Though he couldn't wear any sort of jewelry while working, there was no reason he shouldn't have something for special occasions.

First, though, he must find a way to keep his wife busy, without letting her do anything that would put her at risk.

His gaze darted around the kitchen area, and he spotted a box with bits of hay poking through the slats. "You can rinse and put away the dishes. But only on the low shelves. No balancing on chairs."

"That task will barely take me an hour." She thrust out her chin. "What will I do after the dishes are finished?"

"I'll think of something equally safe."

He unfurled a handkerchief from his pocket and gently wiped the dirt from her forehead. "Be good, or I'll send you back to the Cattleman Hotel."

"I'll be good, *Herr Werner*." She stepped back and saluted. "I promise." Her hand dropped. "I'll go mad if I'm stuck in that room another day."

Colton stilled. Her teasing salute, an echo of the war, had not even caused a twinge of sadness. With Beatrix, he was able to think of the future, and leave the past where it belonged—in the past. Her presence was a soothing balm.

If only he could be the man she thought him to be. Every time he touched happiness, the petals crumbled beneath his fingertips. He couldn't do that to Beatrix. He mustn't be diverted by the vulnerability in her deep brown eyes. She was stronger than any of them. She could build her own happiness—as long as he didn't let himself get too close.

"We're almost finished," he said. "Soon we can both relax."

Noises sounded from the front parlor, and they glanced around.

"The Schuyler boys," Colton said with a grimace. "They've got your trunk and that deceptively heavy musical instrument of yours."

"My armonica!" she exclaimed. "I'd better check on the placement. It mustn't sit too near the window or the sun will bleach the wood."

"How did you manage to move that awkward, heavy piece all the way from Austria?"

"With tenacity and determination and several bribes," she declared. "I had to pay extra every time I changed trains."

"You're very fond of that instrument," he said, his gaze thoughtful.

There was nothing in his life that couldn't be replaced. Nothing he'd bribe people to allow him to deliver across oceans.

Her expression grew wistful. "It's the only thing I have left that truly reminds me of home."

The reminder struck him with a jolt. *Home.* This wasn't her home. Austria was her home. There were times when he felt her presence here was as elusive as the morning mist. That he'd wake one morning and find she'd disappeared with the rising warmth of the sun.

She paused in the doorway, her gaze fixed on the arrival of her precious instrument. Her profile was strong, with a straight nose and a prominent cheekbone teased by a stray curl.

Colton followed her exit with an uncharacteristic touch of melancholy. He was curious about the instrument, and anxious to hear her play. She had little else to her name. During her recuperation at the Cattleman Hotel, he'd become quite familiar with her three serviceable dresses. She owned a wooden brush and comb, as well. She'd whittled her belongings down to the meager dregs to save her instrument.

He turned away from the parlor and set about emptying the last crate.

He'd speak with her again about visiting Hannah's dress shop. Considering her stubborn refusal on the larger house, she was obviously reluctant to spend money. Or at least to spend *his* money. Though not a wealthy man by any means, he was plenty comfortable. A few dresses wouldn't set him back. Would they make her happy? Did she even care about nice clothes? She'd seemed to like that dress she'd borrowed from Leah, but aside from that, he couldn't be sure.

He knew so little about Beatrix beyond the superficial. They'd talked, certainly they'd talked, though they'd each carefully avoided any mention of their pasts. She'd been raised in Austria, and she had family. Occasionally she'd let a name slip. She had sisters for certain, and at least her father was alive, though she'd never mentioned her mother. In the beginning he'd been content with the shallow nature of their relationship.

Colton tipped his head and pictured the sleeping infant in his room on the second floor. She'd survived her journey and delivered the baby boy with only the comfort of strangers.

She deserved more than him and the little he had to offer. He pressed the heels of his hands against his eyes. She had a deep well of courage that she carried effortlessly and drew upon when the circumstances warranted.

Beside her he was but a shadow. Undeserving.

Voices sounded from the parlor, and something in their tone had him pausing. He stepped nearer the door and caught the words spoken by the Schuyler boys in German.

"I don't have to take orders from you," Dirk spoke.

"*Ja*," his brother Eric replied. "We've heard about you. You're a—"

His next word sent a red haze over Colton's vision. His jaw tensed, and he charged into the parlor. Eric caught his angry gaze and assumed an expression of false innocence.

Beatrix glanced between the two of them and splayed her hands. "It was nothing."

Eric swaggered forward and spoke to his brother in German. "Don't worry. He doesn't understand. She certainly won't tell him."

"I understand." Colton surprised the boy by speaking their native tongue. "You will apologize this instant, and then you will leave this house."

"My father gives you much business." Eric smirked.

"You misunderstood what I said. Didn't he?" the boy directed his question toward Beatrix.

She gave a hesitant nod.

"No apology? Fine then. Out." Bigger and stronger, Colton snatched the boy by the scruff of his shirt and frog-walked him to the front entrance. Keeping his anger in check, he kicked open the door and shoved Eric onto the front porch. "Tell your father why we'll no longer be doing business."

Less arrogant than his brother, Dirk meekly scuttled past Colton and onto the porch. Eric stumbled down the stairs and turned with a heavy scowl. The boys were too used to getting their own way. Because of their father's wealth and power, folks in town turned a blind eye to their misbehavior. Colton had no such compunction. As the only blacksmith in town, Colton needed Mr. Schuyler less than the man needed him.

Eric stumbled backward down the front stairs, his fist raised. "My father will hear of this treatment."

"Come back when you're ready to be a man and fight your own battles, son."

Colton slammed the door, rattling the glass panes. He took a deep breath, trying to calm himself. The boy was a child. A child who'd been given too little supervision over his actions.

He turned and discovered Beatrix staring at him, her face ashen, her hands wringing.

"Don't be angry with them," she pleaded. "You don't understand. There was war in Austria, like there was war in America. They are German. They won. They don't have respect for the Austrians anymore."

"I understand war," Colton bit out through gritted teeth. "I understand victors and vanquished. I will not let a boy insult my wife under my roof. They believe they are invincible. Young men aren't invincible. Their actions are nothing but a match on dry tinder."

The truth tore through him like a bullet. Foolish boys playing with fire.

His anger strangled in his throat.

The Schuyler boys were no different than he and Joseph had been all those years ago.

Chapter Eight

Alarmed by the angry grimace distorting her husband's face, Beatrix took a hesitant step forward and reached out one hand.

The Schuyler boys were bullies, and she'd grown a thick skin against bullies of late. Their words had bothered her considerably less than the thought that they had upset her husband—and forced him to end a profitable business relationship.

"You mustn't lose Mr. Schuyler's business."

She took another step closer, placing her hand on the tense muscles of Colton's forearm.

The tendons beneath her fingertips flexed.

"Eric is a selfish child," he said, "who knows nothing of life."

Colton made a frustrated movement of his hand. Conditioned from years of living with her father, Beatrix flinched instinctively and flung up her arms, shielding her face. Blood roared in her ears. His breath hissed, and she braced for a blow.

A moment passed, and the expected pain never materialized. Heart hammering, she forced the air from her lungs and slowly lowered her arms a notch. Colton stared at her, a blank look on his face.

"Beatrix," he said, his voice deceptively calm. "Did you think…did you think I might hit you?"

He reached for her, but his movement was too sudden, too unexpected. She stumbled back and bumped into the wall, her body quivering in anticipation of a blow.

She cowered away, loathing her own weakness. "Don't use your fists."

He was so much larger than her father. He'd break her bones.

Her whole body quaked, and the more she tried to hold herself in check, the more she trembled. Except nothing happened. He'd gone ominously still, and his unpredictability frightened her more than his anger. She forced open her eyes, and the room reeled.

The pulse in his temple throbbed violently. "I would never strike you. I would never harm you. Please, understand that."

Her head buzzed with tension. "I'm sorry."

She was bone tired, grimy and sticky with sweat. She didn't know what else to say. She couldn't tell if he was sincere, or if he was luring her into a false sense of security.

"Shhh," he soothed. "Let me come nearer. Let me show you there's nothing to fear from me."

She pressed her back tighter against the wall. The old fears remained. She'd angered him. He'd lost a valuable customer because of her. He was so much larger. He'd always been kind to her, and yet she hadn't known him for long. Maybe she'd just never pushed him to his breaking point before. She had Joseph to think about…

"I can't," she choked out, her voice barely more than a sob.

She wanted so badly to be brave, but in the past, her boldness had cost her a blackened eye—sometimes worse.

"You can." He took another slow step forward. "If we don't do this now, you'll never completely trust me."

She cringed. "I trust you."

The heightened tension sent her muscles aching. She'd put her life in this man's hands. Leah had assured her that Colton was a good man, and she trusted Leah's word. And yet men were deceptive, with their honeyed words and false promises.

"No," he said. "You don't trust me."

One of his arms slid around her waist. With the other he dragged the limp handkerchief from her hair and smoothed the strands from her face. His touch was cautious, feather light and achingly gentle.

"Let me hold you," he soothed. "Let me show you there's nothing to fear."

She glanced at his hands. His fingers were not curled into fists.

A small part of her anxiety eased. She rested her cheek against his chest. His heartbeat thumped against her ear, strong and restful. She sensed no coiled tension in him. He didn't force her compliance, merely kept his arms loosely holding her in the circle of his embrace.

All of her experiences over the past weeks came rushing back.

He'd stayed by her side with Joseph when the doctor thought she might not last the night. He'd never once raised his voice or lost his temper with her. Nothing Colton had done since she'd met him had ever given her a reason to fear him. There was no reason to believe he was anything but the gentle man she'd married.

And yet his anger at the Schuyler boys had caused a reflexive action in her.

She closed her eyes and pressed her temple against his shoulder, hiding her face. He cupped the back of her head and murmured soothing words. After a long moment her mind and her body relaxed into the safety he offered. Relief weakened her knees, and she slumped against him.

"You're exhausted," his breath whispered against her ear. "You need to sit."

"There are no chairs."

"Then we'll sit on the floor."

He carefully lowered them both to the floor, his shoulder sliding against the wall, cradling her against his chest. She clutched his collar and rubbed her cheek against the rough canvas of his shirt. Humiliation burned hot in her chest.

"Was it your father?" he asked. "Did your father hit you?"

Beatrix carefully considered her next words. The past was the past, and there was no use dwelling on what had been before. "Sometimes. My father was a kinder man before my mother died. After she was gone, he bore all the responsibility for me and my sisters. There were eight of us." She offered a humorless chuckle. "I don't think he realized how much he depended on my mother. He was a prideful man who took great stock in his reputation."

"He took more stock in his reputation than in the safety of his daughter? He let you travel alone. Pregnant. That's not a prideful man. That's a weak man."

Her father had never said a word against Peter, either for seducing or abandoning her. In his view, men habitually made advances on women, and the responsibility for remaining chaste rested with the woman alone. As though a man's attention was some sort of test of chastity. Except Peter's attention had felt authentic.

She'd been so very alone after her mother's death. She'd felt as though she didn't belong anywhere. Though she often visited her sisters, they had their own families and their own concerns. She hadn't wanted to grow old and alone, waiting for her father to die. She'd seen the fate of the spinsters in the village. Once her father passed away, she'd go to live with one of her sisters. A burden.

She'd been so very lonely and so very angry at the future she'd been dealt. She'd clung to the illusion of Peter's affection and attention.

"I had to tell my father about the baby," she said. "There were rumors already. One of my sisters had told him about Peter."

Colton's arms tightened around her. "He shouldn't have hurt you."

The buttons of his shirt dug into her palm. She tipped back her head and stared into the glittering intensity of his gaze. Her language slipped into the comfort of German once more. "My sisters had warned me. They told me that I was only a challenge to him. My father kept a close watch on all of us. But I was headstrong. As the youngest, with my mother gone, I was supposed to stay home and take care of my father—to never marry or have a home of my own. I wanted more." She choked back a sob. "I sold my future to a fool because I was lonely."

"He took advantage of you?" Colton asked, his voice hoarse.

She pressed her nose against his shirt, catching the faint scent of coal fire and ash.

"No." The responsibility was hers and hers alone. She'd consented to things she'd known were wrong. "I thought myself in love. I was so naïve. I didn't understand love. I was infatuated with Peter because he was the first boy who'd ever paid any attention to me. After what happened, he left for Vienna and refused to answer my letters. I think his father suspected something. When I found out about Joseph, I had no choice but to tell someone." She smiled weakly. "Peter had a choice. He chose to marry a girl from Vienna whose father worked for the government. Peter could be very charming. This union made Peter's father very proud. She was much better than a girl from the village."

"He was a weak fool." Colton drew back. "You're safe here. With me."

"I know."

"You don't believe me yet, but you will." He rested his chin on the top of her head. "Why did you marry me? You must have been terrified of me. Of my size."

She recalled that first evening, the harsh planes of his face thrown in relief from the lamplight. "When people talked with my father, they were tense and wary. No one flinched or cowered when they spoke to you."

He rocked her gently, his enormous hands making comforting circles against her back. Her breath quickened with his touch. As with Joseph, she sensed he performed the soothing movement unconsciously.

"I'm sorry," she said. "I didn't mean to doubt you."

"Don't be sorry. We're both learning to trust each other. Your reaction was natural."

Perhaps, but she'd wounded his pride. This was a man who valued honor, and she'd questioned that honor by flinching away from him, even when he'd told her she had nothing to fear. She smiled up at him, and he brushed the hair from her face, then leaned the back of his head against the wall.

Each lost in their own thoughts, neither of them spoke for a long while. They sat on the floor of the parlor, with Beatrix secure in the cradle of his embrace. She tipped back her head and stared at his lips. How had she ever doubted the tenderness of this man? From those first confusing days when there was nothing but voices and uncertainty surrounding her, he'd stayed with her. He'd married her when she'd been distraught, and he'd kept his vows even when he could have denounced them. She'd repaid his kindness by treating him like a monster.

Without stopping to think, she pushed upright and pressed her lips against his. He remained motionless, then his fingers reached out, caressing her cheek and tenderly adjusting the angle between them. She clung to him, winding her arms around his neck, and strained closer.

He broke away and rained soft kisses down her temple and cheek, taking a soft nip at the tip of her ear. She laughed and rose on her knees, threading her fingers through his hair. The tresses were rough and soft at the same time, and she delved deeper, wanting to feel him, touch him. His caresses weren't demanding, more like gentle explorations, and she felt as though she was safe, as though she could pull away at any moment.

An angry squall sounded from upstairs, and he twisted away from her. "Joseph."

"Joseph." She raised her eyes toward the ceiling. "I know that cry. He must be changed."

"You'd better see to him." Colton stood and reached for her, assisting her to her feet. "Are you all right now?"

"Yes," she said, her lips tender from their kisses. "Promise me you won't make any decisions about working with the Schuylers. It's different in Europe now. Since the war, things have changed. I won't have you losing out on business because of me."

He cupped the side of her cheek, and the sweet shock of his touch sent a ripple of awareness down her spine. "I've chafed your skin."

She placed her hand over his, the nicks and scars raised against her palm. "I don't mind."

"Thank you. For telling me about Peter."

"This is a new beginning for me. Peter is in Austria,

and we are here. He gave up his rights to Joseph. He gave up his rights to me and my thoughts. I don't want him in our lives anymore."

"Neither do I."

The cries from the second floor grew insistent, and she backed toward the stairs, one hand pressed against the wall, the other fisted against her stomach. "Promise me that you will speak with Mr. Schuyler."

"I promise."

She stifled a sigh and made her way toward the crying infant.

Colton caught her sleeve. "I'll see to Joseph. Will you play?" He gestured toward the armonica.

"Would that please you?" She wanted to make him happy, wanted to be a good wife to him—and she knew she was making a mess of it. Maybe this was one thing she could get right.

"Yes."

Preparing the instrument took longer than she'd expected, and she was soon lost in the process. Once she'd arranged her chair and had a saucer of water in place, she worked the pedals, setting the spinning bowls into motion.

The first few notes were off key, but she soon found her rhythm and lost herself in the music. A long while later, she glanced up to find Colton watching her, his eyes rimmed with red, Joseph cradled in his arms.

She lifted her fingers from the instrument.

Colton shook himself, as though waking from a trance. "Don't stop. That's the most beautiful sound I've ever heard."

Pride swelled in her chest. "Then I will keep playing."

Her playing pleased him, but she sensed he was building the wall again. Brick by sorrowful brick. She trusted him, but she feared he'd lost his trust in her.

* * *

Two weeks after the move, Leah opened the front door and waved Beatrix into the parlor of her grand home. "Thank you for coming."

"Thank you for inviting me."

Leah was radiant as always. She wore a soft blue calico gown with a square neckline. Beatrix brushed at her faded green skirts. Leah's dress was casual, and Beatrix was certain she'd worn something simple in deference to her guest.

Of her three serviceable dresses, Beatrix wore her best today. A drab shirtwaist under an olive green jacket. Though the dress Leah had given her was far more suitable for the occasion, wearing the gift in Leah's presence felt odd.

A heavily pregnant redheaded woman seated in the wingback chair near the fire struggled to rise.

Leah flashed her palm. "Don't get up, Tomasina," she ordered. "I've got everything under control. Can I bring you a glass of water?"

Tomasina slumped back in her seat. "That sounds delightful. And a scone if you have one. Or two."

Leah flashed an indulgent smile. "Beatrix, this is Tomasina Canfield. Tomasina, this is Beatrix Werner. I think I might have a scone or two in the pantry."

She disappeared through a door that presumably led to the kitchen.

"Call me Tom," the woman declared. "Everyone else does."

Tomasina Canfield looked completely unsuited for such a masculine name. She was petite and delicate, with a mass of fiery red curls atop her head and brilliant, green eyes. Her pregnancy was advanced, and her high-waisted, brown wool dress fell over the swell of her stomach in a waterfall of fabric.

"I met your husband," Beatrix said. "Mr. Canfield."

The other woman's eyes took on a wistful look. "He's more anxious for the baby than I am, and that's saying something. Will has a weakness for babies." She patted her rounded belly. "He wants ten more after this one. Easy for him to say. All he has to do is rub my feet and order an extra dinner tray when I'm famished."

Beatrix's heart ached a bit. Her pregnancy with Joseph had been filled with worry and trepidation. Those last weeks had been consumed with travel and more fretting. How nice it must be to have a husband who looked forward to the birth of one's child. To be married to someone eager to become a father.

As though sensing the change in her mood, Tomasina gestured toward the settee. "Sit. My neck is aching from looking up at you."

Beatrix took her place on the settee, and Leah returned with a tray. "The housekeeper is watching the baby. We have at least an hour of peace. What about you, Beatrix?"

"Colton is watching Joseph, but I've never left them alone for more than an hour."

"What is he like?" Tomasina asked. "Colton? I don't know him as well as I do some of the others in town."

Beatrix pleated her wool skirts between two fingers. "He's quiet."

"Are you happy?" Tomasina inquired, her expression intense.

Beneath her questioning scrutiny, Beatrix opened and closed her mouth a few times. "I suppose, yes."

"Because if you're not happy, I can have him taken care of." Tomasina winked. "I know people, if you know what I mean."

Chapter Nine

"Tom!" Leah admonished.

She rested her laden tray near Tomasina. With her threat still hanging in the air, the pregnant woman attacked the snacks with gusto.

"You're frightening the poor girl," Leah continued. "Tomasina will not have your husband *taken care of*. She's simply trying to discern if you're content. We women must stick together. If you're unhappy, we can help. In a nonviolent way, of course."

"I'm happy," Beatrix replied, a slight squeak in her voice.

Just in case Tomasina *did* know people. She *was* happy, mostly. Since Joseph slept for several hours at a stretch, she'd gotten more sleep and was feeling more robust. She had no complaints, other than an occasional tinge of loneliness now and then.

Leah patted her arm. "We didn't mean to frighten you. We simply want you to know that we're here for you, if you ever need to talk. If you ever have a problem. Enough jabbering about husbands. With the babies on a time schedule, we'd better work quickly."

"What is this project?" Beatrix asked.

Leah had invited her over, but she'd only given a brief outline of what she had planned.

"I'll take this explanation." Tomasina set down the last bite of her third scone and brushed the crumbs from her hands. "The ladies are putting together a history of the town, and I've decided to act like a lady this once so I can help. Will deserves to have his legacy mentioned, even though he doesn't want the recognition. Most of the men who settled in Cowboy Creek served in the war. We'd like to document the stories of their friendships in an archive."

"They let you do this?" Beatrix asked.

Colton was such a private man, she couldn't imagine him talking about his past, let alone his war experiences.

"They're not happy about the plan." Leah heaved a long-suffering sigh. "But we feel the stories are important. We've promised they'll be placed in a time capsule that won't be opened for one hundred years. That's the only way we were able to convince our husbands to agree."

Tomasina rolled her eyes. "I had to threaten Will."

Beatrix touched her chest. "You threaten your husband?"

"He can take care of himself." Tomasina flapped her hand in a dismissive wave.

Glancing between the two of them, Beatrix frowned. "How can I help?"

"I know you want to improve your English. This is a way for us all to work together. You can help us transcribe the stories."

Tomasina reached for a cookie with a dot of strawberry jam in the center. "Will says that Colton was a hero during the war. Maybe he'll tell you some of his stories."

Learning Colton was a hero didn't surprise Beatrix. There was an inherent sense of honor about him. She didn't doubt he was the same quiet, self-contained man during the war.

"Yep." Tomasina licked a spot of strawberry jam from her thumb. "I guess he's got a whole box full of medals. Wonder if he'd be willing to donate one of those medals to the time capsule."

"I will ask," Beatrix said. "But I do not think he will help."

She was hesitant to press him. There'd been a distance between them since they moved into the house. Colton worked at the shop well into the evenings. They rarely saw one another. She left a covered dish for him in the kitchen each evening, and sometimes she heard his footsteps tread past her room, but they rarely spoke unless she forced the issue. Even then his replies were brief.

"Either way." Leah shrugged. "Colton's memories would be a wonderful addition to the time capsule, but I'll leave that up to you. You know him best."

Did she? Her head throbbed. Beatrix highly doubted she knew her husband any better than the other ladies in the room.

After chatting in the parlor, Leah led them to the dining room where they gathered around the table. Beatrix remained quiet as Leah and Tomasina set to work. They wrote out who in the town had served in the war along with their rank. There was little chance for her to help, but she studied their writing, and recognized many of the words. After forty-five minutes, a knock sounded at the door.

Tomasina pushed off from her chair and staggered upright, cradling her round stomach. "That will be my husband. With my time nearing, he has to check up on me every hour or he frets. Trust me, the sight of Will fretting is not for the faint of heart."

Beatrix smiled despite the prick of loneliness invading

her thoughts once more. Not since the day they'd moved into the house had Colton fussed or worried over her. Lately, he barely seemed to notice she was around.

Tomasina's prediction was correct, and Mr. Canfield was ushered into the entry. Dapper and charming, Will complimented each of the ladies in turn and even spoke a few practiced words in German to Beatrix. After exchanging a few more pleasantries, Will helped his wife into her wool coat, wrapped a scarf around her neck, and carefully led her down the front stairs.

Beatrix followed their slow progress, Will with his cane in one hand and his arm protectively wrapped around his wife's shoulders.

Leah followed her gaze. "They're quite a pair, aren't they?"

"Yes."

"You should have seen them butt heads in the beginning. I wasn't certain if they were going to marry each other or kill each other."

"Really?"

"I'm exaggerating, of course. But they had quite a feisty courtship. They spent the first night of their honeymoon in a posse tracking the Murdoch Gang. Reverend Taggart married them right there on Eden Street, with the rest of the posse lined up behind the couple, and everyone else gawking from the boardwalk."

"This is a story you should write for the time capsule."

Leah grew thoughtful. "You're right. We should add the story of Texas Tom and her Wild West Show. Men aren't the only ones who make history around here."

Beatrix grinned, pleased her suggestion had met with such enthusiasm. She gathered her cloak and thanked Leah for the invitation. "I wish I could be of more help."

"You've been a great help. Next time we meet, we'll

invite a few more of the ladies. We didn't want you to be overwhelmed." Leah tapped her chin. "Oh, before I forget. We're putting together a banquet to celebrate Thanksgiving. Since the whole town is invited, we're hosting the dinner at the Cattleman Hotel."

Beatrix frowned. "Thanksgiving?"

Leah playfully slapped her forehead. "How silly of me. There's no reason why you should—it's only recently become official. Our president has declared that Thanksgiving is a day for giving thanks for the blessing of the harvest, and for our country's peace and prosperity. At least that's what it says on paper. In reality, it's a day for the women to cook up a storm and for everyone to eat like bears preparing for hibernation. I think it's taken on a deeper meaning since the war."

"This sounds similar to the Austrian festival of *Erntedankfest*."

"Tell me about this festival."

"It is a very large community celebration. There is a parade and a dance."

"You've piqued my interest. You should join the committee, and we can incorporate some of your traditions."

Recalling how Eugene and the Schuyler boys had reacted to her heritage, her stomach folded. "This is not a good idea."

"Why ever not?"

"Not everyone is welcoming of immigrants, especially from Austria."

Leah frowned. "That's ridiculous. Everyone in town was an immigrant at one time or another. Except for Sitting Bear, of course, but he's the only one who has any right to condemn an immigrant." She huffed. "It'll be a wonderful chance for you to meet more people in town."

"And practice my English."

"Your English has improved greatly. You haven't met the new doctor, have you? Marlys Boyd? She might speak German, as well. I'll ask her. She knows several languages. I was skeptical at first because her methods are a little different. But after she cured Pippa of her dry skin, I'm convinced. Anyway, I'm babbling. We'd love to see you and your family at the Thanksgiving Festival."

Family. *Her family*. Beatrix enjoyed the way that sounded, and appreciated Leah's thoughtfulness.

"Thank you. Can I cook something for this festival?"

"Do you have a special dish?"

"*Ja*. A torte. A dessert."

"That sounds marvelous," Leah replied with a wave. "Come to the celebration and bring your dessert."

Sun glinted off the snow on her walk home, and her breath puffed vaporous clouds into the air. Wanting to stretch her legs, Beatrix crossed the street and made her way toward the dressmaker's shop. She was sorely tired of the dresses she owned. Colton had offered to buy her more, but she was reluctant to accept any more of his charity. She had a little money of her own left over from the trip, and she wanted to treat herself.

Hannah, the store owner, assisted her with fabric selections and took her measurements. Once outside again, Beatrix whistled a merry tune. Her meeting with Leah and Tomasina had left her more hopeful, more optimistic of the future.

A shadow crossed her path and she stumbled. Eric and Dirk Schuyler blocked her way.

Eric pulled a small knife from his pocket and ran the tip beneath the fingernail of his index finger. "You better talk to your husband."

Beatrix froze. "I already have."

"Our pa is real mad. Colton is the only blacksmith for

miles, and Pa's got no one to do the metalwork. Except your husband is refusing the business."

She glanced around, but the street was deserted against the frigid temperature. "Then you must apologize, no? That is what Colton asked."

"I ain't apologizing to you. Fix this. Lie to him. Tell him we told you that we were real sorry. You fix this, or you'll be sorry."

He pivoted on his heel and his brother followed.

Beatrix stumbled the rest of the way home in a daze. Even if she lied to Colton, he was bound to speak with Mr. Schuyler. What then? He'd know she'd lied. If she confessed to Colton that the boys had threatened her, she'd only escalate the matter and ruin any chance he had of making peace.

Both choices left her trapped.

Colton dreaded shoeing old man Bishop's horse. The animal had never been properly broken and shied at every touch and noise. While some horses were naturally more skittish than others, Bishop's horse was terrified of its own shadow. Walter Frye had volunteered, but Colton couldn't send someone else in good conscience.

"C'mon, Shasta," Colton soothed the agitated animal. "It's all right. Just relax. We go through this every time. There's no need for all the fuss and bother."

The horse jerked its leg, yanking Colton forward. "Easy there."

Two more nails and he was done.

A loud bang sounded, and a small, furry animal darted through the barn. Shasta reared. Colton lost his hold. The terrified animal sidestepped.

A dog barked. Colton braced himself against the rough

slats of the barn. "It's only a dog, Shasta. Surely you've seen a dog before. You're as old as the hills."

The horse must have taken umbrage with the mention of its age. Shasta's eyes rolled back, showing the whites, and the horse's nostrils flared.

The dog dashed from behind a pile of hay. Shasta reared, front legs flailing. Colton whistled, shooing the dog out of the path of the rampaging horse. Shasta whipped around.

Colton slid toward the half-open barn door. The dog scurried through the opening first. Shasta wheeled around and hind legs thrashed. The first blow landed against Colton's ribs. He yelped and automatically covered the spot. The second blow struck his hand.

Pain exploded up the length of his arm. Protecting his ribs with his good hand, Colton knelt to avoid the flailing hooves and crawled his way toward the exit. He slid through the narrow opening.

Once free of the rampaging horse, he collapsed on his back and groaned.

Old man Bishop leaned over him, his forehead creased. "What on earth happened to you?"

"Fetch Daniel," Colton ordered weakly. Old man Bishop lived near the stockyards. This time of the day, Daniel would be checking the accounts. "He'll be in the stock-yard's office."

"Suit yourself." The old man slapped his hands against his thighs and squinted. "But I'd see a doc if I was you. Cuz you don't look so good."

"Fetch Daniel."

"All right, all right. Quit your jibber jabber."

Prior experience told Colton that he had bruised a couple ribs and, judging by the rapid swelling in his hand, busted a finger or two, as well. There was nothing the doc could do for those types of wounds other than order rest and a tight wrap around the injuries. Daniel could accomplish the task as easily. After four years of war, most soldiers could do some doctoring.

The angry horse continued to buck, and sharp cracks sounded against the barn. The dog that had started all the trouble barked at the noise and lunged toward the barn, then darted back again.

Colton groaned. "You're real tough now that he can't get to you."

The dog appeared young, not quite full grown, with a dark brown coat of fur and a pointed snout. The unrepentant animal trotted over and gave Colton a lick on his cheek.

With his good hand, Colton shooed the animal away. "I think you've done enough already."

The pain came and went in waves. Old man Bishop was sure taking his time. He closed his eyes until he heard footsteps nearing.

Two familiar faces appeared above him. "I've seen worse," Daniel declared. "Let's get you home before you freeze to death."

Will tilted his head. "I can't believe you let that tired old nag get the better of you."

Colton grimaced. "This is who you brought for help? He's only got one good leg himself."

"You're in no position to complain, old man." Will poked him in the shoulder with his cane. "Even on one leg I'm steadier than you."

The good-natured teasing had taken his mind off his pain. Temporarily. When together the two men hoisted Colton between them, he hissed a breath. Colton leaned heavily on Daniel and cradled his arm protectively against his chest.

"We'll take you to the doc's," Will said.

"No." Colton shook his head. "That old fool will probably try and bleed me for something as simple as a couple of bruised ribs."

"He's gone anyway," Daniel offered. "I'll leave a note on the chalkboard. He can visit you later."

"I'll be fine. Just take me home."

Beatrix. She already had a baby to care for, and now he was coming home a temporary invalid.

As though reading his thoughts, Will said, "I'll have Simon bring by a tray for dinner from the hotel kitchen. Beatrix will have her hands full for the next few days."

Colton wasn't going to be able to work, and he desperately needed to leave the house. Otherwise he'd be alone with Beatrix. He'd hear her laughter and catch the scent of her rosewater hair rinse. He'd hear the sound of her playing music. He'd never experienced an instrument as beautiful as the armonica.

The next few days were going to be torture, and pain was the least of his worries.

Since the day of the move, he'd kept their schedules separate. Every time something good started between them, they were interrupted. If circumstances conspired against them, that was probably for the best.

He was little more than a bad seed from which nothing of value could grow.

A few broken fingers were the least of his worries. Being around Beatrix was going to be the true torment. She was so close, and yet just out of his reach.

Chapter Ten

Beatrix heard the commotion from the second floor. She rested Joseph against her shoulder and rapidly traversed the steps. The back door flew open, and Colton stood on the threshold. He was flanked by Will Canfield and Daniel Gardner, who held him propped up with their hands around his shoulders.

His face was ashen and contorted into a grimace of pain. Her hand flew to her mouth. She beckoned them toward the bedroom on the first floor, the room she'd been preparing for the future visit from his grandparents. A visit he hadn't agreed to yet.

"This way," she ordered.

The men half carried, half dragged her husband behind her, his heels scuffing along the floor. His strained face was set against the pain. They rested him prone on the bed, and he threw back his head, his eyes closed, his lips pinched together.

Her questions tumbled over one another, and she tentatively reached for his hand. "What happened? Where are you injured?"

Daniel reached for the baby. "Why don't you let me hold Joseph while you sort out Colton?"

She hesitated only a moment before handing over the baby. Her gaze swung between her prone husband and Daniel. The blond-haired man was about Colton's age, though a full head shorter. Then again, most men were a full head shorter than her husband. Daniel appeared comfortable with the baby, and she turned her attention to Colton once more. Daniel had his own child, and his wife served as midwife. He must have plenty of practice with infants.

Colton's jaw was clenched, and one hand gripped the edge of the mattress. Assuming her calmest demeanor, she lowered one hip to the bed next to his fisted hand and brushed the tumbled hair from his forehead.

"There was an accident, ma'am," Mr. Canfield spoke. "He was shoeing a horse at old man Bishop's place, and the horse spooked. Colton took a hoof to the ribs. They're just bruised, I think, but he's busted a couple of fingers."

The hoof had torn his shirt, and she peeled back the layer of canvas and tucked aside the rip in his union suit. An enormous purpling bruise was rapidly spreading over the lower half of his chest and side.

She felt the blood drain from her face and swallowed convulsively. There'd been a boy in her village who'd fallen from his horse and broken his ribs. They'd punctured his lung, and he'd died the next day.

She rested a trembling hand on Colton's chest. "Can you breathe?"

A jerky nod met her words. "Hurts. I can breathe. Just need to rest."

"Fetch the doctor," she ordered Will.

"The doc isn't available."

Her ire rose. "What do you mean he isn't available?"

"I mean to say that he's not at his office. We left a note on the chalkboard."

She pursed her lips and muttered in German. "A fine lot of good it does to have a doctor who isn't even there when you need him."

"I'm all right," Colton told her with a shuddering gasp. "Just knocked the wind out of me."

"You're not all right. You've got broken fingers. You can hardly draw a breath." She pressed her fist against her mouth and chocked back a sob. "Someone find that doctor."

"Dr. Boyd," Daniel chimed in. "She can help."

Will Canfield scratched the back of his neck. "Are you certain you want us to fetch Marlys Boyd? She's got some odd ideas."

"If she's a doctor," Beatrix spoke, a shrill edge in her voice, "she's the best choice we have right now. Fetch her."

"All right, Mrs. Werner." Will removed his hand and took a cautious step. "I'll fetch her and return in a lick."

"*Danke schön.*" She drew in a deep, calming breath. "Thank you. I did not mean to yell at you."

"I've got a wife, Mrs. Werner. I know you're worried." The man tipped his hat and backed out of the room.

Daniel gently wiggled the baby against his shoulder. "I'll leave you two alone for a moment."

Beatrix brushed her quivering fingers over the rapid swelling of Colton's bruised ribs.

He clutched her wrist. "I'm fine."

"You're not fine. I know you've been avoiding me, but I won't allow you to push me away now. You might recall that we're married, and I'm your wife. I'm going to take care of you whether you like it or not, Colton Werner, and there's nothing you can do to stop me."

"Beatrix—"

She pressed two fingers over his lips. "No words. I must see to Joseph. Daniel can stay with you until I return."

There. Let him argue with her now. He was flat on his back, and entirely at her disposal. There'd be no more slipping out before dawn and returning after sunset. "Bea—"

"Not one word!"

She slammed out the door and smoothed her hands over her hair, then down her apron.

He was about to get a taste of what it felt like to be a captive audience. They were married. There was no point in the two of them behaving as though they were strangers.

If she had to force the issue, now was as good a time as any.

Daniel glanced up from his seat, Joseph nestled against his chest. "Everything all right, Mrs. Werner?"

She set her jaw. "*Ja.* No more work for Colton."

"I've seen that look on my wife's face before." Daniel stood and handed her the baby, then patted her shoulder. "I'll just give Colton my sympathies."

He returned to the sickroom with a cheerful grin and a wink.

Beatrix rocked the baby and watched for the doctor. Why was the foolish man happy? There were times she did not understand Americans.

"You're a fortunate man, Mr. Werner," Dr. Boyd said. "Your ribs are only bruised, not broken. I'll give you something for the pain. You'll sleep through the worst of it."

"I can't just laze around here all day," Colton interjected. "There's work to be done."

"Then you shouldn't have let that horse kick you. You've got bruised ribs and two dislocated fingers. You're fortunate there, as well."

Recalling the pain of *re*-locating those fingers, he bit back an oath. "I don't feel very fortunate."

Beatrix pulled open the door, then in an attitude of pure exhaustion, leaned her head against the frame.

Immediately concerned, he attempted to rise and winced. "Is something wrong?" he demanded.

There were dark circles beneath her eyes, and even her delightful curls appeared to droop a bit.

"Nothing is wrong." She glanced between him and Dr. Boyd. "I've simply been worried about you."

"Then stop being worried." His order sounded more petulant than threatening. "I'm fine. All this fuss is for nothing."

She ignored him, just as she'd ignored every variation of those words he'd said all day. "I've made you two lunch."

She disappeared and returned a moment later holding a tray stacked with sandwiches. She set the offering on the table near his headboard, then backed away.

Marlys smiled her appreciation. "*Danke schön*, Frau Werner. *Wie geht es euch?*"

Colton collapsed onto the pillows and gaped. He'd heard the doc was smart, but he hadn't realized she spoke German, as well. Her accent was impeccable.

At the sound of her own language spoken with such perfection, Beatrix's face lit up as though she'd seen the first tulip of spring.

For the next twenty minutes, the two women completely ignored him. They chatted away as though he was invisible. Despite the improvements he'd made with his German since Beatrix's arrival, he could barely keep up with them. The more they spoke, the faster the words tripped together.

To the best of his ability, he followed the conversation, using all his powers of concentration. Marlys asked about the baby and Beatrix's health. She gave orders for him to rest and to visit her offices for a mineral bath once he was able.

Not likely.

He wasn't lounging around in some mineral bath like a pampered heiress.

Watching the two of them together, a painful weight settled on his chest. He hadn't taken into consideration how Beatrix had been suffering with isolation and homesickness all these weeks. Because of his own experience growing up, he'd treated their tribulations as though they were equal, but the reality was far different.

Sure, he'd struggled with the language barrier when he'd first lived with his grandparents, but that experience paled in comparison to what Beatrix was going through. His grandparents' farm was only a twenty-minute ride from town.

He'd been twenty minutes from immersing himself in his own language once more. Beatrix was worlds away from anything familiar.

Dr. Boyd stood and removed her white apron, then cast him a withering glance. "I won't tell you to rest, because I know men. The more I order you to rest, the more determined you'll be to work. Instead, I'll simply ask that you perform only light duties for the next few days. Though your ribs are only bruised, they're vulnerable. Another blow and the bones will snap. Then you'll truly be laid up for a week, doctor's orders or not."

The mattress depressed beside him, and Beatrix touched his cheek. "Promise you'll be careful?"

Her thumb caressed the side of his jaw. The motion was relaxing...hypnotizing. "I always follow doctor's orders."

"Liar."

Her eyelids lowered at his touch, and he felt her lean slightly toward him. The look was unconsciously inviting, alluring. He longed to pull her into his arms but refrained because of the doctor's audience.

Dr. Boyd, always brisk and efficient, lifted her leather bag and crossed to the door. "Call on me if you need anything. Remember, don't wrap the bindings too tightly. Only light activity. Come by the office for a mineral bath when you're feeling up to the journey."

She and Beatrix spoke a few more words of German before the doctor quietly exited the room.

He reached for Beatrix, but she scurried out of the room. "Rest. The doctor has ordered you to rest."

The remainder of the day passed with boredom punctuated by Daniel and Will who gave him no end of teasing for his predicament. He spent a sleepless night, each toss and turn pressing against his bruised ribs, waking him. The following morning he managed a few chores before the pain caught up with him.

In deference to Beatrix, he crawled back into bed after lunch. There was no use making her sick with worry.

Except there was something decidedly determined in the set of her jaw this afternoon. Something that didn't bode well for him.

She paced before the foot of the bed, her lower lip pulled between her teeth. "The ladies in town are working on a time capsule. They are writing down the stories of the war."

"I heard." He reached for the coffee she'd brought him. Some parts of being laid up weren't half bad.

"They have asked me to help them."

"Good." He liked the idea of her having a hobby. "I'm sure the ladies are pleased with your help. Is Marlys involved?"

"Yes."

Even better. Beatrix would have someone near who spoke her language, and could help her navigate the new culture.

"I want to tell your story," Beatrix said softly.

Colton's hand jerked, sloshing the coffee, and he winced. "That's not a good idea."

"Will says that you have many medals."

His throat worked. The mere idea of someone writing down his experiences filled him with revulsion. His knuckles whitened around the handle of his mug.

Beatrix took a cautious step back. Was his expression that terrifying? He felt a rush of remorse. After the incident on the day of the move, he was fearful of frightening her.

"The war isn't something I like to talk about." He forced calm into his voice. "I'm sure you can assist the ladies some other way."

"Is there something you'd like to donate? A piece of memorabilia?"

"I burned my uniform."

At his harsh tone, her face paled.

"Beatrix—" he held out his hand, then let his arm drop against his side with a wince "—nothing good can come from digging up the past."

"But if you had medals, you must have earned them with your courage. Don't you want someone to understand your sacrifice?"

"There was no sacrifice. The medals, the stories. Everything is a lie. They'll still be lies in one hundred years."

"I don't understand."

"Help the ladies all you want, but I want no part of the project."

There was no way to explain, no way to tell her without bringing up the past.

She perched on the bed beside him and gently rested his injured hand in her palms. "How is your hand?"

"Better."

"I'm sorry I brought up the project. I don't want to argue."

"We're not arguing." He cupped her cheek. "I'm being surly because I let old man Bishop's horse get the better of me."

"Dr. Boyd seems like a very good doctor."

Colton flexed his fingers. "I guess it wouldn't hurt to follow her advice. The salve she gave me has helped."

Beatrix rubbed one of the scars on the back of his hand with the pad of her thumb. "I don't think a mineral bath can hurt anything."

"I'm sorry about the project."

"I don't mind. I promised the committee that I would ask. I have done what I promised."

She'd asked so little of him, and yet he must refuse. There was no way of telling her the war stories without telling her about Joseph. No way of being totally honest with her without digging up the past.

The memory of her joy at speaking with Marlys the previous day lingered in his memory. Beatrix deserved some comfort. She deserved some news from home.

He placed his hand over hers. "I think you should write to your sisters."

She looked away. "They don't want to hear from me."

"You don't know that. Your father sounds like a very strong man. While your sisters were reluctant to face him, I'm certain they're worried about you."

Her face brightened. "I almost forgot. Leah is organizing a Thanksgiving celebration in the ballroom of the Cattleman Hotel."

"Leah keeps busy, and you're changing the subject."

"Yes."

"All right." They both had a stubborn streak. "Tell me about this celebration."

"There will be food. And Piper Kendricks is going to do a stage show."

"I think her name is Pippa."

"Ah, yes. Pippa is going to do a show. They say she is very beautiful and very talented."

Having Beatrix near was provoking all the longings he'd feared. Everything about her drew him to her—her touch, her smile, the way she cared for Joseph. Yet with each joy came the same guilt. If he allowed himself this slice of happiness, what did that mean for all the people he'd hurt with his actions? What did that mean for Joseph's memory? He felt the pull toward happiness, but shied away, fearing that his joy would be snatched away again.

He didn't believe a higher power was preventing their happiness, which meant he was sabotaging his future because of the guilt he carried from his past. Always before the consequences of his youthful actions had been his alone to bear, but now he had Beatrix to consider. Now his actions punished them both.

She unconsciously rubbed the back of his hand in tantalizing circles, and he struggled to recall what they'd been speaking about. "Pippa organized a show at the opera house last spring."

Pippa had been a darling of the mail-order brides from the first bride train. She was beautiful and vivacious, and more than one man in town had fallen for her before she'd married Gideon Kendricks.

"You like this Pippa person?"

"She's an excellent actress. Personally, I don't know her very well. As far as women are concerned, she's not my preference."

He didn't want to think about the past anymore. He didn't dare ponder the future. He simply wanted this moment. If his happiness was fleeting, he'd take what little he could grab. He caught her gaze and something flared between them. A reckless anticipation took hold of him.

Winding his free hand around the nape of her neck, he drew her close. Having her near incited an unbearable longing. Beatrix trembled, and she moved her hands tentatively, sliding her fingers up his shoulders. He pressed closer and felt her soft whimper against his lips. His hands caressed the delicate skin behind her ear and moved down to cradle her side.

A knock sounded on the door. He pressed his forehead against hers and bit back a curse. Perhaps he wasn't meant to be happy. Each time he and Beatrix came together, something always drew them apart.

She tsked at the frustrated look on his face and muffled a giggle behind one hand. "It is always something with us, *ja*?"

"*Ja*."

"That will be the Walter Frye, from the livery, I think," she said. "He has some questions for you."

"I'd better speak with him."

The work didn't stop simply because he'd been laid up.

Beatrix blew him a kiss from the doorway. "We can finish our…ahem…discussion later."

Heat flooded his face. "Yes."

No doubt they'd simply be interrupted again.

His past would always stand between them. He was starting to believe he wasn't meant to be happy. And if he wasn't meant to be happy, what did that mean for Beatrix?

Chapter Eleven

"Beatrix!" Leah called from the door leading into the ballroom of the Cattleman Hotel. "This way."

She waved her hands over the crowds, drawing their attention. Beatrix made her way toward her friend, pushing through the good-natured jostling of people swarming into the ballroom for the Thanksgiving celebration. She carefully guarded the cake she'd slaved over for most of the morning.

The friendly chatter spilling from the enormous space was nearly deafening. Colton hoisted Joseph higher on his shoulder and placed a protective hand around her waist. Beatrix smiled at the baby. His eyes were wide, and he stuffed a fist into his mouth. He seemed to be enjoying all the commotion.

Using his superior height to his advantage, Colton led them toward where Leah and Tomasina stood.

"I'm so glad you could make it," Leah said once they'd navigated the crowd. "The parlor has been set aside for the children." She indicated the room opposite where they stood. "Once Joseph is situated, you can help with the buffet table. We have more food than the table will accommodate."

Beatrix strained for a view of the ballroom. The ladies on the Thanksgiving Committee had outdone themselves. A stage had been erected at the far end of the room. Row upon row of tables and chairs had been situated lengthwise from the stage. Each table had been set with centerpieces at varying intervals. There were heaps of gourds and cornucopias brimming with nuts. Candles scattered throughout the space gave the room a warm glow along with the light from the enormous chandeliers hanging overhead.

"This way," Colton said. "I'll forge a trail."

Beatrix smiled and shouted her thanks over the noise.

The parlor had indeed been cordoned off for all the children. There were cradles lining the walls for the babies, and the older children had been recruited to watch the younger children. Hannah Johnson, the owner of the dress shop, had taken the first shift overseeing the chaos.

Colton handed over Joseph to Hannah. The dressmaker patted the head of a young boy, no more than eight years old, with dark eyes and curly dark hair.

"This is August," Hannah said. "He's been helping me out today." She leaned closer and lowered her voice. "His father is Sam Mason, editor of the newspaper. You didn't hear this from me, but I think there's a romance brewing between Mr. Mason and Dr. Boyd."

The crowd surged around them once more before Beatrix could even digest the shocking piece of gossip. Dr. Boyd seemed so independent and solitary, she'd never considered her courting someone.

There was little time to ponder Hannah's announcement. Beatrix clutched the edges of the cake pan and made her way toward Leah again. She'd woken up an extra hour earlier to work on the cake, and her effort and paid off. The torte had turned out beautifully. Colton had begged for a slice, but she'd held him off.

Once, she'd even had to slap his fingers away from the edge. He'd laughed and made her promise to bake two tortes the following year.

Leah glanced at the cake and clasped her hands, exclaiming in delight. "Oh my, that's too pretty to eat."

She led them toward a buffet brimming with food. The sight was magnificent as well as overwhelming. The scent of roasted turkey mingled with the various pies and side dishes.

Beatrix laughed. "Who will eat that much food?"

"Don't worry." Leah joined her laughter. "Nothing will be wasted. We'll eat what we can, and send the rest home with the bachelors and the drovers. There are always plenty of men to feed around Cowboy Creek."

Beatrix carefully set her cake toward the back of the table.

Colton leaned over her shoulder. "You have the prettiest dish on the whole buffet."

Her chest swelled. Though not as accomplished a baker as some of her sisters, she knew she'd done a fine job on the cake this morning.

"Thank you," she said. "You look very handsome today."

He'd worn the somber gray suit and string tie he'd donned the day he'd brought her the wedding ring. While he was handsome in his work clothing, he was devastating in a suit. Without pausing to think, she reached out and adjusted his tie, then smoothed his collar.

His face flushed, and he covered her hand. "Thank you, Mrs. Werner. I have the prettiest girl in the room on my arm."

She glanced at his hand and her heart stuttered. "You're wearing a wedding ring."

"Yes," he said. "I can't wear a ring for work, but nothing says I can't have jewelry for special occasions." He tugged a box from his pocket. "You should wear yours. I wanted to surprise you."

She hastily slid the ring on her finger. "Thank you."

Hope stirred in her heart. He'd remembered her ring, and he'd even bought one for himself. That had to mean something.

"You are quite welcome," he said.

The next half hour passed in pleasant chaos. Beatrix was introduced to so many new people, she'd never remember all their names. When she was introduced to Mr. Mason, she made a point to remember him. He seemed like a nice man. Dr. Boyd had been such a help to Beatrix over the past week, she felt protective toward her.

Dish after dish was passed around the table. Pippa performed her show to a standing ovation. The room heated from all the bodies, and Beatrix's face flushed pleasantly. Colton tolerated the crowds, greeting people and ensuring she had everything she needed.

When the ladies broke away to serve the desserts, he clasped her hand. "Would you like a breath of fresh air?"

"Please!" she exclaimed.

Laughing, they fought their way through the maze of tables and emerged triumphant into the lobby of the hotel.

Colton grasped her shoulders. "Beatrix, I—"

"Mrs. Werner," a male voice called. "I have something for you."

Colton's hands dropped away. He rubbed his forehead. "I should have known."

"You should have known what?"

"Mrs. Werner!" Beatrix turned toward the insistent call and discovered a young man with a tin star pinned to his wool vest.

The man held out his hand. "Buck Hanley, Mrs. Werner. I'm the sheriff here in Cowboy Creek. I haven't had a chance to greet you properly."

The sheriff was an average-sized man with brown hair and blue eyes. He wasn't as tall or as well built as Colton, and still held the faint callowness of youth. His expression was open and friendly, and she shook his hand.

"It's a pleasure to meet you, Mr. Hanley," she said.

"A letter came to the sheriff's office for you."

"The sheriff's office?"

She glanced at Colton, and he shrugged.

"Care of Quincy Davis," Buck said.

The blood drained from her face. There weren't many people who'd write to her care of Quincy Davis. She glanced at the letter and recognized the sharp scrawl of her oldest sister.

"Thank you, Sheriff Hanley."

"No problem."

The sheriff tipped his hat and excused himself.

Colton stuffed his hands in his pockets. "Why don't you read your letter? I'll check on the baby."

Beatrix gave a distracted nod and searched out a quiet corner, a difficult task. She finally climbed the stairs to the second landing and leaned against the railing. She ran the tip of her thumb beneath the flap, and several bills fluttered out.

Frowning, she knelt and gathered the money. Quickly scanning the contents of the letter, tears sprang into her eyes.

She stood motionless, losing all sense of time and place until a hand settled on her shoulder.

"Bad news?" Colton asked. "You haven't moved in the time it's taken me to check on the baby and return. You're pale as a sheet. You need to sit."

"I'm all right," Beatrix replied, still lost in a daze.

Colton pressed two fingers beneath her chin and gently forced her to meet his gaze. "Is something wrong? What's happened?"

"My sister has written to me."

Relief shifted across his face. "That's good. You should keep in touch."

"Peter is dead."

Colton went still. "Dead?"

She sniffled. The emotions swirling around her head were too confusing to sort. "There was a train accident outside of Vienna."

"I'm sorry, Beatrix. This must be a terrible shock."

"Now that Peter is gone, my father says that I may come home." She held up the fistful of bills. "He's sent money for our travels. For me and for Joseph."

"I don't understand." Anger flashed in his eyes. "What does one thing have to do with the other?"

She snorted softly. "I guess with Peter gone, there is less shame for my father. He wants someone to take care of him."

Colton rubbed his forehead with his thumb and forefinger. "Is this what you want?"

"I can contact my sisters now—my family will no longer shun me. I am happy about this."

"Will you return home?"

As she stared at the wad of bills, Beatrix fought back a sick feeling. "I don't know." She'd left under such strained circumstances, the thought of returning home held a certain appeal. Those first few weeks, she'd been so homesick, she'd ached. She'd left part of her heart behind. Yet here in this vast prairie land, she'd discovered a new home.

Austria was in her past. And though she might visit someday, she knew in her heart she'd never stay. Cowboy Creek was her future.

* * *

Colton felt as though all the air had been suctioned from the room. He couldn't think. He couldn't breathe. In an instant everything made sense. Beatrix should go home. She should go home to everything that was familiar, to her family, to her homeland.

She wasn't here because she was supposed to find happiness with him; she was only here waiting until she could finally go home.

He swallowed around the lump in his throat. "Will you at least stay until Christmas?"

Her face grew ashen. "You think I should go?"

"I think you need to do what's best for you and Joseph."

"But what about you?"

The pressure built behind his eyes. "I want what's best for you."

"But you would like me to stay through Christmas?"

"The weather," he said, his voice husky. "The weather is bad for travel this time of year."

He was being unbearably selfish. The weather in January was bound to be worse, but he wasn't thinking straight.

"Yes."

"You shouldn't travel alone. We can hire someone. That will take time."

"I don't mind traveling alone."

His vision blurred. "I mind. Can you do those two things for me? Can you wait until after Christmas, until after we can find someone to accompany you?"

"If that is what you'd like."

He cleared his throat. "Yes."

She folded the letter and replaced the money in the envelope. "It's time for dessert."

"I can't wait any longer. You made the most beautiful dessert on the table." He held out his elbow. "A beautiful dessert made by a beautiful lady. You made me wait all day for a slice."

She hooked her arm over his sleeve, her gaze quizzical. "Will you miss us?"

He stared straight ahead, seeing nothing. "Every day."

All around him people laughed and joked, while inside his world crumbled. He wouldn't allow himself to hope that she'd change her mind. He'd been selfish enough in asking her to stay another month.

Each opportunity he'd had with her had been interrupted. Even today. He'd hoped to tell her he loved her, but fate had intervened. This time he was grateful. He didn't want any lingering guilt over his declaration of love clouding her decision.

A line had formed for the row of desserts. Colton and Beatrix joined the queue.

Will jostled in beside him, balancing two plates in one hand. "I'm here for a second serving."

"Tomasina?"

He chuckled. "Sometimes I think she's having twins."

His obvious joy was almost unbearable in the moment. Colton was glimpsing everything his life was missing.

Engrossed in his task, Will hadn't noticed Colton's sadness, for which Colton was grateful.

They'd nearly reached the front of the line when a crash sounded.

Several people gasped and formed a circle around the source of the commotion. Leah searched the room and caught sight of them.

Her hands flew to her mouth. "Oh, Beatrix. I'm so sorry."

The crowd parted, revealing the spattered remnants of the cake Beatrix had labored over all morning. Instantly alert, Colton searched the faces of the group. He caught the back of Eric Schuyler's head near the end of the table.

Glancing around, he spotted Eugene, his arms folded over his chest, a smirk on his face.

Colton angled his body, shielding Beatrix from the store clerk's view.

Will followed the direction of his gaze and placed a restraining hand on his arm. "It might have been an accident."

"Maybe."

Leah and several other ladies were rapidly cleaning away all evidence of the mess.

"He's a boy, Colton." Will spoke near his ear. "He's not worth it."

Beatrix clutched his arm, and he caught the tears shimmering in her eyes.

"I'm tired," she said. "Can we go home?"

He nodded and ushered them from the room.

She gathered her coat and donned the fur hat he'd bought her that first week after she'd recovered. She was wearing one of the new dresses that had arrived from Hannah's dress shop. She was beautiful. She was radiant.

She was leaving him.

He quickly fetched Joseph, shielding Beatrix from the curious eyes of the Thanksgiving crowd.

Leah caught them at the door. "Are you all right?"

"She's a bit worn out," Colton replied. "Will you make our excuses?"

"Of course," Leah said, appearing as though she wanted to say something more. "Your cake was beautiful," she added, her words rushed. "There's a service on Christmas Eve, with dessert and coffee afterward. I know it's a lot to ask after what happened today, but would you consider making another?"

"I can make another," Beatrix replied softly. "It is not too much trouble."

"I'm sorry," Leah said. "I only turned my back for an instant. I don't know what happened."

"This was not your fault," Beatrix assured her. "An accident."

"Yes," Leah replied, then glanced at Colton.

He caught the question in her gaze. They were both thinking the same thing. Someone had ruined the cake on purpose, and he was fairly certain he knew the culprit. Without proof, there was no use making wild accusations.

Leah pulled Beatrix into a quick hug. "Get some rest." As Beatrix turned, Leah caught his gaze. "Take care of her."

"I will," he said. "I promise."

He'd take care of her for as much time as they had together.

Chapter Twelve

Beatrix giggled at the crooked star swaying atop the Christmas tree. "Leave it the way it is," she ordered. "This angle is jaunty."

"Your decision," Colton replied from his perch on the stool.

Beatrix narrowed her gaze. Her husband didn't behave as though he wanted her to leave. For the past four weeks, he'd been perfectly solicitous. He'd helped her with chores, and he'd assisted her with dinner each night.

The previous afternoon, he'd insisted they find a Christmas tree and supervised every stage of the decorating. The house fairly overflowed with evergreen boughs. They were wrapped around every balustrade and beam.

Even Joseph was cooperating. He was sleeping through the night and took regular naps during the day. With her schedule mostly free, Beatrix baked up a storm in anticipation of her surprise. She'd used the money from her father and purchased train tickets for Colton's grandparents. They were set to arrive late this afternoon. She'd timed their arrival before Christmas Eve as a gift to Colton. She wanted him to spend the holiday with his family, with the people he loved. She wanted to see him happy.

No matter what happened, she certainly wasn't leaving. Cowboy Creek was her home now. Considering the change in Colton's attitude these past weeks, she kept hold of a thin thread of hope that he wanted her to stay. Even the sorrow in his eyes had abated somewhat.

Her trips to town had improved, as well. After Will Canfield had spoken to Mr. Booker, Eugene had ceased taunting her, and the Schuyler boys were too busy working with their father to bother her. Even with everything that had happened, the majority of the people in Cowboy Creek had been kinder to her in her time of need than her own family.

She had friends here. Leah, Tomasina, Marlys and many more. This was where she wanted to raise Joseph. She wasn't giving up on Colton. Not yet. Not when she'd finally discovered the true meaning of love.

The day was clear and bright, and she had a few more supplies she needed in anticipation of the arrival of her guests. Her heart light, she glanced out the frost-covered window panes.

"I'm going to Booker & Son," she said. "Would you like to come along?"

"Yes," he replied easily. "I need some things, too."

Colton jumped from his perch on the stool and examined the Christmas tree. "I think this is the finest tree in town."

"I agree."

After she'd gotten ready and bundled Joseph, Colton paused by the door. "I can hitch the wagon."

"There's no need. It's only a few blocks, and I don't have many purchases. Joseph is bundled, as well."

"I'll carry him."

Beatrix handed over the baby, and Colton tugged back the blankets with his index finger. At nearly three months old, Joseph's face had filled out. Some of his hair had thinned, and he had a perfectly ridiculous hairline.

Colton clearly adored the baby, and hope flared in her chest. From that very first day she'd met him she'd known that something was troubling her husband. Something he'd buried deep inside himself. Perhaps if he shared his burden, there could be a future between them. Until then, she could only wait and hope.

Feeling optimistic, she tugged her fur-lined mittens over her wrists.

"You look beautiful," he said.

Her cheeks pinkened. "I look the same as I do every day."

"You look beautiful every day. I like the dresses you've bought from Hannah's store." Today she wore a wool plaid dress in shades of emerald and pale green. "The color suits you."

Her color deepened. "Thank you."

At his words, her optimism grew. Together they walked the distance to Booker & Son. Colton kept Joseph tucked against his side, with his other arm wrapped around Beatrix's waist. She didn't protest.

Inside the mercantile, she took the baby once more. Joseph delighted in all the sights and sounds of the busy store, and customers stopped her every few feet to exclaim over him. They quickly accomplished their task. Brimming with obvious pride in his family, Colton gathered her purchases. Another sign he was growing to care for them.

He held open the door for her, and she stepped onto the boardwalk. Something slammed into the side of her head. She shrieked and stumbled back. Colton rushed forward and caught her against his chest.

Joseph squalled, and she frantically peeled back the layers of blankets. Snow peppered his hair, but the infant was more angry than hurt. Beatrix touched the side of her face. She'd been struck by a snowball.

Colton gathered them back into the store. The customers who'd seen the prank gathered around them, murmuring their concern.

Beatrix swiped at her face. "It was nothing. A snowball."

"This ends today," Colton declared, his voice ominously low.

A chill rippled over her. "We're fine."

The door burst open, and Mr. Schuyler stomped inside, his hand wrapped around Eric's upper arm.

Mr. Schuyler caught sight of them and shoved the boy forward. "You'll apologize. Now."

Eric shrugged from his father's hold and mumbled an insincere apology.

His father's face suffused with color. "She was holding the baby."

Eric blanched. "I didn't see."

Colton kept a protective arm around Beatrix and the baby. "I need to speak with you, Mr. Schuyler. But not here. Meet me at our house in twenty minutes. Bring Eric and Dirk, as well."

The normally brash man meekly nodded. "We'll be there."

Uncertain of her husband's mood, Beatrix was quiet on their return trip home.

Once inside, he caught both her shoulders. "Are you certain neither you nor Joseph was hurt?"

"I'm certain."

His shoulders slumped in relief. "Good."

She wrapped a new blanket around Joseph and placed him in his wicker bassinet in the parlor. Colton tenderly dried her face and brushed the snow from her hair.

When he'd finished, he sat down beside her at the kitchen table. "I need to tell you something before the Schuylers arrive. I love you."

"I—"

He touched her lips, silencing her. "You have to hear the rest before you say anything. I need to tell the Schuylers a story, a story that may change the way you feel about me. But I want you to know something. I want you to know that I am going to fight for us. I love you, and I love Joseph, and I'm going to fight for the happiness of our family every day of my life. Please, remember that after you hear what I have to say."

Her heart thumped against her ribs. This was the day she'd waited for, prayed for. She'd finally learn what caused the sorrow behind his eyes.

He retrieved a sheaf of papers. "This is your Christmas present. I wrote something for the time capsule."

"You didn't have to do that."

"I did. You were right. Writing down the story of the past was lifting a burden. And now there's another burden I need to lift."

Reverently accepting the papers, Beatrix said, "Thank you."

He'd given her the gift of his past, now she needed the promise of their future.

She sensed something in him had shifted, and marveled at the change. Moments later, the Schuyler boys, along with their father, sat around her kitchen table.

Mr. Schuyler pinched the bridge of his nose. "I'm as much to blame as the boys. I didn't want them to be bullied, so I made sure they knew how to defend themselves. But I focused so much on making sure they were strong, that I never took the time to teach them how to use that strength. There'll be some changes around our house, I can promise you that."

Colton rested his forearms on the table and fisted his hands. "I want to tell you a story."

All eyes turned toward him.

As Colton told the tale of his brother, Beatrix's eyes misted over. When he finished, she cupped her fingers over his clenched hands. He met her gaze, and something changed between them. An understanding.

"You're young," Colton said, his eyes fixed on the boys once more. "But the choices you make have consequences. You have your whole lives ahead of you. Someday you may do something you can't take back, and you'll have to live with that burden. I'm asking you to make some changes now, before it's too late. I promise you this, if you ever target Beatrix again, things will not turn out well for you."

Dirk pushed back his chair and stood. "I'm real sorry, Mrs. Werner. I'm real sorry about everything. I shouldn't have called you that name. I shouldn't have wrecked your cake or hit you with a snowball. I didn't know you were holding the baby."

"I'm sorry, too," Eric added, his face suffused with color. "The stuff seemed harmless. Eugene gave us the idea to hit her with a snowball."

Mr. Schuyler fisted his hand over his mouth and cleared his throat. "I'll speak with Eugene's father. He needs to be apprised of the situation."

The mood somber, the three of them filed out, leaving Beatrix alone with Colton.

"Now you know," he said. "Now you know who I really am."

Chapter Thirteen

Colton took a shuddering breath and waited for her reaction.

Beatrix squeezed his hands. "I already knew who you were, and I already loved you."

Her complete acceptance stunned him into momentary silence. "But I'm no different than those boys."

"Yes, you are. You're different because you've grown and learned from your mistakes. You've punished yourself long enough. It's time to let go."

"I hurt people." But even as he argued, relief coursed through him. For the first time since Joseph's death, he felt as though he could take a full breath, as though the band around his chest had loosened. "I tore our family apart."

"An accident tore your family apart. And then you kept punishing yourself until you tore yourself apart. That accident was not your fault. When you stole those apples, you should have been punished. Your neighbor started the war by retaliating instead of forgiving."

"I needed to give meaning to the suffering."

She traced the rigid scar on the back of his hand. "My grandfather once said that our souls emerge stronger for

suffering. He said that the strongest souls are riddled with scars."

Colton desperately wanted to believe he could be happy, that he didn't need to carry the burden any longer. "How does that make up for what happened?"

"We can never change the past," she replied sadly. "We've all made decisions we regret. I regret the foolish girl who put her trust in the wrong man. But I cannot wish it undone. Even with all the pain I suffered, I'm grateful. I'm grateful for Joseph. I'm grateful for the wisdom that experience gave me. I'm grateful because that heartache led me to you. I know you're a good man. I know the difference now. I didn't before."

Her words filled the empty spaces between the scars in his soul. "I love you, Beatrix. And I want you to be happy. But you're so far away from home, from your family."

"I am happy. *You* make me happy. This is my home, and you are my family."

"Are you certain?"

"I've never been more certain."

He glanced at the baby sleeping in the bassinet. He'd come full circle. He'd buried his brother, and he'd seen this new life enter the world. *Joseph. The beloved.* There'd never be any reason for what had happened to his brother, but along the way, he'd forgotten there was hope. With each new generation, there was life and loss, joy and sorrow. All that had happened before had made him the man he was today. He'd been broken and repaired, he'd been scarred and healed, he'd loved and he was loved in return.

His parents had died unforgiving, shattered over the loss. Their grief had been more important to them than their living son. Yet their bitterness had not changed the past.

Colton knelt before the bassinet. The baby cooed and

kicked at his swaddling. Tears sprang in his eyes, and he didn't fight them away.

He lifted his eyes heavenward. "I will honor you with my joy. I will honor you with the love I share."

Beatrix came to stand beside him. Colton stood and swept her into his arms. Of all the kisses they'd shared, this one was the sweetest, because this was their first kiss without guilt to taint it, or obstacles to overcome. This was the first kiss they'd shared that didn't hold the pall of sorrow for the past.

This was the kiss that started his new life, and he refused to let anything interrupt them.

Beatrix glanced down the pew and smiled. Colton's grandparents had arrived, and their reunion had been a heartwarming combination of tears and hugs. Mrs. Werner, who'd ordered Beatrix to call her Angie, held Joseph during the service.

Her beautiful linzertorte had been set in the place of honor for the gathering after the service. Best of all, the sorrow had finally gone from Colton's eyes, replaced by joy and wonder.

He squeezed her hand. "I love you."

"I love you, too," she whispered back.

Reverend Taggart stood before the congregation. "Please, rise for the singing of the Christmas hymn."

Skirts rustled, voices murmured, and everyone stood.

The piano began a familiar tune, and the congregation sang along.

The words brought tears to her eyes, and she gazed at Colton in wonder. "They're singing in German."

"I know," he whispered back. "They practiced last week after the service was over. I wanted to surprise you."

Beatrix added her voice to the chorus. "*Stille Nacht,*

Heil'ge Nacht, Alles schläft; einsam wacht Nur das traute hoch heilige Paar. Holder Knab' im lockigen Haar, Schlafe in immlischer Ruh."

Silent night, holy night, All is calm, all is bright. Round yon Virgin, Mother and Child.

Holy infant so tender and mild, Sleep in heavenly peace, Sleep in heavenly peace.

Her heart swelled, and she gazed at the row of faces singing beside her. She'd finally come home.

* * * * *

Don't miss a single installment of
COWBOY CREEK

Bringing mail-order brides, and new beginnings, to a Kansas boom town.

WANT AD WEDDING
by Cheryl St.John

SPECIAL DELIVERY BABY
by Sherri Shackelford

BRIDE BY ARRANGEMENT
by Karen Kirst

Find more great reads at www.LoveInspired.com

at her cheeks, helping her to make the decision. Josephine nodded and led the short distance back to the house.

His boots crunched through the snow as he followed her to the kitchen door. She stepped up on the porch but then turned to face him. He deserved an apology. "I'm sorry. I should have done as you asked and stayed inside."

He reached up and brushed a wayward curl from her face. "I understand your need to come outside. I'm not sure I could stay inside for three whole days, either."

The light touch of his fingers against her cheek surprised Josephine. Her gaze met his. She felt the urge to lean her face into his warm palm. He smiled and pulled his hand away. "I best be heading back to the house. I'll see you tomorrow."

As he turned to leave Josephine called out, "Thomas."

He stopped and searched her face.

"I'm glad you are home." She smiled as her mind went blank. She could think of no more words to retain him.

His lips twitched into a grin. "Good night, Josephine." And he walked into the shadows.

She stepped into the kitchen but turned to watch Thomas climb onto his horse and head into the darkness that now enveloped the world. It seemed she was forever watching him leave.

Tomorrow they'd be married. Would they be compatible? Or would he soon tire of her and want to go on with his life, without her? She didn't know why, but the last thought troubled her.

Don't miss
PONY EXPRESS CHRISTMAS BRIDE
by Rhonda Gibson, available December 2016 wherever
Love Inspired® Historical books and ebooks are sold.

www.LoveInspired.com

Finding a husband is the only way Josephine Dooly can protect herself against her scheming uncle, so she answers a mail-order-bride ad. But when she arrives and discovers her groom-to-be didn't place the ad himself, can she convince Thomas Young to marry her in name only?

Read on for a sneak preview of PONY EXPRESS CHRISTMAS BRIDE by Rhonda Gibson, available December 2016 from Love Inspired Historical!

"You have spunk, Josephine Dooly. I've never heard of a woman riding the Pony Express. And now here I find you outside when you know it could be dangerous."

Josephine turned her gaze back on him. Had she misheard him a few moments ago? The warmth in his laugh drew her like a kitten to fresh milk. Was she so used to her uncle treating her like a child that she expected Thomas to treat her the same way? She searched his face. "You aren't angry with me."

"No, I'm not. I am concerned that you take risks but I am not your keeper. You can come and go as you wish." He pushed away from the well. "I came by to tell you that tomorrow we'll go into town and get married, if you still wish to do so."

Josephine exhaled. "I do."

He nodded. "Can I walk you back inside?"

A longing to stay out in the fresh air battled with wanting to please him and go inside. The cold air nipped

Dear Reader,

When Cheryl St.John and I were invited to work together, we knew we had to revisit Cowboy Creek. We knew the town had many more stories to share, and we had a wonderful time working together on this project. My heroine brings a keepsake from Austria. If you're interested in hearing how her beautiful armonica sounded, there are numerous videos on the internet. The craftsmanship of these instruments is incredible!

I hope you enjoy the love story between Colton and Beatrix.

I love connecting with readers and would enjoy hearing your thoughts on this story! If you're interested in learning more about this book, or others I've written in the Prairie Courtships series, visit my website at SherriShackelford.com, or reach me at sherrishackelford@gmail.com, facebook.com/SherriShackelfordAuthor, Twitter @smshackelford, or regular old snail mail: PO Box 116, Elkhorn, NE 68022.

Thanks for reading!
Sherri Shackelford